PRAISE FOR *THE VICIOUS DEEP*

"This mythical tale is a great read told on land and below the sea. These mermaids are not the lovely creatures you know—they may be beautiful but they are also deadly."

—*RT Book Reviews*

"An authentic 16-year-old male voice and viewpoint…the great title, killer jacket, and edgy portrayal of the mythical creatures should cast a wide readership net."

—*Booklist*

"*The Vicious Deep* is incredibly original and is plump full of funny, witty, charming, likable characters."

—Night Owl Reviews

"A delicious debut that pulled me in and kept me entranced."

—Leanna Renee Hieber, author of *The Twisted Tragedy of Miss Natalie Stewart*

"Original sea creatures, fun side characters that heighten the adventure, and a deep, memorable romance that made me ache…This is a must read for every YA lover out there."

—YA Bound

The Vicious Deep Series

The Vast and Brutal Sea

ZORAIDA CÓRDOVA

WITHDRAWN

sourcebooks
fire

Copyright © 2014 by Zoraida Córdova
Cover and internal design © 2014 by Sourcebooks, Inc.
Cover design by Sourcebooks, Inc
Cover illustration © Tony Sahara

Published by Sourcebooks Fire, an imprint of Sourcebooks, Inc.
P.O. Box 4410, Naperville, Illinois 60567-4410
(630) 961-3900
Fax: (630) 961-2168
www.sourcebooks.com

Library of Congress Cataloging-in-Publication data is on file with the publisher.

Printed and bound in the United States of America.

BG 10 9 8 7 6 5 4 3 2 1

For Adrienne Rosado, my best friend and soul sister.
All of this is possible because you believed.

Part I

"Now put me into the barge," said the king...

"for I will into the Vale of Avilion to heal me of my grievous wound;

and if thou hear never more of me, pray for my soul."

—FROM *Le Morte d'Arthur* BY
SIR THOMAS MALORY

LONG AGO

The Daughter of the Sea would never be loved.

She was the first child of the Golden Queen and King Elanos of the Erabos Kingdom. King Elanos, descendant of the first Kings of the sea, watched his daughter tear free from the birthing sac without the help of the midwife. She slithered between her mother's split tails, silver and pale as the face of the moon, haloed in blood and flesh.

They called her Nieve.

Her sisters needed help. For long, painful hours, six more daughters followed, wailing and ripping their way into the sea. Nieve grabbed one of her sisters' hands, curious at the strange face that shared her crib, and sunk pearly teeth into her golden flesh.

The midwife reeled Nieve into a crib of coral, separating her from her sisters who bloomed like violet and turquoise jewels in the quiet darkness of Glass Castle.

It was the Golden Queen's first pod with the king. Her voice echoed in the new, shining halls, not in pain like the queens before her, but in happiness. She was his prize after the war with the rebel tribes, and together they would birth a new reign in the deep, ignoring the whispers of distant enemy shadows.

Merfolk came from all the oceans, bringing precious gifts for the princesses. They stayed, wonder struck at how the little ones shone with the queen's golden skin and the king's eyes, one turquoise, one violet.

Then there was Nieve, with a paleness that radiated like starlight. She brought awe, nestled in her mother's warm arms like a pearl.

And as she grew, fast and strong, she reached and reached for the brilliant fissures inside the quartz scepter of her father's trident. The court smiled tightly at the brazenness of the tiny mermaid. Gasped in awe at the silver princess swimming with wild white-bellied sharks, taming them with the tender pads of her fingertips.

A thousand eyes trailed Nieve around the walls of Glass Castle. A thousand whispers always present, yet always at a careful distance, not knowing the extent of the curious sparks of her hands. It was magic—so rare that it had never presented itself in the royal family. Not since the legends of Eternity, when the children of Triton fought the winged fey. With each battle, the Sea Court moved deeper into the coldest breaches of the seas.

King Elanos recognized it. Magic, like the core of his trident, the spark that could summon storms and tear into the rocky beds of the ocean floors. But in a mermaid, the magic was uncontained and unpredictable. The king watched as the spark grew in his silver daughter's eyes until, in a fit of anger, she killed.

It was an accident.

The palace guard would not let her swim to the surface. She thought she was old enough to see the world alone. The guard grabbed her and pulled her back down to court. She pressed her hands on his chest for a moment, just a moment, and stopped his heart. His body froze, eyes gaping at the princess, until a current carried him away.

An accident.

The court watched her, unsmiling, unnerving, unloving.

He watched her, the king, sleeping with eyes open, ears open, to the murmurs of his daughter's sleep talk, and he knew what he must do.

His enemies came in the night.

But in the dark of the deep, it was always night—rebel tribes against his door—the sea people of warmer oceans with copper scales and onyx weapons. They sought retribution for the Golden Queen stolen from them by King Elanos so long ago. But the queen had grown to love her captor, her husband, her king, and she wouldn't go—wouldn't leave. She was pregnant once more, and this time, she was certain it was a son.

King Elanos had waited for this day. He knew their kind was dwindling in numbers. The blood of war was no longer as appetizing as in his youth. It was a queen they wanted and a queen the rebel tribes would get.

And so King Elanos took his first daughter from her single chamber and led her to the rebel Southern King.

Nieve screamed, as her mother had screamed when she was taken so long ago, the sound echoing through the ocean, the current yielding to her palms, and at once, King Elanos took Nieve's face. He had never held her, not as a child, not as a daughter. But she wasn't a child any longer, and he held her then, looking into her pale moon eyes, and said, "Daughter, do this and you will save your kin."

The kin who turned away, relieved that the silver princess would no longer grace the court. The kin who peered between glass pillars as she was taken away. Some crying. Some smiling.

And without looking at her weeping sisters or her mother, Nieve took the hand of the Southern King.

She could hear the sigh of relief, like the last breath of a tempest. She looked at her father, dark hatred slithering into her heart and she promised, *I will save my people, Father. But who will save you?*

chapter
ONE

NOW

Layla is gone.

Layla is gone and there's a chance I may never get her back. That she's dead. That I'm two days away from losing her, the throne, and my life because for a moment, I wasn't strong enough and the silver mermaid knew it.

She knows me in ways that I don't even know myself, knows the paralyzing fear that swelled in me when I thought I could lose the girl I love.

The ship hits a wave and heaves. I grab on to the table in front of me and drop the knife in my hand. I can hear Brendan and Kai on deck moving weapons around. They'll come checking on me any minute and I know I have to hurry.

The pressure on my temples builds like tiny land mines going off in my head. I press my palms and squeeze, but the image doesn't go away. I see Gwen. Gwen putting a pale hand over Layla's mouth and diving off the pier into the water.

Layla can't breathe underwater.

I hold on to the basin in front of me, face myself in the scuffed mirror, and examine the damage. My skin is peeling over my nose. Salt water stings the thin cuts on my face, trickling down my neck and down my chest. I can feel the ghost of an injury where Nieve's fingernails cut me the first time she found me. Was it only eighteen days ago? Eighteen days ago that I washed up on Coney Island after the freak storm created by the arrival of the Sea Court's Toliss Island.

Now, despite everything I've been through, my journey is far from over. Just a little bit more, just a little bit, I tell myself to keep going. I have to wake the Sleeping Giants, powerful creatures that once belonged to the first kings of the sea. They're my best chance at defeating my enemies. Their strength is legend and we're heading to a place that will help us find them.

I pick up the knife again and get to work. My body shakes like a house during a hurricane every time I exhale.

I can do this.

I'm psyching myself out.

I jog in place like I'm warming up before a meet. But the combination of jogging and the waves lapping around the ship knocks over the jars of healing gunk the urchin brothers applied to all my wounds, as well as the last of my fresh water.

I hear my buddy Angelo's voice in the back of my head saying, "Get your head out of your ass, T."

Do it, Tristan, I tell myself.

I grind my teeth, and staring at myself in the mirror, I let the blade slice through the hair bunched in my fist.

I haven't gotten a haircut in more than three years. I love my hair. I grab another bunch at the nape and hack. The wet, brown waves fall to the ground and coil at my feet. When we were in junior high school, I tried to spike my hair because that was the scene. Layla took one look at me and said I looked like a Dragon Ball reject. I went right to the bathroom and washed off the glue gel. I let my hair grow longer and longer until the girls started coming up to me and running their hands through it. All of them except for *her*.

It seems stupid. It's just hair. It'll grow back. It's not like I lost my fighting arm or my head, though in the five hours since we left Coney Island, I did come pretty close. I refuse to let anyone else take something from me. I have to take matters into my own hands. Brendan promised me that the Sleeping Giants and their primitive strength would help me with this war. But to do that, I have to change. I am a different guy than I was three weeks ago. I'm a merman. I don't know if I'm a better person, but I want to be. I have to be.

When I'm done, I run a hand across the surface. The stubble is foreign against my calloused palms. I turn my face from side to side. My cheekbones are more pronounced from the weight I've lost and muscle I've gained from miles of swimming and sweating under the sun. The only things that haven't changed are my eyes, turquoise like my grandfather's—the Sea King. I touch the soft, purple bruise ringing my eye and wince.

I drop the knife on the floor and use a brush I nabbed from the urchin brothers to get rid of the loose strands sticking to my skin.

The door swings open and Brendan runs in.

"Are you all right? I heard a noise."

His shoulder-length red hair is tied back. His turquoise eyes flick from me to the knife on the ground, then back to my head.

"Who are you," Brendan says, "and what have you done with my cousin?"

"He's still here," I say. "And he's ready."

chapter
TWO

Brendan, Champion of the North and my cousin, is the reason I'm here now. After the fight against the merrows on Coney Island, after Nieve took Layla, after Kurt—after all of that, I was a mess. Brendan showed up and, along with Princess Kai, hauled me onto Arion's ship. We started sailing north right away.

I'm like, "Say something, man."

"I'm not entirely certain what I'm looking at." He leans against the door frame. Behind him I can see a lunch spread and my stomach roars. He points a finger at the brush in my hand and says, "Vi's been looking for that to scrub the deck, you know."

"That bad?" I rub my hand on my head.

"I didn't say that."

"A bunch of it kind of burned off on one side during the fight." I brush stray hairs from my chest and re-strap my sternum harness. I keep Triton's dagger sheathed on my chest and the Scepter of Earth between my shoulder blades.

"It's—it's nice." When he says that, it reminds me of every time my mom asks for my dad's opinion on her hair, her clothes, her garage sale trinkets. I shake my head—like that'll stop me from thinking of my family.

"You don't have to like it."

"You look like a different person."

Good, that's what I'm going for. "Are we at the Cry Me A River Island yet?"

He jumps around me, still staring at my head. "It's the Vale of Tears. We're not far."

Brendan whistles and holds his arm out north. His shoulders are tanned dark from days of sailing before meeting up with me. He's still got a black and blue shiner around his eye. Before now, he was down south in search of some magical city in the sky. Whatever was guarding that city really did a number on his face. So we've got that in common.

I check my waterproof watch, a gift from my coach for being captain of the swim team last year. "You said it wasn't a long trip."

"It's still morning, Cousin Tristan. The end of the fortnight isn't 'til Saturday night. Tomorrow."

We let a moment of silence pass for the things that don't have to be said. When the moon is full, it will mark the end of the championship. Not that the quest is going by the same rules. We started out with five champions—Adaro of the South and Elias of the East are dead. Brendan is on my side. Dylan of the West hasn't been heard of since the day my grandfather broke his trident into three pieces and set them loose for us to find.

The pieces have been found all right. I have the Scepter of Earth. Nieve took the Staff of Eternity. Kurt has the Trident of the Skies. The rules have gone to shit, and if no one else is going to follow them, then I won't either. We're going to visit the river merpeople to get some power. I'll fix the throne and I'll save Layla.

Piece of cake, right?

"Worry not, dear cousin." Brendan pats my shoulder. "Once we reach the mist, we know we have arrived. Then we sail right into it. It's a bit of a fright at first. The mist will try to push us back, to make sure we have the will to pass. Then," he claps his hands hard, "we're in."

Cake.

"Yeah, fog and mist have done wonders for me in the past."

"That's the spirit!" He smacks my back.

Kai smiles at us from the quarterdeck. Her long, blond curls are wild, and she wears the metallic armor of the Sea Guard. For a scroll nerd, she's taken to weapons really well. She and Arion stop speaking.

"Don't stop just because I'm here," I say. But I know I've given them reason to think I'm not okay. For a moment back there, I thought I was legit insane. Like, put a crazyjacket on me and lock me in a white padded room. I was tired and delirious. I was going to jump into the sea and follow the silver mermaid. It took Kai and Brendan to sedate me with some bitter liquid that let me sleep. When I came to, Brendan told me of the Sleeping Giants.

"Where we at?" I take the heavy metal telescope from Arion

and peer through the glass. Blue and gray, endlessness like there is nothing wrong with the world.

Arion, the captain of the ship, is mystically bound to the vessel with black ropes that stretch as high as the masts but never into water. He moves his arms in the wind, carefully steering across rough waves. "Just passing Greenland."

I turn my face into the salty breeze and breathe deeply.

"The change suits you," Arion tells me.

I smirk at Brendan. "Arion, have you heard of the Sleeping Giants?"

He nods, keeping his dark eyes on the horizon. The urchins load us up with food. I take a seaweed chip and crumble it in my hands. Brendan shoves more food down his throat than my entire swim team during Thanksgiving.

"Aye, Master Tristan," Arion says. "Only tales from when I was a guppy."

"I can't picture you as a guppy," Kai says.

Arion laughs. "I believe this is a compliment, Lady Kai, yes?"

Her cheeks turn red. "What I mean is, I've read the accounts of when you were a warrior. How you were the best dragon slayer in the whole Sea Guard."

Arion looks away from the admiration on our faces and into some memory. "That was long ago."

"The Sleeping Giants?" I urge.

"Aye," Arion says again. "Some legends say our kind was as big as the beasts that roamed the earth and seas long before humans did. When the sea oracles created the trident pieces, they used the blood of three fierce animals as their core. The hippocampus."

"Hippo what?"

"Really big sea horse," Kai whispers to me, "with webbed claws."

"The kraken," Arion continues, "whose ink and blood also give us the ability to walk."

All four of us have ink tattoos in the shape of a trident between our shoulder blades. My mom, once a mermaid princess, had one too. Now that she's been stripped of her tail, only a white scar remains.

"And the giant turtle."

I laugh, picturing the baby turtles I got for my seventh birthday. "How bad can a giant turtle be?"

"Its teeth could bite through rock, its shell covered in spikes three times taller than you, Master Tristan."

"All right, so pretty bad."

"Once they roamed the seas freely. To possess the Giants of the Sea would be like having thousands of guards at your disposal. The creatures became coveted by our enemies, so the king sealed them with a key no one has ever found."

"And you're sure the River Clan can help us find the key?"

Brendan mutters indistinctly.

"Don't talk with your mouth full," Kai scolds. Because she looks no older than me, I keep forgetting that she's Brendan's aunt.

Brendan wipes his lips with the back of his hand and pats his abs. "I'm certain they know about the key. We have to convince them to help us. That's the challenge."

"Why wouldn't they help?" I ask.

"We merkind don't do anything out of the goodness of our hearts," Kai says.

"Everyone wants something," I say. "I'll find the thing they want."

Arion is going to speak. Then his dark shoulders flex as he struggles to control the wheel. The ship tilts to the side so far I almost fall over the starboard. I grab on to a rope and brace myself as Kai falls into me. Brendan clings onto the rigging like a monkey, shouting as he hangs over the water, then rocks himself back onto the ship.

"What was that?" I shout.

"I've never lost control over the stern like this," Arion says, wrestling to right the ship.

Kai lets go of me and her face scrunches against the sun. "The binding of the king is almost gone. The last days of the championship are unstable. Can't you sense it? Soon, you will be free from your father's punishment."

Arion looks down at his wrist where the black rope has left a pearly scar where it rubs. A bald patch of scar tissue has formed at the base of his tail where more black rope winds around his black and white scales.

When he sees me staring, a sad smile appears on Arion's severe face.

"What did he do?" I ask. I never have. Arion has been with me this whole time. This is the ship that ferries the landlocked from the shore to Toliss Island. Looking at his face, the new redness on his tail and around his wrists makes me angry. I should have asked every time.

"My father fought alongside Nieve when she rebelled against

16

King Elanos. When she was a princess, there was no one like her. Men wanted her and feared her at the same time. It was the king who kept away from the people. Then she became a queen, given to the rebel tribes to keep the peace."

"It didn't work, I guess," I say.

Arion shakes his head solemnly. "Now she's a monster. After her rebellion failed and King Karanos took over, he couldn't kill his own blood. He banished her beneath the sea. Those who didn't surrender were killed. Those who surrendered were either indentured to the throne or sent off to the coral cave prisons. Others were stripped of their tails and left to swim ashore."

"That's where the landlocked come from," I say.

This isn't exactly news to me. I know that the landlocked of the court, the banished, are left landside as a punishment. Every time the court makes a stop on the shore, the landlocked are forced to give tithes in exchange for the court's protection.

"You're still a hero," Brendan says to Arion. "My father says you saved his life. That you killed the leader of the dragons, Akos, the largest dragon in the New World."

Guilt tastes like bile on my tongue. I don't understand how my own family could be responsible for all of this. Now it falls to me to make it right.

"I've always served the crown." Arion lets the black ropes hoist him up and away from us so we can't see his eyes, only hear his voice. "My father was a lost soul. I know exactly who I am. There is honor in that."

"Things will change in the future. I'll make them change." I bang the end of my scepter on the deck. It feels strange to hold, lighter than usual. Or maybe I'm overthinking what Kai said about everything being unstable.

Two blue and violet blurs appear in front of us, brandishing more trays of food.

"Don't make easy promises, Cousin," Brendan says as he bites into a seaweed wrap.

"It isn't easy." I push my food away. I can't eat, not after Arion's story.

Still, Blue stands beside his brother. They are carbon copies of each other, apart from the brilliant inky colors of their skins. Heads with long, spiked points and big, black eyes. Layla used to say they're so ugly they're cute and kept threatening to take one home as a pet.

No matter what is happening on the ship, the urchin brothers fix loose ropes and tears in the sails and keep us fed. I'm not hungry, but Brendan's stomach is a black hole. Even on my best days after swim practice, I couldn't eat as much as him. Blue tempts Brendan with a tray of oysters, a grilled fish with a face like a bulldog, and pickled sea veggies.

I try not to grimace. "I'm good, thanks."

"Lord Sea must eat!" Blue begs. "Kings must be strong." He smiles with his black teeth.

I take another chip and let it melt onto my tongue. It goes down like a mouth full of seawater. True. Kings must be strong. No weaknesses. And I have to get rid of mine.

It's Brendan who says, "Kings must also be terribly attractive. If that were the case, it'd be me on the throne and not you, Cousin."

Kai throws her head back and laughs. Arion grins down at us. Even Vi smiles bashfully. It's the first time anyone has laughed in a while, and if it's at my expense, I'll let them have it.

Then there's a wet splash and the sharp whistle of an arrow. Vi's face is spotted with black freckles that begin to drip. The smile is still on his face as he turns to his brother.

My insides feel cold. My ears ring.

I reach out to him—the ship heaves as something crashes into us. Blue falls to his knees, black blood streaming from the arrow piercing his forehead.

chapter
THREE

Vi's shriek is piercing.

Kai rams into me. Another arrow slices past my ear. The ship tilts sideways. Dozens of arms reach over the sides of the ship and pull themselves on board. Armored mermen in half shifts surround us. A whirlpool spins off in the distance. They must've come from there because there isn't another ship in sight.

And then there's Vi, shrieking and grabbing at Blue's limp, dissolving body. He holds the golden arrow in his purple fist.

I roll over and try to reach him, but arms pull me back. It's Brendan pulling me up. My vision is dizzy and warm; sticky blood trickles down my spine. I grip my scepter, aiming it outward at the mermen intruders. I try to concentrate on the scepter's familiar humming current, but it isn't there, like the batteries have run out. I unsheathe my dagger. Try to keep my hand from shaking as panic floods my body.

"Who the hell are you?" I ask.

They don't answer. On their breastplates is the symbol of a

kraken. Scarlet scales cover their brown forearms and shins. Their hair is long and tied down to their backs. They all wield swords except for one, who readies another arrow.

But he's not the leader. Standing on the ledge is a familiar face. The same amber eyes, like melting fire. The same stubborn frown between the brow—Adaro's father, herald of the Southern Seas. His face is crushed, furious. I had that face when Kurt let Layla get away. The deep grooves around his eyes mark his ancient age.

"Leomaris," Kai says breathlessly.

"Lord Leomaris." One of the warriors takes the end of his spear and points it at Kai's face.

"You killed my son," Leomaris says to me.

The gold band around his head glints. He points his sword at me. He's too far to stab me with it, but the intent is clear. There are ten of them and three of us. Blue is dead, and Vi wordlessly holds his brother's body.

Two men have taken hold of Arion's ropes, stretching him as taut as possible, immobilizing him.

"That's not true," I say. "Adaro was my friend." Then instantly I wonder, was he? His cousin Sarabell did try to convince him to kill me. He refused. We were going to join forces against Nieve. But she got to him first. Nieve killed him and took the staff of the trident.

"Lies!" His warriors shout. "They saw you on Adaro's ship. They told us."

"Since when do you take the word of our enemies?" Kai asks.

"It is Karanos who betrays the throne," Leomaris says. "He didn't listen to my counsel. Adaro should be on that throne. Now because of you, he's dead."

"I didn't kill him!"

No matter what I say, it isn't going to matter. He blames me for their deaths. And really, could I have saved Adaro? I stopped myself from giving Nieve my scepter. I wouldn't do it for Adaro, but I would have for Layla.

"We're doing you a favor, land mutt," one of the guards shouts.

"Yeah, how's that?"

"There's a bounty on your head from the sea witch herself. The whole of the oceans will be looking for you."

"Then it's in your best interest to take us alive," Brendan says.

Leomaris holds his sword steadily. "Treasure won't bring my son back. What will I take from you, Tristan Hart?"

"That's really brave," I say, glancing at the urchin, now clutching a decomposing mound of flesh. "Going after someone less than half your size. He was innocent."

"None of them are innocent." His eyes flicker to Arion. "Besides, I've found bigger targets."

I shouldn't turn my back to Leomaris, but I do. Arion pulls and pulls on his ropes. The ones on his left hand are loosening. Their archer raises his bow to our captain.

I run up the deck and aim my scepter at the bowman. A weak burst shoots from the quartz, but it's enough to knock him overboard.

"Tristan!" Kai shouts.

Leomaris's shadow looms over me. Kai blocks his blow. He raises his knee into her gut and she falls back.

"Didn't your mother teach you not to hit girls?" I flip my scepter like a bat and slap it across his face.

"Do not speak to me about mothers," he says, "when yours is a disgrace to our kind."

I lash out blindly, but he throws me off balance with the flick of his wrist. I roll onto my knees swinging my scepter upward, but I hit air. Leomaris is gone.

Brendan dances around the biggest guards. The smile on my cousin's face hides the sheer panic in his turquoise eyes. Brendan is fast, and he rolls between the merman's legs. With two small blades, he slashes at the opponent's ankles, and the giant crumbles.

A sharp blow knocks the wind out of me. Leomaris appears once again. I block his sword with my scepter.

"You've got the wrong guy!" I try to reason with him. "It's Nieve you want. It's not too late. We can defeat her."

There's something electric in his eyes. Sarabell had it too—the dark spark of the magic in their family. Leomaris smiles cruelly. He raises a hand and a wave rises up in the air, following his movements. It crashes over the deck, washing Blue's body away. Vi picks up a discarded weapon on the deck, a spike carved of stone. He stabs a guard in the thigh. But the guard turns around with a fierce growl.

Leomaris is on me, pressing his hands on my chest. My body seizes, and for a beat, my heart stops. I blink. See black. The guard raises his sword and brings it down, cleaving Vi in two.

"No!" Kai shouts.

Leomaris electrocutes me. I'm shaking, crying, convulsing. My muscles lock, fingers gripped tightly around my scepter. I search for the power inside my scepter but all I can do is scream in frustration because when I need the power the most, it's failing me. Leomaris lifts his hands off me to watch me choke. He reaches back down for my throat, but the ship heaves under a wave. I roll out from under him and onto my knees. I stab the scepter into his thigh. Leomaris screams at the same time his fist hits my face. My head spins as I land on my back, my entire body shaking.

Beside me, Kai is screaming, pinned under a merman with muscles like boulders. Tears spill from her face as if her strength is leaving her, and her eyes focus on the bloody mess of the urchin's body beside her.

Brendan loses his grin and uses all his strength to drive a sword through the warrior pinning Kai down. The body decomposes into a messy splash over her face and she chokes.

Two remaining guards flank a bleeding Leomaris, balancing like statues on the side of the ship. They've let go of Arion's restraints and the captain rises up beside me.

"Are you all right?" I ask.

"The mist," Arion hisses. "You must swim to it."

The air thickens around us. I step forward, keeping my friends behind me. My head is a jumble of words. What do you say to a man dead set on killing you?

Leomaris pulls out a slender flask with a liquid that radiates neon blue. Blood trickles down his leg, but it doesn't stop him from smiling.

"Combat fire," Kai says breathlessly. She takes a step back.

The last time I came across combat fire, I saw it consume a Brooklyn street.

"Don't do this," Kai pleads. Her fingers are white, pulling at Arion's ropes. Brendan slashes with his sword but it won't cut. I can't concentrate enough to channel the scepter, and as a last resort, I stab at the rope with the crystal end.

"I didn't," Leomaris says, pointing a finger at me. "He did."

"We have to get off the ship," Brendan hisses. "Now."

"Arion," I say.

"Go, all of you. Go now!"

I can't. It's caught in my throat when Arion takes Brendan and Kai and flings them overboard. It makes Leomaris chuckle. He wags the vial in his fingers.

"Even after all the court has done to you, you spare them?"

Arion won't answer. He grabs me with the full intent of throwing me off the ship. It's for my own good. I have to get to the mist. But I won't let him, and neither will Leomaris's guards because they launch themselves on me, pulling me back and out of Arion's grip. I lash out but I slice at air. The merman hits me so hard that I wonder if my head's been split in two. I fall forward on my face and brace for the next hit that never comes. The mermen retreat beside Leomaris.

"I will destroy everyone you love," Leomaris tells me. "And it gives me great satisfaction knowing you won't be there to save them."

Then the herald of the Southern Seas dives backward into the whirlpool he summoned. His men follow and then the sea is still. The vial spins in the air, suspended, until it shatters onto the deck, bleeding blue fire.

The explosion burns black and blue. The flames are living things, slithering along the deck, up the masts and chomping away at the sails. I try frantically to make my scepter work, but with every heaving breath, my insides ache and fill with smoke, and I know the power is gone. I don't understand what I did—

A ringing fills my head, the aftereffect of the first blast. I grit my teeth to stop myself from screaming. Arion isn't screaming. In fact, when I open my eyes, Arion isn't beside me.

He hangs from one hand that looks broken. Blasts fill the morning sky as the combat fire eats our powder keg. It's like the Fourth of July. The contents of the ship are like shrapnel. Something hot stabs my thigh.

Get up, Tristan, I tell myself. Get up or die.

"Leave me," Arion yells, hoarse desperation in his voice.

But I can't leave him behind. I can't leave him like this.

I push myself up on the side of the ship for support. Blue flames crackle and devour the deck, licking at my heels as I make my way to where Arion hangs at the masthead. The sound of wood breaking is like the tick of a time bomb. The ship snaps in half, and I slam into the knobs of the steering wheel.

Arion is screaming.

My blade slices through the ropes tying down his right hand. It gives! His hand hangs broken and he slumps against me.

"I got you," I say. "Just two more."

But when I look into his onyx eyes, I know he heard it too—the sizzle of fire as it consumes our weapons hold below, followed by a blinding white-blue light, a deafening silence, and then our screams as the rest of the ship blows up, and a gust knocks me into the waves.

chapter
FOUR

The first time I was lost at sea, I was unconscious.

Now, I snap awake with the knowledge that I have no idea where I am. I taste blood in the water and know it's mine. A few feet ahead is the shipwreck. It's the same ship that took me to Toliss Island to present me to my grandfather and the Sea Court. That took me to the Vanishing Cove. That brought me back to Coney Island.

Tumultuous waves pull me in different directions, but I keep my eyes trained on the burning ship and swim around it. All of its contents are spilling from the seams. Silverware, cannon balls, daggers, and the glass jars the urchin brothers collected. The rest is burned beyond recognition.

I see a familiar black mound and swim to it, each flick of my tail sending an agonizing shock through my body. Five, six, seven, I reach it. My backpack. I sling my arms through the straps. It's a tiny bit of hope, and I let it fill my head. I watch the wreckage, trying to spot Brendan or Kai or Arion. I wait and wait, but soon the flames eat at the wood like a match igniting a cigarette.

I want to shout their names, but I know better. My ears perk up at a distant echo. I haven't spent much time communicating underwater, but I know it isn't friendly. Poseidon, Vishnu, sweet Baby Jesus, I say. Please, please let my friends be safe.

The sharp cry gets louder. Nieve's merrows have found me. I can finally understand what they're saying. They can smell combat fire and my blood. They've found the champion's ship.

I swim up to the surface where it feels like I'm in the middle of a cloud. With the best breaststroke that won All-City Champ three years in a row, I head right into the mist.

When Brendan said the mist was terrifying, I didn't think he meant this.

The change is unnoticeable at first. Fog, thick and wet, envelops me. The cries of my hunters are replaced by whispers along my skin. Fish the size of marbles rise up from the depths and jump all around me. This is not a good time to be attracting fish like I'm the Snow White of the seven seas. Except these fish bite. The first one doesn't hurt, but then their white shimmering bodies become a swarm. I pull out my scepter and concentrate on its energy connected to mine. I thrust it outward and wait for the blinding white light to come from the crystal but it doesn't. The cold gold feels like lead in my hand, and the swarm comes down on me one more time, pulling me under.

I flash back to this one time at the aquarium in Coney Island. One of the demonstrators threw a hunk of bloody meat in the piranha tank, and within seconds, it was clean. If I don't get these things off me, I'm going to bleed out. I swipe at them with my tail, breaking their formation, but they come back together, pulling me down. I'm going to lose the mist. I scream in frustration as more of them appear out of thin water.

I give my scepter one more try, and this time I let everything I've been trying not to feel wash over me. I think about Layla, her eyes full of rage as Gwen held a knife to her throat. I think about Nieve, her moon-white face waiting expectantly because I was going to surrender to her. I think about the very first time my grandfather showed me the history of the kings in the pool of his chambers, my very first time at Toliss Island, and I know that I'm stronger than this. With a shudder, light bursts from the crystal of the scepter and the mass of marble piranhas dissolves into foam.

I look down at my arms and the red bites are gone.

It wasn't real. It wasn't real. It wasn't real.

But I'm farther down than I thought. I race back to the surface. I kick my tail as hard as I can, pushing against the pain in my bones, my arm stretched out for the finish line. The moment my hand breaks the surface and I touch the mist, I get sucked into its current.

chapter
FIVE

I can't remember the last time I went through a portal, but this one feels like I'm getting squeezed into a compact little box. When I come out in one piece, my whole body sighs.

I let the water push me onto the sandy shore.

I roll over and throw my backpack off.

The sand is white and soft and dotted with smooth oblong stones. I pick some up and sift them between my fingers. I shut my eyes and brace against the rip of my tail. Fiery numbness coats my skin and then stops at my upper thighs where I leave the scales because, even though I'm alone, I don't feel like running around an unknown island buck naked. I rub the scales on my knees and they dissolve into blue sand. It takes me two tries to stand up, and even then my legs shake.

I take it in. A white sun and purple moon hang at opposite ends of the sky, creating a gradient of night and day, as if the heavens are stuck. I suppose in a land hidden from the human plane, it's about right. A sea breeze guides me inland where patches of grass rise to calf length and a forest fans as wide as the shoreline and beyond.

I empty my backpack and take inventory of my weapons. A tiny knife that can fit in my palm. I won it from a redheaded demigoddess with an attitude. Some wet shirts and underwear—thanks, Mom, but I prefer my tail. Rope. Empty water bottle with my school's logo—the Thorne Hill Knight. A flattened bag of chips. And a red stone from Shelly, the sea oracle of Central Park.

I don't know what the stone does, but it was enough to raise the stakes of our poker game, which means it has to do something. I hold it in my palm and envision the source of its magic. Before I can stop myself, I imagine Gwen saying that magic is gradual and not instant. I roll my eyes at no one, and because the red stone does absolutely nothing, I throw it back into my bag. I readjust my harness, the wet leather cold on my skin.

I take a precarious step on the grass, hoping it doesn't give beneath me. The ground is solid, the grass dewy, like it rained not too long ago though there isn't a single cloud in the sky.

I wait for the call of birds, the whisper of insects, the rustle of hooves behind bushes. Something, anything that would let me know I am not alone in this place.

But I am alone, with only the trail ahead of me, a clear dirt path leading inland.

With every step I take, I wish for the familiar sound of Brooklyn sirens—the ambulance kind, not the magical kind—blaring down Surf Avenue.

I use my dagger to hack off a branch. In two strikes, the wood breaks and falls at my feet. Shimmering liquid seeps from the wound like honey. I let it fall on my open palm and it spills until the bark starts to heal itself, and slowly, the limb shows the tiniest sign of growth.

The branch at my feet has lost the color of the tree it was a part of. The leaves wither instantly and I slice off the bark so it feels like I'm holding a super long bone. A smile pulls at my mouth when I think of what my friends back home would say of my oversized staff. Then I keep walking, periodically hitting my staff between bushes to check for wildlife or anything else that might be looming in the shadows.

I walk.

And walk.

And wait.

And think. Maybe I should go back and search for my friends. Maybe I'm on the wrong island shrouded by magical mist. What if Kai and Brendan are still out there? No, they'd want me to keep going. What if Arion is dead and washed away to surf and tiny bits of flesh? Why don't we leave our whole selves behind? Why do we become nothing?

My head snaps up when I hear the rush of water. There's a waterfall nearby and waterfalls mean rivers. So then where the hell is the River Clan?

The waterfall is a spill of sunset colors. I scoop some water in my hands. It smells of the most intangible things, like dreams and promises. My tongue is as dry as bricks, and my throat raw and scratched. I drink the water in my palms. I fill up my bottle for later. I stick my head right into the waterfall, the weight of it pushing down and beating over my head. I let myself sink down on the slick boulders, and when I move my hands to push my hair back, I'm surprised at the stubble and remember that it's gone.

When my skin begins to feel numb, I make my way back to my backpack and freeze. I can feel something or someone watching me. I hold out my dagger and wade toward the bank. A panic floods me when I start wondering what kind of creatures live on this plane. I've seen shapeshifters and dragons and manic, crazy-ass split-tailed mermaids, so why not a ten-headed bear with a unicorn horn?

"I know you're there," I say.

Then I notice the strange ripples on the bank. Tiny frog-like creatures tinkle like glass when they hop. One of them breaks from the pack and lands in the water in front of me. I scoop it up. Its strange rubbery skin tickles. It stares at me, like it wonders who I am and what I'm doing here. I can see its insides, the tiny heart and lungs, and whatever fly it just ate. It ribbits then jumps back into the water. So much for my multiheaded unicorn bear.

But there's still a lot of land that I haven't seen and I don't know what's waiting for me there. For all I know, I'm not headed in the right direction. For all I know, everyone I know is dead and I'm never going to find the River Clan or get out of this place. My watch is dead at 11:53 a.m. and the white sun and purple moon haven't moved an inch, but it's still getting dark. Maybe there's a dimmer switch somewhere.

When I realize I'm talking to myself, a wet splash catches my attention. A fish, long and large like salmon but with rainbow-colored scales, floats on the stream. Bubbles trail out of its gaping mouth. The eye is the size of a quarter. It's dead. It had to come from up there in the waterfall because it surely didn't fall from the nearby trees.

"Great," I say, holding it across my palms. "I'm making the fish suicidal."

This is so fucked up but I'm hungry. I should have eaten when Blue offered, and the guilt is a knot in my stomach.

I pick a spot inside the first line of trees where the spray from the waterfall doesn't hit and a row of boulders make a natural fortress. Inside this forest, I stand and look up at the canopy. The trees go up for what feels like miles, hiding the bipolar sky.

Okay, you got this. For a fire, you need some wood. I didn't come all this way to freeze and starve to death on an island outside of time. The leaves are still damp, which will prove the most difficult. I lay my fish on a flat stone the size of a dinner plate. A real merman would sink his teeth into the fish, but I've never been a fan of sushi. I gather large rocks and make a ring around my pile of sticks.

I stare at my fish.

I stare at my rocks.

I have this sinking feeling of inadequacy.

And then I grab my scepter and hold it by the hilt, pointing it at my unlit fire pit. I search for the spark, the power, the thing that has made me special for the last couple of days, and it isn't there. When

Kai said unstable, I didn't think that would apply to my big, ancient weapon. It was working just fine when I fought with Kurt—

"Why are you doing this to me now?" I ask it.

Then I throw it on the ground.

I grab my backpack and fling it away from me, the contents spilling over fallen leaves and wet moss.

I take a swing at the tree.

What the fuck has this tree ever done to me?

Nothing.

But I hit it again. It hurts like hell. But this is the kind of pain that I can take. I hit it again and picture Kurt's face. Nieve. Archer.

Warm blood trickles down my hand and wraps around my wrist. I picture my grandfather, the king—his face that looks just like mine. My eyes. My mother's eyes. Everything he told me was a lie. He didn't choose me because he wanted to. He chose me because he couldn't choose Kurt. Instead, he made Kurt my guardian. Some guardian he turned out to be.

I'm spent. And I can't feel my hand. The tree is untouched, unhurt. The bark is red with my blood.

I can't uncurl my fingers. Shaking, I go back to the water and wash my wound.

I go back to my camp and retrieve my things. I hold the red stone, wondering why Shelly would want me to have this. She must have known I would need it. I rub it, feeling stupid at the thought that it'll produce a genie. Instead of a cloud of smoke that grants me wishes, I feel its heat. I strike it against a stone on my fire pit and there it is—the spark. I strike it again, and the spark turns into a flame.

My non-cut-up, non-bruised good hand is on fire.

I drop the flaming stone into the fire pit and make a second trip to the waterfall. The breeze carries a strange sound with it—soft laughter. I concentrate on singling it out, but there's still no one. I settle on the fact that the breeze is alive and laughing at me.

I can feel the dregs of the healing water from the springs of Eternity healing my burn. The water here doesn't heal instantly the way the water from the Springs did. And the last bits that I drank before the battle seem to be exhausted. That's the end of Eternity.

Back at my camp, I take Triton's dagger and scale the fish, as best as I remember from the time I worked at Poseidon's, a seafood market in Coney Island to pay for the dent I put on my dad's Mustang. Poseidon's is closed and boarded up, but I still remember the gist. It makes my stomach turn, and the scales around my wrists and ankles run for cover.

By the time I chop off the head, I don't have much meat left. I find three thin, sturdy branches for skewers. I flash cook the fillet and sink my teeth into it. I'd kill for some Chulita hot sauce. My buddy Jerry's mom always keeps a large bottle on her table. I could drink it like water.

I don't know if it's the comfort of the food or the warmth of the fire, but my eyelids are heavy. An alarming jolt shoots through my skin. What if the fish is poisonous? The drowsiness a side effect? Leave it to me to eat a poisonous fish. My throat feels itchy, my chest tight. I lean back into the soft grass. I can't keep my eyes—

chapter
SIX

A thousand ants are biting at my skin. I try to brush them away, but when I touch my arm, I find I'm weightless, see-through, and back in the sea. The edges of my vision are hazy, like looking through foggy glass.

Though there's nothing foggy about Kurt—swimming right in front of me.

Kurt looks behind himself, then forward, and says, "I can't."

Can't? Can't what? Can't betray your nephew, your friend?

Ex-friend.

Then he starts going back to Coney Island. I know it is Coney Island like I know the sky is blue. He's going back to Lucine. After all of that, he's going back to his thousand-year-old oracle girlfriend.

I guess I can understand. If it were Layla, I'd go back to her. Only Layla isn't crazy or on a power trip. She's just a girl.

She's just my girl.

I try to swim toward Kurt, but I'm immobilized. I have no voice. And yet the urge to knock his teeth out is overwhelming.

Kurt swims over a large rock formation and freezes. Something is stirring nearby. He can smell them. I can tell by the way he lifts his nose toward the surface and the cloud of bubbles trailing from his quickly shutting gills.

The surface is a thin beacon of light that barely makes it down here. Kurt's shoulder-length hair is tied back, the ends billowing in the soft current. For a second I think he's looking right at me with those bright violet eyes. But my vision pans farther out and I can see what has his attention—a group of merrows with clawed hands and feet that are climbing over boulders. Their slick bodies are deceptive. I've been on the other end of their punches, and their skin is like sandpaper. Nieve's children, fully grown with hammerheads and strong bodies. Some even have the tails of sharks, others the hands of humans or the heads of eels. They smell the blood trickling from the nicks and cuts on Kurt's forearms.

They circle him, snapping at the space between them and their prey with those sharp, yellow teeth. Kurt doesn't move.

Kurt is a warrior. If that were me, I'd swim up and have them chase me until I found a diversion and could take them out one by one. Not him though. I recognize the smirk on his severe face from our own fights. The kind of smile that tells his opponent he's going to win and they're going to lose. He raises the Trident of the Skies. The merrows swim back a foot, but they hold their ground.

And then nothing.

Kurt is holding one of the most powerful weapons in the seas. It's the head of the trident that gives the Sea King his power. The same weapon he used to get rid of our enemy hours ago, the same weapon he used to stop me from saving Layla. It sparks and sizzles like the last burst of a firework. Then it dies. The three prongs are an oversized fork in his dumb hands.

It's the same thing I discovered when fighting Leomaris. The trident has lost its power. Hey, at least it's not just me, and I feel a little better watching him struggle. But why can I see him? Am I making this up?

I reach for a weapon at my side that isn't there. He can't possibly take on all those merrows at once. And then I panic, water filling my lungs as my gills shut. I'm sinking, the sea floor opening beneath me. I shout his name— *"Kurt!"*—and he snaps his eyes in my direction. I feel his eyes on my face as the merrows attack him. And Kurt, with the Trident of the Skies in one hand and a broadsword in the other, swims headfirst into their jaws.

chapter
SEVEN

The water in my lungs is real.

It's raining.

I roll over on my side and cough.

What was that? The last I saw was Kurt's sword impaling a merrow. I could feel myself there, lurking like a shadow. Now I'm here in my camp, holding the scepter in my hand. The fire has died. I sift through the wet ashes for the stone and it's still there, good as new. I check my watch, but it's still 11:53 a.m.

A swift movement catches my eye. A bright green leaf full of nuts and berries and a fuzzy orange worm, not the gummy kind, are carefully placed on a slab of rock beside my fire pit.

"You can show yourself," I shout to the woods and the river. The only sign of life is in the brush of wind on leaves, the constant rush of stream into the waterfall, and my heart beating at an irregular pace. Still, I felt something—someone—nearby. Or maybe it was the effects of dreaming of Kurt. Maybe this place will make me crazy before I find the River Clan. Before I can find the key to the Sleeping Giants. Before I can save the day, save the girl. I stare at the woods and the sky like they're an optical illusion and I'm the one who can't see the hidden image. Then I whisper to no one, "Please."

I grab a berry and hold it between my fingers. I squeeze too hard, and a clear, syrupy liquid oozes down my hand. The thought that the berries are poisoned crosses my mind. Then again, if someone took the time to gather me some breakfast, they could have killed me in my sleep. I pop it in my mouth, mostly to get rid of the terrible taste of morning breath, but also because the scraps of fish I ate before I crashed were not enough. When I reach out to grab another berry, a strange bird swoops down and snatches it.

"Hey!"

A head with a long, golden beak and glossy black eyes is attached to a six-inch neck. Its shimmery feathers remind me of oil slicks after it rains in Brooklyn. Then its body becomes hard, like lizard skin in bright yellow and green splatters that change with the light. The berry goes down its gob and it grabs another, this time giving it to me.

"Thanks," I say.

He nods. I swear the dragon-bird nods at me. It pecks at the boulder a dozen times and then flies into the air, swooping into an arc and stopping on a branch. The bird makes a deep sound, like the lowest B flat on a piano, and flaps thin, filmy wings. I strap on my weapons and gather my strewn possessions back into my backpack. The dragon-bird returns to the rock, this time swallowing the fuzzy orange worm in one gulp.

"Gross," I say. "I'm coming, I'm coming."

See, this is the kind of sidekick I needed from the beginning. Animals are much more trustworthy than mermen or people. You have your singing dragons, your loyal crabs, your helpful mice that can sew. I mean, I'm a sea prince, for fuck's sake.

I break into a run on the flat, green path between the forest and the river. Tiny shimmering insects rise from the stream and swarm around me, curious but non-threatening, then fall behind. The land goes on for miles. The sky has its blend of sunsets. The moon and sun and stars hang like mobiles waiting for a breeze. I keep my breath steady and my eyes on the lizard-bird. I can hear drums in the distance and I know I'm on to something. The clan is so close—

Then my foot gets caught and I tumble forward into a pool of mud. I remember the obstacle course at the end-of-the-semester gym class. The mud pit always gets me. I kick but the mud pit feels like suction, pulling me down a drain. My lizard-bird chirps happily nearby. I spit out the mud and shout, "You little shit! You led me here!"

He cocks his head and snaps at me before taking off from his perch and heading all the way into the sky. The last sound the bird makes definitely sounds like a laugh.

"Wait! Come back!"

I shut my mouth because I'm sinking more. My skin is starting to itch. Long branches poke my legs. At least, I hope they're branches, not the bones of other poor souls that met the same fate. Because this is not how I plan to go. Not in a mud pit. I stab my dagger as far as I can out of the pit and try to pull myself up. The ground is so soft that I might as well be slicing pie.

I calm my breathing and grab at the long grass around me. It comes out from the roots, but the sinking feeling loosens up.

I've got this. I get into the rhythm of grabbing and pulling and grabbing and pulling. It occurs to me that I'm running out of nearby grass when a growl rumbles through the forest. Birds take flight. Glass frogs jump away from the stones and into the river. The forest's edge moves. Something snarls in the shadows.

This is it's trap and I'm in it.

I can smell the dried mud on its fur, the fresh blood on its teeth.

No, the mud isn't going to take me.

The beast is—

Long talons grab for my outstretched hand, and I jerk back into the mud. The B flat of the lizard-bird rings in timeless day. I grab my dagger and swing out, but it slices through air and I can't reach much further.

A body—thank Poseidon—a human body lunges at the beast. He tucks and rolls between its hind legs, then jumps on the creature, which throws him right off in a second. The beast leaps over the blond guy. It lays a scaly paw on his chest and lowers its face so I can finally see it—a creature I have no name for. The head of a dragon and a reptilian coarse hide, with long claws that could shred a mountain to a pebble. I blink to make sure I'm seeing straight. From the belly on, the beast has the golden hind legs of a lion and a sea serpent's long, curling tail. It opens its long snout over my rescuer's face, saliva dribbling all over him. I try to grab on to solid ground, the suction of the pit pulling on me like the tide. Between Blondie, me, and the lizard-bird, I can't tell whose screams are whose as we wait for the death bite that never comes.

The beast leaps sideways and dashes back into the forest, disappearing into its shadows.

Blondie gets up at once, readying his staff to chase after it.

"Hey!" I shout. "Come back!"

He turns around. I'm hit with a wave of familiarity. I know his face. And from the shock on his, he knows mine.

"Lord Tristan," he says, kneeling.

"Save the formalities for later, Dylan," I say to the until-now-missing Champion of the West. His blond hair falls over his blue eyes, and I wonder if he's been here all this time.

I grab onto the staff he extends, and he pulls me onto solid ground.

"Best wash this muck off," he says. "It'll burn your flesh right off when it hardens."

Then he points to a spot on his leg where the scales don't grow around the burn.

"Good to know," I say, then jump into the river.

chapter
EIGHT

How did you find me?" Dylan asks, ripping the meat off the bone of a rabbit-like creature he caught in one of his many booby traps. About a mile from where the mud pit is, Dylan has made a fort in a small clearing. He's got a proper roasting spit and a hammock of woven vines. It's like he's hiding from the wild right smack in the middle of it.

He looks slimmer than the last time I saw him. What is it about this championship that takes the life out of us? The thin platinum band on his forehead is tarnished, and a long, pearly scar marks an X on the right side of his chest. The firelight makes the powder blue scales on his arms glisten. Even though we're not in the water, we wear them on our shins and forearms like banner shields.

"No offense, man," I say, "but I wasn't exactly looking for you."

He holds his hands over the flames and stares. The red stone is a bright ember in the center, like an all-seeing eye.

"Right." He forces a smile. "I thought that since I've been here for, what? Months? A year? Can't keep track of the days when the sun and moon don't move. I have no knowledge of what's happening out there—"

I cross my hands into a T. "Hold up. Months? Are you kidding? You think you've been here for months and you haven't gone back?"

Dylan shakes his head. "I can't find a way out! Every time I swim into the ocean, it spits me back onto the white beach. I've walked all over the island, and nothing. There was supposed to be a clan here, but if there is one, they haven't shown themselves to me because I've tried. I have."

The last bit sounds more like he's trying to convince himself rather than me. Dylan slumps a bit and I can see how tired he is. He's a full beard away from being a castaway.

"Then the championship hasn't ended." Dylan looks behind me to where the quartz scepter is strapped to my back. "Of course it hasn't or you wouldn't be here."

"You haven't been here for months," I tell him.

His head snaps up and confusion makes his face scrunch up.

"Twelve days." I stoke the fire and eat some more of the rabbit. It's sweet and tender.

He holds his head in his hands. "He should never have made me come here."

"Who?"

Fire crackles and pops. I use my staff to turn the logs.

"My father." The lion merman swallows and starts. "After we left Toliss, my father—the herald of the Western Seas—had everything planned out. He said the oracles were in the most obvious of our sacred places. We would start at the Glass Castle. But when I got there, the oracle was gone. Instead we were attacked by a sea dragon—"

"Been there," I say, laughing.

"I knew there was something strange about all this. Why wouldn't the king simply give you the throne? You are his true kin. My father said it was because he would—he would not allow it. None of the heralds would have a human-raised boy on our throne."

I nod, keeping my eyes on him. He looks broken. Something inside him is changed forever, and he doesn't know how to deal with it. That's why he's here. Because he's got a good heart, a fighting heart. I could use a merman like Dylan on my side.

"So we kept searching for an oracle. My father's councilman thought about this land. The Vale of Tears. What better place to hide an oracle but a place outside of time? But on our way here, we were attacked by dozens of merrows. I didn't know what they were at first. I'd only heard about them. They're not supposed to grow so large. They were on their way landside and I couldn't—I knew the terror they'd wreak on land so I turned my army from my father's and followed them. That's when more of them arrived and took my father's ship. I barely got away, swimming right into the mist."

"What did you see in the mist?"

But he doesn't answer. Instead his eyes flick around the dark then back at me. "What about you? Have you seen the merrows?"

I laugh again. I can't help but laugh. Champions. We're supposed to be kings and here we are, eating skinny rabbit creatures and hiding from beasts. So I tell him. All of it. From the moment I shifted in the bathtub and Kurt and Thalia came into my life to take me to Toliss. Looking for the oracle, the merrows attacking my school. How the princesses showed up and made the student body crazy. Gwen and how she helped me find Shelly. Shelly giving me the scepter. The strange marketplace at the Vanishing Cove. The promise I made to the nautilus maid—that part I keep to myself.

The rest comes pouring out of me. I tell him of my courting the mermaid princesses. How Adaro came to Coney. How Nieve killed him. How we found the eldest oracle, Lucine—then Kurt.

By the end of it, I'm spent. I stare at the fire, the red eye, the wood consuming itself, and I wonder if I could have changed any of it.

"Kurtomathetis is King Karanos's son?" Dylan marvels.

I nod once.

"There were rumors of how strange Kurtomathetis was in that family. Thalia had their mother's gift of speaking to sea animals. Their father could control fire, a gift so rare it was only passed on to sons. But it died with him, didn't it?"

I don't want to talk about Kurt. "So you've been here all this time and you haven't found the river folk?"

"More like they don't want to be found." Dylan shakes his head. "The tribe is hidden in the center of the land, but I can't get deep enough into the woods without arriving back where I started. It's like I'm going in circles! There's the beast, which the councilman failed to mention. It nearly got me when I first got here. But there are plenty of fish in the river. Game in the forest. Berries in the bushes. It rains and I believe that marks the beginning of the day."

"Then it's a good thing I showed up. You saved me from the lion-dragon-beast thing, and when I get out of here, you'll be able to go back home."

"The trident pieces have been found, Lord Tristan," he says. "I don't think I'll be much use as another champion."

I give him a light punch on the shoulder. "You are seriously not seeing what I'm seeing. You're a great fighter. Better than Kurt. He's like a ballerina with a sword. All you had is a carved piece of wood! Consider yourself hired when we get back to our world."

Dylan smirks at my words. He holds on tightly to his staff, looking up at the mobile sky. At the tiny home he's built for himself. Then it hits me: it's not that he can't get out. It's that he doesn't want to.

I say, "Time out. You've been here playing survivor this whole time while the rest of us are trying to see this championship through, and now that I'm offering a way out, you'd rather stay in the Land before Time?"

"You don't even have a way out! You're barely in!" When Dylan shouts, the vein in his neck pops out.

"Oh, it's like that, right?"

"It's like what?" He gets up and takes a step out of our circle. "I didn't ask for you to come here. I didn't ask for my father to choose me instead of my brother. Now they're both dead because I failed at the one thing I was supposed to do as his heir. I can't go back to my people."

He sits on the ground with his back to me. Something stirs out there. Perhaps it's the beast and its trusty lizard-bird. Or maybe it's the Vale itself giving me a warning. Either way, I keep my dagger in hand and rack my brain for something good to say to Dylan.

"I'm sorry about your family," I say. "But you still have the people of your court who are fighting the silver mermaid. Family is a lot more than blood and DNA. Not that you would know about DNA because merpeople don't have biology class. And I'm not entirely sure what they would teach you in mer high school other than advanced swimming and sword fighting and that nobody likes dragons."

"I don't understand the things you say, Lord Tristan," Dylan says, trying to suppress his laughter. He gets up from his self-imposed time-out then comes back to the fireside. "Do you know the last thing my father and I fought about?"

I shake my head. My dad and I have only had one fight. It was over whether or not I should get a summer job as a lifeguard. I never understood why my parents got so nervous when I kept pushing to see how far out I could swim until now.

"We fought about my place in our court. I told him I didn't want to be like him, with the next thousand years of my life mapped out for me." Dylan takes the platinum band off his head and holds it in his hands. "He even had a princess all picked out! And she moved right into my chambers without even asking if I wanted her there."

The forest has gotten so quiet that not even the wind makes a peep.

"What did she have, bad teeth?" I set down my dagger. "Oh man, was she one of those octo-maids, because multiple hands might not be a bad thing."

"Lord Tristan!"

"Just call me Tristan."

"The problem with the princess—" Dylan seems to be listening to voices in his head. He looks down at his feet and swallows the dryness from his tongue. "The problem was that she was a princess. My father turned down my choice of stethos because he was from a lesser family."

I raise my hand. "What the hell is a stethos?"

That word sparks a memory of Sarabell. The minute I think of her, I think of Adaro, then Leomaris. The blue flames. Arion.

Then Dylan pushes me on the ground.

"What the f—"

"Tristan," Dylan says, but he's not looking at me.

A dozen warriors surround us, their skin as see-through as glass and their bows pulled tightly, arrows aimed right at our heads.

chapter
NINE

Warriors surround us. Their armor is green leather. Their skin is nearly translucent. I can see the outline of ribs, lungs, and hearts beating. The River Clan.

I raise my hands, but that makes half of them turn their arrows on me.

"Wait a minute, guys," I say. "We've been looking for you."

"I don't think they want to talk," Dylan warns.

"I'm Tristan Hart and this is Dylan of the Western Seas—"

One of the warriors steps forward. I wonder how fast I can reach for my dagger. She raises a blade and, with one swipe at me, cuts the leather bound around my chest. My harness falls off into her hands. My weapons clink against each other.

Not fast enough, I guess.

"We know who you are, Land Prince," the girl says. Her face is no longer translucent but brown. Her irises are like the black and amber swirls in tiger stone. She knocks the wind from me with a single hit in the solar plexus.

While I choke, someone pulls my arms back and binds my wrists together. Dylan falls beside me. She pokes me with Dylan's staff.

"If you wanted to tie us up, you just had to ask," I say.

She hits me again, and this time it hurts too much to speak. Her warriors laugh. One lights a torch with the flames from our fire. Another blindfolds us.

"Thank you," I say to the blindfolder. "I forgot my sunglasses at home. Damn UV rays, really bad for you."

That elicits another blow to my back.

"A little lower," I say. "I have all these kinks from my last explosion."

I feel hands pushing me forward and hear the quick feet of Dylan beside me. "Do you want them to tear you apart?" he asks.

"Can't make it too easy for them," I say.

"You guys should try out my weapons," I shout to the leader. "They slice through bone really nicely."

"And have my flesh burned off when I touch one of them?" she asks. "Keep walking."

"Damn, there goes my maniacal plan," I say as hands shove me. "What's your plan? My parents are pretty middle class so we don't have much in the way of ransom. My college fund won't get you much in this economy."

"Can I put an arrow through his jaw?" A dude's voice comes from somewhere in the back. "His babbling offends the river gods."

"Sorry, river gods!"

"Lord Sea," Dylan hisses.

For his benefit, I stop talking. Brendan didn't mention anything about angry see-through people. What have I gotten myself into?

A hand presses against my chest. We must be at another waterfall because it sounds like water rushing everywhere. When my blindfold is cut off, I know I'm right. Here the trees grow thicker and lower to the ground.

"Where's your merry band of lost boys and girls?" I ask.

The others have vanished, but Tiger Eyes is beside a wall covered in ivy.

"You talk much for someone who's lost the things he loves the most."

Her smile grows bigger when I don't have a comeback.

"I didn't lose things," I growl.

"So you *can* be serious."

When she stands directly in front of the ivy, it parts like a curtain.

"A tunnel," I say. "Of course."

"You first."

I hesitate.

"You haven't spent much time in darkness, have you?"

"Only at the water park," I say, swinging my feet into the opening. "The Slip 'N Slide is my favorite."

"Then slip and slide, Land Prince," she says.

"Will you untie my hands at least?"

"Of course, Land Prince. But first get in."

I sit at the mouth of the tunnel. It angles down and off to the side. She slices through my ropes. Before I can say another word, she shoves me down the hole.

chapter
TEN

I must've hit my head. The numbness on my skin returns. My temples throb, and the foggy edges of my vision are back. I instantly recognize my grandfather's chambers in Toliss Island. This time I'm looking at Gwen. Her face is pale and sad. Gray eyes are cast down at her lap. She's in human form with white and black scales at her ankles.

"Gwenivere!"

She snaps her head up and stands. Her hair is gathered into a braid at the top of her head. Pearls and shells are woven like a crown. Her dress is an ivory sheath that shows her scales at her calves. Princess Gwenivere in all her splendor. The daughter of the silver mermaid.

"Are you listening to us?"

I know that voice anywhere by now. Nieve's slithering voice fills the cave of the room.

"Forgive me, Mother."

Nieve swims in a backlit pool. The Staff of Eternity is in her hands. She's not the weak and frail mermaid of weeks ago. A blush colors her ivory cheekbones, and her pale eyes spark with frenzied energy. But when she tries to channel her magic through the staff, nothing happens. Her forehead crinkles with concentration, and I want to laugh because her third of the trident is failing too.

"Mother, what is it?"

"Something is wrong—the boy must be doing it."

Gwen shakes her head. "We both know Tristan isn't capable of that."

I resent that.

"Perhaps you exhausted yourself with the battle, taking the island, keeping La—the girl—conscious. Even you have your limits."

"I don't want to have limits," Nieve seethes. "I want to be limitless."

Archer runs into the room. His jaw is bruised where Kurt hit him the day before, but the rest of him is patched up. He kneels before Nieve and she strokes his patchwork face, her own creation. "It's done, Mother Queen. Anyone who has opposed us is in the cells."

"And my brother?"

"The king is gone," he says nervously. "There is no sign of him."

Nieve reaches into her well of power. It fills me with a rage I've never felt before. Then she releases it at Archer. He slams into the white stone wall. Gwen stands to tend to him, but after one look at Nieve, she sits back down.

"What was that, my child?"

"Karanos," the merrow groans, standing at attention. "The leech Karanos is gone."

Nieve holds her hands to her face. "You see what he makes me do? He makes me hurt my own children."

Archer comes back for more, this time on both knees, placing his head on his mother's lap. He's so big. He could squeeze the life out of her with one hand. But despite all of it, she made him. She saved him when the Sea Court decreed that all children born deformed—merrows—would be executed or left in caves where they would not be able to survive in the wilderness.

I try to shake Nieve's thoughts out of me, but it's like we're one person.

She moves her tail in the pool, as if she sees something in the water. "I know my brother. I know where he will go. Gwenivere, you will go after him. As for the girl—"

The girl. The girl. The girl.

"Is she awake yet?"

Archer nods. "Do you want me to break her?"

"No!" Gwen stands. "She'll be worthless unless she's untouched. Tristan—"

"Tristan will do as I say as long as I have her. Her condition means nothing to me."

"But—"

"Your infatuation with the boy is clouding your better judgment," Archer says.

Gwen steels herself. "I am not infatuated."

Gwen and Archer are face to face. He's twice her size, but Gwen is drawing on her magic. Sparks fly from her fingertips.

"There's that fire, my darling girl." Nieve chuckles. "We'll need it to bring our people together. For too long we've cowered before my brother and his love of humans. Send out more search parties for Tristan. He can't have gone far."

"What about Kurtomathetis?" Gwen says.

Nieve keeps her hands on the staff, gripping it and searching for the magic. "My allies tell me he will bow to me before sunrise."

"What allies?"

Nieve studies Gwen's beautiful face. The thin, pearly scars that run down the right side of her face, shoulder to hip bone. "You have never questioned me before."

Gwen lowers her head. She takes Nieve's hand and holds it to her face, kissing the center of her palm. "I mean no offense, Mother Queen."

Nieve looks at Archer and Gwen in a way that makes my skin crawl. It's the way that my mother looks at me, like no matter what I do, she'll love me forever. I didn't think the silver mermaid was capable of feeling. I don't want to think of her this way. I don't want to think of her at all.

"Go now," Nieve tells Gwen.

And she does, leaving Archer in the glittering room that once was my grandfather's chamber.

"The girl, Mother Queen?"

Nieve winces. Presses her hand to her forehead. A drop of red stains the pristine blue of her pool. She rubs the red stain between her fingers. Their voices become distant, like we're on opposite ends of a dark tunnel.

"Break her."

chapter
ELEVEN

L ord Sea."

Hands lift my face and smack my cheeks.

"Lord—Tristan, wake up!"

I open my eyes to Dylan looking over me. Tiger Eyes is at his side. The white sun beats down on us. I sit up and my head throbs where a bump has formed beneath a gash. Bright red blood comes away on my fingertips. I smear them on the grass.

"Where are we?"

"You weren't breathing," Tiger Eyes says. "The Lion breathed air back into your body."

CPR. Dylan gave me CPR.

"Thanks, man."

"Are you going to tie us up again?" I ask, willing my head to stop spinning. I stand and dust grass and pebbles off my ass and legs.

"I think we understand each other now." She slings her bow around one shoulder and holds my belt of weapons firmly in the other hand.

Dylan and I walk on either side of her. Since neither of us know where the hell we're going, we should just let her lead, even though I have a tendency to walk ahead. She didn't answer when I asked her where we are, and I know she's not going to tell me. My best guess is we're in the middle of the Vale of Tears, where the River Clan is. Here the sun is brighter, at a high noon, and the moon is a crescent resting on the horizon.

Everything is the new, wet green of spring. The earth is soft, almost too soft for my quick, heavy New York City footsteps. Countless thin streams run like snakes across the ground. I can't see where they end, but I bet I could walk for miles and still not find it.

"At least you ditched your toy soldiers," I say, wanting to keep our conversation light.

But I've spoken too soon.

Figures rise out of the stream, liquid molding into the flesh of men and women. They're translucent at first, like glass mannequins with their insides showing. Then they're solid, skin ranging from pinks and algae blues to browns and white. All of them, men and women, braid their long black hair in thick braids that end at their tailbones.

"That's different," I say.

"Come," Tiger Eyes says.

The warriors walk around Dylan and me. I liked it better when it was just the three of us. At least Tiger Eyes throws me a smile every now and then.

"Finally, he's shocked into silence," one of the guys says.

But it's not them that keep me quiet. It's the thought of Nieve telling Archer to break her.

And me here, unable to go to her.

My insides are painful, bloody knots ready to burst.

So I focus on our footsteps. The trees are wilder here, tall and weeping over scattered ponds of water and the snake-like streams. The rush of the river is close by. And the sun is a white disk in a cloudless turquoise sky.

"Are we there yet?" I ask three times until I can pinpoint the guy who wanted to shoot an arrow through my jaw. I make a mental note of him—the one with the greenish pallor and muddy brown eyes. My hand itches for my dagger.

"We're here," Tiger Eyes says. Here is a stone and wood archway.

A curtain of vines gives way to our troop, and when we walk in, a small village of people is waiting for us.

They're wonderful to look at—some in their semi-fluid form and others in solid colors that match the woods. I suddenly imagine being a kid and trying to play hide and seek. No one would win.

A woman with skin like beaten leather, eyes as dark as earth and violet hair braided to her hip bones, breaks from the crowd.

"Land Prince," she says to me, her voice thick like smoke. The kind of voice that can soothe a child's ache but then turn around and sentence a man to death. "Son of the Western Seas," she says to Dylan. "I am Isi, leader of the River Clan."

"Ih-sea," I repeat.

She nods gracefully. "Welcome."

"Welcome?" I ask. "Do you bind and blindfold all your welcome guests?"

"You cannot blame us for wanting to keep our home secret and safe."

A hundred eyes descend on me.

I straighten my posture. "I would have come willingly. I came here for you."

Isi nods. "You want our secrets."

"Yes."

"There are many steps to this, Tristan Hart."

"I will take them."

The old woman and Tiger Eyes smile at each other, like they're sharing an inside joke. "So eager. Eagerness is foolish. Though I am told it's part of your charm, as far as charm will take you."

I like making jokes, but I don't like being the butt of them. "Good men died to get me here. I won't leave until you help me."

"Men?" Isi repeats it like she's not sure she heard me right. She stares at me for a long time. They all do. I've spent my whole life trying to be in the spotlight, but this kind of scrutiny makes my insides shake because I want—no—I need their approval.

"Come," Isi says finally. "Be judged by our Elder Council."

I swallow. "Judged?"

"Make yourself at home, Lion," Tiger Eyes tells Dylan. Then she throws my weapons on the ground and I pick up the cut harness.

Dylan looks like he doesn't know whether to stay or take his chances with the beast back on the outer ring.

When Isi steps into the village, the crowd parts for her. Tiger Eyes follows and I'm a close third, keeping my eyes on the back of Tiger Eyes' head. I feel like schoolyard rules apply to islands outside of time. Don't look at anyone the wrong way, and you'll live another day. I could be looking at the scenery, but I'm sure I'm not missing much other than trees, and we have those back home. I don't realize how nervous I am until we reach a giant tent.

Isi holds the flap-door aside, and all I can think is that it leads into a black hole. But like all things, this is a test. A judgment. I have to see it through.

Plus, they gave me my weapons back, so they're okay, right?

I step inside and am overcome by the smell of old leather and herbs. A hunched figure with a black veil sits at the center. My heart is racing like a jackrabbit in mating season. I'm covered in a cold sweat.

Isi and Tiger Eyes sit on either side of the veiled woman. Then they're joined by a fourth shape that slithers from the ground, first liquid, then changing into the warrior that wanted to skewer me on the way here. By the look on his grumbly face, I can tell we're going to be fast friends.

"Do the rest of you have names?" I ask.

The veiled woman nods. "As the tree and the sky have names, we are called many things."

"I just need one."

"Sit, Tristan Hart," Isi says.

So I do.

Tiger Eyes is fighting a smile as she says, "I am Yara."

Grumble says, "I am Karel." But I much prefer Grumble or, you know, Hater.

I wipe my forehead with the back of my hand, but it doesn't help much. "Has anyone ever told you that you guys come on a little strong?"

"Has anyone ever told you that you talk too much?" Grumble says.

"Yes," I answer honestly.

Isi wants to smile. I know she does. Instead, she gets down to business.

"You are here to attain something from us."

Maybe my body is getting used to the heat in the tent, or maybe as my eyes adjust to the darkness, I'm not as nervous. "How'd you guess?"

"No one comes to the Vale of Tears without wanting something. We're a cursed land."

"Cursed by—?"

"King Karanos. Your grandfather."

I look down at my lap. "Of course. But you're not exactly merpeople. Unless you have tails somewhere down there."

Yara lifts her chin. She wants to smack me but can't. If I've learned one thing these past few weeks, it's that sea people take their secret meetings seriously. "We are older than the children of Poseidon. We are of the river. We are eternal."

"So you can go from water to solid. But you're not merpeople. But you belong to the Sea Court." I nod, trying to make sure I got it all straight.

"You make our trials sound trivial," Grumble says.

"I'm not. I'm trying to understand."

"When the silver princess rebelled and attacked the crown," Isi says, "we were caught in the middle. We helped her control her magic, and as punishment, the court claims one of our daughters every mortal year."

"And we have to hide here and lose more kin to the beast," Karel adds.

"That charming thing that almost ate me and Dylan?"

"The Naga. She is also part of our punishment. She eats more and more of our warriors when the dark falls over the Vale."

"None of you can kill her?"

They shake their heads in unison, but it's Isi who speaks. "She is cursed to roam the forest until we are freed of her by a direct child of Triton."

Their eyes settle on me. Is it getting hot in here? "Me."

If it gets them to help me with the Sleeping Giants, save Layla, and beat my enemies, I'll go get that beast right now.

"What are we doing here then?" I unsheathe Triton's dagger. "Point me in the right direction."

Grumble chuckles. Then it catches on with the others, even the woman under the veil, and all four of them are seconds from melting into laughing puddles.

"I wasn't being funny."

They go on laughing.

"I'm serious!"

"Our warriors have been after the Naga for endless days," Isi says. "Do you think a boy could do better?"

But I know the answer she wants. She wants a yes, because I'm pretty sure this boy is the one they've been waiting for.

"You just said—"

"We said 'a child of Triton,'" the veiled woman says in her raspy voice. "That is you."

"So—"

Isi cuts me off. "That doesn't mean you're ready to go against the Naga."

"I'll get ready. As we speak, Nieve is doing more and more damage. She's taken over Toliss Island." I point to the tent door, but I might as well be pointing to the North Pole because direction means nothing here.

"The Silver Queen will get nowhere without that—"

They look at my scepter.

No, but if I don't show, she'll get Layla. Break her.

"Tonight we will welcome you to our people," Isi says, holding her hands out to touch my face. "Then you will give yourself to us, body and soul, for training. Your world is not going anywhere without you. Not while you're here. Do you accept?"

I'm not sure if they are the kind of people you shake hands with. But I know that words mean a lot more in these strange worlds than they do back home. "I accept."

chapter
TWELVE

The village is riled up after our arrival. The electricity in the air reminds me of the minutes before prom. Girls with crowns of leaves and branches walk past me whispering behind their hands. They could make themselves invisible, but they want to be seen. And I've never been one to shy away, so I offer my best Tristan Hart smile.

The judgy elders don't follow me out of the tent, which makes them the worst hosts in the Vale of Tears.

Or they trust me enough not to raze their village when left to my own devices.

Even though I'm miles away from Coney Island, I still feel like one of the freaks on display at the sideshow. Hundreds of eyes follow me as I walk through the tents, along paths lined with smooth stones.

When I hear my name, I freeze. I'm dreaming. I have to be.

Brendan and Kai—clean and clothed in the green leather of the tribe—push their way through the scattered throngs of villagers to get to me.

"You're alive!" I say, seconds away from pulling them into an after-school-special group hug. But I'm keenly aware of the villagers watching our every move.

"Can't let you have all the fun, now can I?" Brendan says, patting my back. "Arion?"

I shake my head. We look down at our feet. Kai holds on to my hand and squeezes for a while.

"Have either of you seen Dylan?" I ask. "I found him on the outer ring. How did you guys get here?"

They lead the way through the clearing. They're so—happy. Unburdened. How can they be, with all that's going on?

"Dylan is pillaging the food supply," Brendan says. "Cousin, this place is marvelous. These people are marvelous. Everything is—"

"Marvelous?" I finish for him.

He nods rapidly. His turquoise eyes are glossy and dilated. Perhaps it's all this fresh air.

"I've nearly forgotten," Brendan says. "It's time for the falls!"

"Time for what falls?" I pull him back from the direction he's going and close our triangle so I can whisper.

"We've been invited by the daughters of the tribe to attend. Come now."

"We can't go to any falls." I hold his arm so he won't run off. "We have to figure out what's going on here."

Brendan slings his arms around Kai and me. His smile is infectious. "What did Isi tell you?"

"She said they would welcome me to the village tonight and then start my training to kill the beast."

He smacks my back. "See? Let's go to the falls."

"Why don't you go," Kai says playfully, "and I'll take Tristan to our tent. We'll meet you there."

Brendan gives us a thumbs-up then sprints down through the trees, his red hair a beacon in the green.

"Did he smoke their magic mushroom?" I ask Kai.

"It's this place, Tristan," she says. "Ever since he was a guppy, he's talked about finding fantastical worlds outside our own, just like this one. Isn't it beautiful?"

"It's something all right," I mumble to myself.

She leads me to a tent just like the one we left. There are furs and cots that look inviting.

"Isi has been very kind to us," Kai says, sitting on one of the four cots. "The minute we got here, we told her you wouldn't be far behind. What happened there?"

She points to my sternum harness hanging on my shoulder.

"They were just being very welcoming," I say, using the same wondrous tone she was.

She rolls her eyes, a habit she picked up from Layla. "Take out the weapons, please."

I do and hand her the leather straps. She pulls a thick needle and thread from a wooden box in the corner of the room. There are other supplies there—fresh fruits, a wooden comb (not that I need one anymore), and folded throws. It's a five-star magical-island hotel.

I sit beside her while she sews. "Kai, what do you know about the trident?"

She sticks the needle into the leather and snaps the string with her teeth. "I told you all I know when you put me in that Wonder Wheel contraption that nearly killed us. Why?"

"I've been having these dreams. It's like I'm watching Kurt and Nieve and I'm right there, but they can't see me. Sometimes it hurts when I wake up, like a side effect."

Kai pricks her finger and curses. "I'm not very good at this."

"Just leave it."

"I can't. It was made for you." She shakes her head. Threads the needle again. "I can't say why you're having visions of the other champions. Perhaps it's brought on by the trident pieces."

"Then they can have visions of me too."

Kai yelps when she sticks her finger again, but she doesn't stop. "I doubt it. In the Vale of Tears, the outside world exists but with a thin separation and at a different pace. Life goes on here forever, while only seconds pass in our home. Only one is unaware."

"Like a two-way mirror. So when we go back home, Kurt and Nieve will be able to see me."

"It only happens when you dream?"

I nod, rubbing my aching head. "So far, yes. I can't control it either."

She smirks. "Then try not to fall unconscious."

"Real funny."

"Perhaps Isi can help."

"Yeah, they were really helpful to Dylan and me when they sneaked up on us." I run my hand on the soft animal fur on the bed and think of the Naga. Where do creatures like that come from? How do a lion and a dragon and a serpent get together to make that beast? How do half humans and half fish? Then I count. One, two, three, four beds. They were expecting us.

"Tristan," she says in that warning way of hers. Like I'm the one being unreasonable.

"Did they greet you with bows and arrows?"

"They did. But they can't be too careful, Tristan. That terrible creature is out there. We tried to go with them, but they told us we'd slow them down. But they've kept us safe. They gave us this tent."

"Not many tents to go around?"

"Many of the river people don't have beds." She bites the thread then restrings it. "They sleep in the river. If they sleep at all."

"Makes sense." I don't want to come right out and say, "Hey, I don't trust these people." For all we know, they could be listening to us, and as of now, I don't know where the Exit sign is.

"Did they know Dylan was out there with that beastie?" I ask.

She doesn't respond because she knows that they knew. That they left him out there. So much for their hospitality.

"The warriors are making a bow for Brendan," she says lightly. "They've even let me look at their scrolls."

"When I go to new places, I also love to check out the library," I say. *Not.*

She has a curious look in her eye. "It's the best way to learn about your hosts. Through their history."

"What have you learned so far?"

She smiles. "Tristan—there's an oracle here."

We're silent, looking at the silhouettes that pass in front of the tent like our own black-and-white movie.

"The trident pieces have been found," I say. "Does it matter?"

"When one of the five oracles is dead, and another is trying to shape our future to her own liking? I'd say it's worth a small conversation."

"I'm tired of chasing them." I sit up. "All I want is to drive this pointy end through Nieve after I get the staff and Layla back."

"And Kurt? Will you be able to do the same to him?"

I open my mouth to answer the same question I've been asking myself since I found out who Kurt was—what it would mean for us.

"I beg your pardon," Kai says. "I shouldn't have asked."

I let it go for now. "Is time moving back home?"

"The way I understand it, if we go back now, seconds will have gone by. How do you say, 'Take it easy, dude'?"

I laugh. "I can't take it easy. Not 'til this is over. How can Brendan go to a pool party at a time like this? Let's snoop around."

"Snoop?"

"I have a feeling Chief Yoda is hiding something from me." There, I said it.

Kai gives me a sideways glance, like she's expecting watery shapes to materialize and take us away. But she doesn't disagree. "I can't. I can only look at their archives when one of the elders is there."

"Then I have to snoop around myself."

She snaps the needle from the thread. "My work is not as good as Blue's is"—she catches herself— "was."

I strap the leather across my chest and over my shoulder then sheathe my weapons. "Fine. You read. I explore. I'm serious Kai. My merman senses are tingling."

She gives me a small smile. I want her to see what I see, beyond the hospitality and land of paradise. I want her to be careful.

"I'll see you then." I grab a fruit from the tray of supplies. It's as hard as an apple, with deep violet skin.

"Tristan," Kai says. It's the smallest of movements, her head cocked to the side, as if she's playing with her hair. But her eyes are steely, warning as they look to me then to the outline of a guard standing outside our tent. Totally betraying the smile on her lips as she whispers, "Whatever you do, don't eat that."

chapter
THIRTEEN

Rule number one: Don't eat the purple fruit.

Got it.

Rule number two: Don't underestimate the book nerd.

Rule number three: Don't act suspicious.

Sure, I'm making these up as I go along, but if we're going to survive the Vale of Tears, I have to play along with whatever games they're setting up.

As I walk, more and more villagers seem to turn into their translucent selves, hiding behind trees or just standing with their moving eyes and guts showing. I swing by the elders' tent to see if the oracle is in there, but when I peek my head inside, it's empty. A warrior sees me and starts advancing on me so I smile like I got lost and keep walking.

There's a main square where people trade everything from food and cloth to weapons. Fuzzy green things that look like coconuts and dozens of leafy greens. Linens and silks and shields made of copper and wood. I don't spot the purple apples from our tent.

I walk through the aisles and pick up an arrowhead. When I touch the tip, I yelp as it pricks my skin even though I barely touched it. The vendor chuckles as I put it back and walk away.

Rule number four: Don't. Touch. Anything.

A pretty girl tempts me with a string of honey-colored beads. "For your heart's desire."

They remind me of Layla's eyes.

"I don't have any money."

She shakes her head. "Trade."

I pat down my body, but I have nothing to trade with. Nothing that I'd part with.

The girl takes my arm, her touch soft as feathers on the scales on my forearms.

"They turn to sand."

She shakes her head again. I'm starting to think that she thinks I'm a moron. "Yes?"

"You can try, I guess."

Then she plucks two of them. It stings as much as the time I let Layla manscape my eyebrows. The river girl holds one scale on each earlobe and smiles.

"That's a little gross," I say, but I take the glass bead necklace and wrap it around my wrist twice until I can give it to Layla.

"Where's the armory?" I ask her.

"That," she says, "I will tell you for a kiss."

My tongue is tied and I back away slowly, realizing that half a dozen girls materialize behind her and burst into giggles.

An old woman one stand over sucks her teeth. She beats a stone over a fresh leather hide to stretch the material. "Armory is down river. Watch your head."

I follow the river until I get to a clearing in the woods. The sun is blocked by long weeping trees, like a natural barrier for the warriors training within. I try to approach slowly, wishing I were part ninja in addition to the whole merman thing. But with every step, I'm keenly aware of stray branches snapping under my feet, and for a moment, I let myself think of Gwen and her pink smile while telling me how clunky legs were.

She's not wrong.

An arrow hisses past my ear the minute I step into the clearing. My hand instinctively goes to my right ear to make sure it's still there. The last time someone shot an arrow at me, it went straight through my palm. This one sinks into the tree behind me.

I slice it in half with Triton's dagger. Grumble is standing smugly between Yara and Dylan. They don't think it's so funny, and so Grumble, outnumbered, bows in a mock apology.

"You missed," I say, putting my dagger and his bow between us. I wonder how fast he can draw an arrow from his quiver before I raise my dagger.

"No," Grumble says. "I hit just where I meant to."

Dylan tries to form some sort of polite conversation. I need to get him alone and tell him not to eat the purple apples, but he's giddy from something else. "Tristan, Karel and Yara were showing me some of their weaponry. It's truly fantastic work." He holds out a fighting staff with an intricately etched design. He spins it between his hands. He bats at the air in front of him, his movements precise and calculated. When he switches sides, he finds he has an opponent. One of the warriors is challenging him.

At first Dylan hesitates. But when he sees his opponent's playful smile, he relaxes, and they break into a blur of hits that are too fast for me to follow. As they fight, I feel Yara and Grumble's eyes on me, the way my chemistry teacher watches me when I start mixing things that I'm not supposed to be mixing. Except maybe I'm the experiment here.

"Impressive toys," I say.

"We were sent here without weapons," Grumble says. "But we made our own to protect ourselves from the beast."

He hands me a spear. The wood is light but solid with thin vines carved all over. The spearhead is glass. Sharp. I picture it going through Archer's gut.

"When do we start my training?" I say, my knees almost shaking. "Dylan gets to train."

Yara nods in Dylan's direction. "Dylan isn't training. He's flirting."

"Before, when we lived on the human plane, we supplied weapons to the court," Grumble continues. "But they prefer their steel and combat fire now."

The blue flame surfaces in my mind, and then I shove it away before it can consume me the way it did the ship.

"Are you so eager to feel pain, Land Prince?" Grumble says,

walking slightly behind me. I turn because I don't like anyone at my back.

"I can handle it."

He sniffs the air around me. He presses a finger on my chest, and even though he barely touches me, I can feel a force push me back and the weeping vines whip the air around us. I step back, back, back until we are outside the circle of trees. Dylan and Yara and the others are a distant echo, and there is only Karel pushing me. Why does he hate me so much? I'm a pretty nice guy. But it's like a lion realizing there's an intruder in his pride.

He shakes his head, dispelling all of my confidence. "You do not know, Land Prince. You hide behind a mask of strength, but I can see what you keep underneath. You are cloaked in fear, and that fear will break your human heart until there is nothing and you are alone in the dark."

I stumble back. He gives me one last push, then he's gone, but his laughter lingers in the wind. I break into a run.

chapter
FOURTEEN

Rule number five: Don't piss off Grumble. I mean Karel.

As I run back to the village, I notice the soft change in the moons. They do move. Not very far, but a purple light falls over the village, which is as dark as it ever gets down here without being pitch black.

Leaves crunch hard in front of me and I draw out my dagger. She chuckles in her translucent form.

"I know you're there, Yara."

I turn, but I don't know if I'm turning the right way because I can't see her. Then when I look closely, I see the soft ripple in the air. She blinks her tiger eyes and then shows the rest of herself.

"Put that away, Land Prince." She walks ahead of me with her quiver full of arrows and bow around her arm.

"Do you always walk around here fully loaded?" I jog to keep pace with her.

She looks at my harness with my dagger in the front and the scepter in the back. "I hope Karel hasn't made you change your mind."

"He's not that scary." I shake my head, but I'd be a fool to say Karel doesn't rattle me. So I'm going to be the fool and not say it, just think it. "I have to go through with this, Yara. My people, the ones here, the ones on the other side, they depend on it."

She doesn't say anything for a long time, just walks alongside me even though I don't know where I'm going.

"Why aren't you as angry as Grumble?" I ask. "I mean Karel."

She stops and watches the sky as the purple darkness deepens around us. "I was much younger when we came to the Vale of Tears. I've grown up here. It is my home, more than the river I was born in. For Karel, for many of the older generation, it will always be a place of banishment."

I think of Coney Island, the beach, Layla sitting on our lifeguard tower with the sun in her wavy hair. No matter where I end up, that will always be my home. The thought of it weighs down on my chest. I breathe fast, like it's going out of style.

Something falls from above, right at my feet. I pick up the purple apple and brush the dirt off the skin. Unlike the weeping trees, this one holds its branches up, reaching toward the sky. Its leaves are as dark as the skin of the fruit it gives.

"The goddess tree," Yara says. "The only one we've found in the Vale."

I hold it out to Yara.

She shakes her head, but I see her body stiffen. "Too sweet for my taste. The kids gobble it up."

I hold it closer to me to see if she'll stop me from eating it.

"It's time to eat," she says, pressing her hand on mine until I lower the fruit from my lips. "You'll spoil your appetite."

I throw the fruit behind me.

We pass the tent where I'm staying on the outside of the village square, and I'm feeling a little bit better because at least I can trust Yara. There's a massive fire pit that looks like it gets regular use, and people are surfacing from the river, from tents, hopping out of trees to gather around for dinner. Off to the side there's a wooden dais that looks like it's hardly ever been used.

"This is the town square. We have dinner collectively every night."

"Is that like a family tradition?"

She shakes her head. "To make sure we're all accounted for."

I follow her as she walks past the tent they shoved me into when I first got here. "The tent of the elders. Isi is our leader. Karel and I are in charge of training our children. The Tree Mother is—"

"The oracle," I offer. She doesn't deny it, but she also doesn't confirm what I've said.

"You don't look so old," I joke. "I mean, to be an elder."

"You should know better than anyone else how deceptive our exterior is."

We walk in silence for a bit, passing eyes that follow us with unabashed curiosity.

"I feel like I have something on my forehead."

She licks her finger and rubs it between my eyebrows. "It's gone now."

"That's gross."

"You asked," Yara says. "We haven't had a court visitor in—ages. You have to understand that to us, there isn't a world outside here. There's the outer ring where the beast lives. Then the inner ring, where we live. This is it."

Suddenly the warriors start marching past us. They form a circle around the border of the village where the tree lines start.

I'm about to unsheathe my dagger, but Yara places a hand over mine. "It's okay. It's just our guard."

"Does this happen often?"

The warriors of the clan ready themselves, facing the darkening forest.

Yara nods. "The Naga doesn't come here, but it's a precaution."

"Then how does she take so many of your people?" I don't realize how crass that sounds until after I say it.

"The bigger game is on the outer ring. We have to hunt."

I stop when we've made a complete loop around the main village. The fire pit is lit and older women bring out trays of food. Kai and Brendan and Dylan emerge from their paradise getaways ready to stuff their faces.

"If you knew Dylan was out there, why didn't you get him before?"

She walks past me, ignoring the question, but looking back to say, "Best eat and get some rest, Land Prince. You have no idea what you've agreed to."

The breeze brings a soft drizzle from the weeping trees, and I know why they call it the Vale of Tears. I shiver at Yara's words, because I know she's a hundred percent right.

chapter
FIFTEEN

You aren't going to help anyone if you can't sleep," Brendan says.

His feet are at my head, and he's wiggling his toes every ten minutes. It's a mer thing.

"You aren't sleeping, either."

"Can you sleep with Dylan's lion roars?" Brendan says.

Dylan is on the other end of the tent beside Kai, who emits a whistling sound every time she breathes.

"You'd think, with how big this place is, that they'd give us our own tents."

Brendan scoffs. "I don't mind it so much."

"Surrounded by every girl in the tribe, including the old lady with the missing front teeth? Of course you don't mind."

"Really, Cousin, you underestimate me. It's part of my plan. They want us right where they can see us."

"Easy for them to say. They're see-through piles of water."

We chuckle then listen to the white noise of foreign insects and waterfalls and rivers.

"Karel wants to kill me."

"Did you tell him there's a very long list?"

I snort. "And that's just my ex-girlfriends."

Brendan chuckles, but he's fading fast.

"And Yara is hiding something."

He mm-hmms. "They all are. Must keep"—he yawns—"eyes open."

A snap makes me sit straight up.

Brendan follows suit. He presses a finger to his lips, and his turquoise eyes turn to the tent flap.

I think I see a shadow walking past, but there are a million shadows in this place. I grab my dagger at my side. Brendan is on his feet. We lift the flap to peek outside. The fire pit is long gone. The weeping trees dance in the breeze. And then there's Isi standing at the edge of the forest.

There are no guards around her. She's still, head bent to the ground. Then up to the purple moon. Her hair whips around her. Then she starts to fade, becoming water, moving in a rush where we can't follow.

"Is that a normal River Clan custom, praying alone in the woods?"

"I'd say not," Brendan says. "However, your presence has given them hope of being free of a monster they've known too long. You worry too much, Cousin Tristan. All will be smooth as the seas."

Except that he doesn't worry enough, so I have to worry for both of us. Smooth seas means the storm has passed, or is only just arriving.

Cold water to the face wakes me.

I jolt up, grabbing my dagger. Karel is standing over me. I take a swing, and he ducks out of the way before I can follow through. He laughs and that makes me swing again. This time, he laughs when I miss, and we topple out of my tent.

Where the hell are my friends? Oh, that's right. Brendan has his girls, Dylan his boys, and Kai her books. Me? I have Grumble and a new bruise on my cheek.

"You may be fast landside, Prince, but in our world, you're still catching up."

And so it happens. Me throwing punches. His shoulders lean back, but I don't give him time to catch his step. I cross punch. My second hit lands on his solar plexus. His breath catches. I grab a branch from the ground and turn it to feel its weight. "I'm a fast learner."

The thing about fighting someone who doesn't exactly want to be your BFF is that he's not going to go easy. He doesn't slow down or hold back his punches. We fall back, narrowly missing a woman carrying a basket of fuzzy green coconuts. I block Grumble's stroke with my dagger. He's strong as hell and I can't hold him off, falling back. The wood digs into my throat. I bring up my knee for a cheap shot, and he rolls off me.

"You're strong, Land Prince," he says, standing back up. The villagers have stopped their day-to-day activities to watch us. "But you have to be stronger."

"That's why I'm here."

"To wake the Sleeping Giants, yes. But that's not the same kind of strength I mean."

"I don't even know what you mean."

"You're resisting me."

"I'm fighting back. Isn't that the point?"

"You're fighting like a human. Your lineage is ancient as the seas, and yet you still haven't discovered what it means."

I'm panting, but I don't stop. "Show me."

Grumble nods. He turns and I race him into the trees. The ground is wet and our bare feet squish against the soggy earth. "Are we going back to the outer ring?"

"Scared of the beast, are you? You should be."

The lush, green forest starts thinning out. The trees grow sideways, elongated like they're trying to stretch and break away from the ground but can't. Then we reach the bottom of a cliff.

"What the hell is this?"

There are carvings in the stone.

"Do you know what we did before the court took us?" Grumble asks.

I shake my head once, feeling red at my ignorance.

"We lived in the rivers of the world. We kept the waters clear, safe from beasts. We lived every day in peace."

"Don't you have peace now?"

"We have warring children that will grow into soldiers like me. They will hunt the Naga until they fall."

"Not anymore they won't," I remind him. "I'm here now."

He cocks his head to the side, studying me like he wants to believe me, but years of fighting won't let him. Like I'm something rotten that washed up on his shore.

Suddenly I stop taking all of the happiness in my life for granted.

"Climb," he says, becoming translucent, then water moving into the trickle running through the stone.

"Easy for you to say!" My voice echoes *Say. Say. Say.*

The first half is easy enough. The words "death wish" come to mind. I have no harness. One time, I did the rock-climbing wall for my buddy Angelo's birthday and they were all, oh, finally we can do something better than Tristan. I remember reaching for the red and yellow hooks and sweating bullets, even though I was safe, and Layla climbed past me like a squirrel on a branch. She blew me a kiss, her helmet too big for her head, and said, "Bet you can't catch me!" And maybe it'll always be like that, me a step behind.

I can't think that way. I have to keep going, reminding myself that this is a test.

Now, I grab hold of the edges jutting out of the wall. I'm a merman. Mermen don't go rock climbing. But that's the thing— this is the fear I have to get over. Climb to the top of the mountain. Step by step. My bare feet burn and get cut on the sharper edges of stone. My hand slips and I swing outward. They say, "Don't look down," so I keep my head up. The pit of my stomach plummets. *Don't let go, Tristan.* The day is bright with white sun, and I pull myself one more time. The top of this cliff is flat. Chipped stones litter the ground, and I inch my way up.

"I made it!" *It. It. It.* "Take that motherf—"

Hands, wet and fluid, press down on mine.

I lose my footing and bang my knee, dangling off the side of the cliff.

"What are you doing?" I yell.

Grumble's face is in his water form right in front of me. His breath is like wet soil. "Getting rid of your fears, Land Prince."

"Don't—" *Don't. Don't. Don't.*

His fingers are solid around mine, crushing, lifting, and pushing me off the edge.

chapter
SIXTEEN

I scream for hours.

At least, when you're falling off a cliff as tall as the Empire State Building with nothing to cushion your fall, it feels like hours.

Perhaps I should rethink words like "forever."

I feel like I'm sifting through the air, screaming until my throat is raw. I hate this. I hate Grumble. I hate, hate, hate heights.

But the one thing I hate more than this free fall is that I lost control. I let him get to me.

With all the strength I can muster, I flip myself over, facing the oncoming ground, my arms waving like a flightless bird. I can see myself in the reflection of the ground, and as it comes closer and closer, I'm relieved it's water.

This is not to say that belly flopping doesn't hurt. I choke hard, swallowing a mouthful before my gills flare open.

This is not the ocean.

This is not a pool.

But I taste the salt and I'm overcome with a loss I can't shake.

Images appear in the water—faces that seem like ghosts made of light. I kick up, running my hands along the stone wall to find some sort of opening. I'm inside a sphere. A goddamn fishbowl.

"Mom?"

I see her. Her stomach is unnaturally big—I know she's pregnant, but I left hours ago and she had only just found out. I'm going to be a brother. My folks are going to get another chance. She's trying to swim up. Her red hair floats around her, and I see my dad. His glasses float off his face and into the dark. I scream for them, but when I swim, they get farther away. Someone yells my name, and I flip around and swim to the other end of the sphere. I push my hands on it.

Then I'm surrounded by familiar faces—Angelo, Bertie, Coach. They materialize around me holding their necks, their cheeks full of air.

It isn't real.

I repeat that over and over, but being surrounded by my drowning parents shakes me. It's like I'm retreating into a part of myself, shrinking into a useless, helpless kid.

Then it happens. My gills shut. My legs rip, bloody and raw, and I join them. I join my family in drowning.

There's got to be a switch somewhere. Then the bottom becomes black, a void sucking everyone downward.

I hold my breath until I'm sure I'm blue. I grab my mother's hand, and she, in turn, holds on to my dad's. I try to pull them up, against the current taking us into that darkness.

"Let go, Tristan," she says.

I shake my head. Her hand feels so real in mine.

"Please," she whispers.

But I hold on. I hold on to my mother's hand as my vision starts to blur because my fear isn't falling. It isn't the dark or heights or Nieve. My fear is this.

"Let go, darling."

"I can't!"

"You have to."

It's not her, but it's her voice, soothing and familiar, singing to me. And I remember, before I was chosen, before I was grown, when she held me and pushed away the darkness that crept in my room. I remember that my dad always said her voice could change the world. Her voice made everything feel right.

And so I close my eyes and let go.

chapter
SEVENTEEN

As soon as I let go of my mother's hand, I get pulled upward until I breach the water's surface. I float on the river by the inner ring. The air is sweet with pollen and laughter.

My body is frozen. I don't want to even paddle. I want to let the river take me away.

"Cousin!" Brendan yells. He walks to the bank and extends a hand to pull me out. "You've found the falls."

I make to run my hands though my hair but then remember. Plus side of a buzz cut is less time air-drying. Brendan pats a dry hand on my wet back.

"Grumble threw me off a cliff." He did something to me. My mind is a mess of thoughts and voices and the dark shadows he keeps rubbing in my face. Those aren't his fault though. They must have always been there.

"Ah, spirit quests," Brendan says. "My father made me try once. Couldn't get over the first hurdle. But d'you know what I've decided?"

"What?"

"I was never lost. My father always told me I could do great things, if only I changed my ways. Yet, deep in my heart I know all the great things I'm meant to do in my life, and I can only accomplish them as the terrifyingly handsome merman you see before you."

I shake my head, though I can't help but laugh. "So I'm lost?"

"No. You're just a very long way from home."

"At least you're having fun," I mutter.

"Worry not, dear cousin." He taps his temple, stepping close enough so that I can hear him whisper. "You carry out your mission. Leave the rest to us."

He turns and, with a flourish of his hand, directs me to the falls he's been talking about. The green grass is lush and radiant, and the flowers bloom with light. Strange glass animals perch on boulders. Naked and see-through guys and girls jump from the top part of a waterfall. From this far I can see black marks of tattoos, and I wonder if they're anything like the trident on my spine.

Dylan is kissing the guy who challenged him at the armory. And then it hits me.

"Oh," I say. "Oh! That's what he meant by stethos!"

Brendan elbows me.

"Sorry, I just put two and eight together."

"You were right, Tristan," Brendan says, resting his hands on his hip bones. His eyes are closed and his chest expands with deep breaths. "There is something about this place."

The soft spray from the waterfall feels nice. At the bottom of a fall, the river forms a small basin where the young girls and guys swim lazily, freely.

"The Goddess Falls are the most beautiful falls on this plane or any other. And there are some truly beautiful places in this world. There's a lagoon in Galapagos that is the closest thing to paradise I've ever seen. But this…" he says, his face full of wonder as he runs to his new paradise. "This is better!" he shouts.

Brendan grabs a blue-haired girl around the waist. She stands on her toes, wraps her arms around his neck, and kisses him. Then together they jump off. She lets go, dissolving into a splash. He flails like a baby bat that can't control its wings. But it doesn't seem to matter because he bops back out of the water unscathed, with the blue-haired girl attached to him once again.

I look at the waterfall. What makes it so much better than any other place? What makes it so special? It's not very high—certainly not after the cliff Grumble pushed me off. But the thrill is not about the height. It's about the redheaded merman who chases them off the ledge.

Fine, I'm jealous.

Not of the blue-haired girl.

Not of my cousin Brendan.

Not exactly.

It's all of them, really. I've never been this—alone. And with my girl being held hostage by my enemy, yeah, I feel pretty damn shitty.

I want to be mad at Brendan because he's so happy when we've had so many of our friends die. But maybe there's a reason merpeople don't leave behind traces of their bodies. It's so that they won't mourn. So they can move on faster. That has to be it, right?

Music fills the Goddess Falls. It comes right out of the air—the long, weeping vines trickling with water, the birds flitting about as if they could sing for always. There's a different kind of magic in this land. It's as if there isn't a care in the world, and I bet if I let myself, I'll forget about my own cares. About getting out of here and being the hero of the day.

Like Dylan. He's been here for nearly two weeks, and I'm not convinced he's ready to go back.

I hold my toe over the ledge.

"Cousin!" Brendan shouts. "What's taking you so long? Jump in!"

The girls around him echo him. "Yes, jump in!"

But there's something I have to do. It's whispering in the wind. "Maybe later!"

They boo and call out my name as I turn around and walk away.

I know I'm right. There is something about this place. It's perfect. It's eternal. And if I'm not careful, it won't let us go.

chapter
EIGHTEEN

I t's not polite to stare," I tell Isi. She's watching the frolicking in the Goddess Falls from behind a tree.

I wonder if she's pissed off that her daughters are so attached to Brendan.

"I'm not staring," she says indignantly.

"I'm sure you can jump right into the fun."

She ignores my jibe and uncrosses her arms. Her long, white dress is dirty where it trails on the ground. I want to ask what she was doing last night at the edge of the woods. I don't know much about religion, but it looked to me like she was praying. I decided it's not my place to ask so I leave it alone.

"I wanted to walk you to your next session," she says, heading away from the music and laughter behind us.

I want to say that I'll find my way, but all I see is tall tree, slightly taller tree, tree that looks like all the other trees.

"So, do you normally let your emotionally unstable warrior shove your visitors off a cliff?"

I think she chuckles, but it could also be the squirrels in the trees.

"Only when they ask," she says. "You asked to be trained. So you are being trained."

"I guess I was picturing a montage with a sweet eighties hair band in the background and my friends cheering at the finish line."

She stares at me blankly, all, What planet are you from?

I'm from Brooklyn, lady.

"Just out of curiosity," I start. "How many days are we talking about? I'm in a 'places to go, sea witches to kill' kind of situation."

"You have just faced your greatest fear," she says. "But you still haven't discovered patience."

"It's hard to be patient when lives are in your hands."

"Nieve has been patient, and look where it's gotten her."

"Yes, because I should take life lessons from a mass murderer," I say, but I've clearly offended Isi. She clenches her jaw and keeps her eyes trained on the path ahead.

"Hey, where does the oracle go? Every time I go by her tent, she's not there. Do I need, like, an appointment?"

Isi's eye twitches a little. I can't get a read on her. I think she likes me better when I don't ask questions. "The Tree Mother makes her presence known when she feels it is needed."

"So no?"

"No."

"Hey, what else can you tell me about the Naga? Is its saliva poisonous like a sea dragon's? Can it breathe fire? Can—"

She holds up her hand to cut me off. The topic of the Naga ruffles her. I guess if a monster was picking off my people, I'd be short tempered too. I think of Nieve. See her face when I close my eyes.

"Tristan, please know we are preparing you to fight her."

"Got it." I say it to appease her, not because I do, in fact, have it. I've seen this thing in the flesh, and while I know anything can be killed by chopping off its head (I hope), I want more details. Details they aren't giving me. "I won't fail you."

She moves aside a curtain of weeping vines, letting me into the armory. She takes my chin and looks into my eyes. "I believe you."

I walk into the armory and training grounds. When I turn around, Isi is gone.

An obstacle course has been set up overnight. Round stones where car tires ought to be, tall poles lined like monkey bars. A large barrel is full of spears with glass arrowheads, and beyond that, a really big target for them to hit.

Yara jumps in front of me, hands on her hips, that defiant grin on her face. She's painted a series of rectangles and circles on her body. Up close I can see the tattoo on her shoulder, a perfect circle with a wavy line through the middle.

"Am I supposed to be painted too?"

She smirks but tries to hide it by turning around and walking away.

"Is it too much to have a conversation? You know, 'Follow me, guys!'"

She comes to a stop. "If it would please you to have me treat you like a pup, I could do as you ask."

I don't respond, and she keeps walking until we are alone in a field. I take in the trees, the pristine bright greenery of it. It almost makes me feel at ease, and I'm afraid this is going to be one of those "inner peace" moments.

"Just so you know, I hate yoga."

Then Yara gets into a crouching position, hands at the ready, urging me to strike.

"I can't hit you. You're a girl."

Standing in the clearing, Yara screams, springing at me with a kick that leaves me breathless on the ground.

I roll over and cover my face with my hands as she brings down the side of her hand on me. I block it. Hot damn, she's strong.

"I am no girl, Land Prince."

"No offense, but you've got all the girl bits."

She laughs but doesn't stop advancing. My dad taught me never to hit girls. That's not what men do, ever.

"I'm a warrior," she says, "and if you can't fight back, you will hurt."

She chases me down, along an offshoot of the river. I block, block, block, and she brings her strikes with more precision each time. It's like she finds the spots that bruise the fastest and then digs into them.

"I admire you sticking to your human code."

"Morals, my dad likes to call it."

I grab her wrists in the air and squeeze. She's surprised by how hard I hold her. She pulls, but I don't loosen my grip. She turns to their little magic trick, the melting thing. Soon I'm grasping water, and she slips through my hands.

"That's cheating," I say as she resumes solid form.

"Your code will get you killed. Assume I want to kill you. Assume everyone is out to kill you."

"That's called paranoia."

I lean back so far to avoid her punch that my thighs burn as I hold the pose to keep from falling backward. I throw my weight forward. Yara moves back to kick. I grab her leg before it hits my thigh and flip her so hard that she smacks into a tree.

"Yara?"

She doesn't move.

I race forward and kneel down to her. Her head hangs slack, untucked hair from her braid covering her eyes. I reach a hand out to touch the pulse on her neck.

She grabs my arm and pulls me forward.

Few types of pain are as bad as hitting your face smack into a tree. I can feel my septum crack. Blood gushes into my mouth.

"Only assume your opponent is not getting up if you have a sword through their head."

"What about their heart?" I say.

She shrugs. "Not everything has a heart in the same place."

"Can you go all see-through again so I can see where your heart is?"

Yara goes to the stream, but first she shoots me an evil glare, much like the girls in school. I lean my head against the trunk, moving the blood down my throat. Yara comes back and kneels beside me and drops the handfuls of water on my head.

"You're a tough chick," I say. "And I mean it in the best possible way."

"I'm not a chick." She stands over me. "I am Yara, maiden warrior of the River Clan." She holds her hand out. The bleeding has stopped. I take her hand and stand in front of her. No weapons. Just the strength of our fists. She leans back. Her stance is strong. I realize she leans too much on her right side. I can use this.

She motions me with her fingers. "Again."

chapter
NINETEEN

W hat happened to your face?" Kai shrieks.

Not the usual response I get when girls see me. After days of rock climbing with Grumble—I throw myself off now—and hand to hand with Yara, my face has taken a good beating. I've gotten so good at disarming her that she smashed my face into a tree again. I have a new cut on my eyebrow.

"Good thing they don't have mirrors," I say, throwing myself on the furs beside Kai. She has taken the river people's history scrolls and has been reading them nonstop.

I press my finger on the sensitive bruise on the bridge of my nose and wince.

"This is strange," Kai says. She retraces the lines she just read.

"What is?" I press my hands on my face. "Is it that bad?"

"In the records of the clan's people, there is mention of Amada, daughter of the leader Isi. But we haven't met her. And she isn't on the list of the daughters sent to court."

"Maybe she died?"

Kai shakes her head. "They keep records of their dead as well as their living. Their numbers are less than ours."

"I thought they were part of ours."

But I've stopped listening. The ache of my body, the adrenaline buzzing through me, is strong. I know I'm ready to fight the Naga. I know it in my bones. As if sensing my thoughts, Kai says, "You're in no shape to fight anyone, Tristan. Least of all the Naga."

"They're stalling," I say. I can lift a whole tree pole with my bare hands and throw it. I can do handstands for hours without toppling over. I can run across a field with stones draped over my shoulders. I've wrestled their best warriors and won. "Why are they stalling?"

I shake my head. "They haven't even gone hunting since we got here."

My stomach twists into knots. They remind me that we're outside of time, but I still feel like I'm missing it. Like I'm going to return home and it won't be there.

Brendan sticks his head through the tent door. "Come, you two. The feast is about to start. The daughters of the tribe are putting on a dance in our honor."

Kai arches her eyebrow. "Our?"

"Fine." Brendan sighs, tucking his hair behind his ear. "Tristan's honor. Dylan's already there."

"We're having a debate," I say. "Come in here."

Brendan looks over his shoulder to make sure the coast is clear then joins us. "Do tell."

"I think the clan is stalling my fight with the beast. Kai thinks I'm not prepared."

"I didn't say that!" She shuffles her papers so hard that she nearly rips one in half.

Brendan smiles easily. He reminds me of me three weeks ago. "Do you feel ready?"

"A hundred percent. A hundred and ten percent."

"I'll take that as a yes," Brendan smirks. "Then do it."

"But Isi said—" Kai argues.

Brendan holds up a finger. "Isi left us a basket of goddess fruit, which makes the children here happy and carefree and forgetful."

We sit in silence. I realize Brendan might act the fool sometimes, but he never stops observing people.

"If you feel ready, then go. You are a prince of the Sea Court. Besides, with me around, no one will be looking for you. That's a promise." He winks.

Kai shakes her head. "Tristan, be careful. We still don't have a way out of here."

"One thing at a time," I say. "Let's go pay me some honor."

Kai and I follow Brendan to where the whole village is gathered around a tall fire. Old men blow on wooden pipes that remind me of the pan flutes Layla's dad brought back from Ecuador. After weeks of trying to learn—poor Mrs. Santos—he finally hung it on his kitchen wall along with his Panama hat. The river people's music sounds like mountains whistling down their valleys, along with the rustle of rainstick and tambourines. Instead of metal, the cymbals are made of hard shells and rocks that tinkle like wind chimes.

Isi stands over the fire. Her long, violet hair is braided down to her hips on either side. She looks like a phoenix in her long, feathery robes. Beside her, Yara wears an intricate leather dress. Her brown skin shimmers like light on water. Beside her is the veiled woman I have only seen once in the tent of council elders. The oracle. Standing up, she is hunched like a question mark, with long hair the color of moss peeking through the bottom of her black veil.

"Land Prince, Tristan Hart," Isi speaks to me. "You honor us here. By taking strength from us, you have accepted the challenge of the Naga who roams the outer circle of our plane. Her talons have ripped our children to shreds. Her teeth have devoured generations of our warriors."

I swallow my drink down the wrong hole and cough-choke. Brendan punches it out of me.

"That's comforting," Dylan mutters beside me, adjusting the platinum band around his head.

"Tonight, we gift you and yours with the symbol of the river goddess, who refused the salt gifts of Poseidon and chose the shade of trees."

I look at Kai. "Gift?"

Kai shrugs then turns her back to me, showing where her trident tattoo is located between her shoulder blades. Yara lifts a copper branding iron, and the oracle holds a jar filled with some red stuff.

I think of the time I first met Kurt. He showed up in my bathtub. He held a slender vial of ink between his fingers and said some magic words. Then blam! The tattoo was burned into my skin to help me control my shifting.

The iron is held over the fire. It lights red like the end of a cigarette. Kai takes my hand eagerly. Brendan hesitates but tries hard to maintain his smile. Dylan fidgets but won't back out. The four of us approach in a line.

I should go first. I bite down hard, preparing myself for it—the music gets louder, thickened by the voices of the clan.

"Tristan Hart," Yara says. "Your honor, strength, and valor are admired by our people. Come what may, you always have a place here."

She looks at me the entire time she says that, and I believe her. Her words are so nice that I stop clenching my teeth. The iron digs into my skin. I whimper but stare straight into the brown and gold swirls of her eyes. Burning skin smells like bacon, and then I remember that's me.

There's nothing quite as gratifying as someone listing your good qualities and having the end of it be a poker to the chest. She pulls it back, cool wind kissing the sting off my skin. And then comes the pain.

Oh.

I shake so hard that I take a knee. The old woman is unveiled, a face like tree bark staring right at me with pitch-black eyes reflecting the fire pit behind me. Her hand is on my chest, patting red powder into the outline of the iron burn. The stuff cools the burn, and then I stand back up.

Next in line is Kai. She concentrates on a spot on Yara's forehead and tenses for the iron. Her face is serene, probably way more than mine must have been. Then she moves on to the old woman, who presses the red powder into her shoulder. When it comes away, I can see the design. It's the same as Yara's—a circle with an undulating line going through it. At first I think it's a snake, but on second thought, I realize it's a river.

Then it's Brendan's turn. He doesn't even flinch! His red hair is tied back at his nape. He winks a turquoise eye at me. Show-off.

Finally Dylan, who cries out once, then falls on his knee at the oracle's feet. His golden hair sweeps across his face. The mark burns just above the pearly scar left by the Naga's claw.

The four of us stand shoulder to shoulder. Isi talks about how brave we are, how much she's seen all four of us grow and become part of their people. I'll never graduate at the top of my class, and I might not know much about the world I've become part of, but I'd like to think I know how to read people. And as much as Isi means some of what she says, I can't shake the thought that she's doing it to keep me at ease.

The training, the tattoo, everything they've done to accommodate us—it's not working on me. My eyes keep wandering to the black outline of the forest. The guards aren't in their usual formation. They're scattered around the feast, their weapons leaning against the wooden dais, but their attention is on the clan's daughters who form a circle around the fire. Their faces shimmer in the reflection of the flames, their hair as green as the forest, white as the river, purple as the apples on the goddess tree, black as the shadow of the woods. They dance the song of the river, a movement that mimics the stream, and their bodies flow, translucent, then fluid, then solid.

Brendan holds the purple apple between his hands and smells it. He looks at me and tucks it under his seat.

"This is kind of them," Brendan says, "to take the time to honor us."

"Honor me," I correct him.

His turquoise eyes dance with the kind of happiness that comes from timeless days of swimming and eating and kissing girls. But still, his shoulders are tense because no matter what face this paradise shows us, he has to be ready in case it changes. Even though my time with Brendan has been short, we really get each other, like we've been swimming side by side our whole lives.

"You can have the honor," Brendan says. "We both know I'm more irresistible. All eyes will be on me. You can count on that."

A sound I haven't heard before in the Vale joins the music. Laughter.

Yara was right—the kids do eat the goddess fruit. They gobble it up, the sticky, sweet liquid dripping from the corners of their mouths.

Sure, I've seen the river kids laugh. But not like this—it's full of happiness, like there is no darkness in the woods, no monster on the outside. They dance around the fire. They grab Kai and Brendan and Dylan into their circle. They try to pull me up. "Join, Tristan. Come on." But I've never been much of a dancer. Kai shoots me a glare that says, "Get up." So I do, but I'm going through the motions.

My eyes keep going to the edge of the forest where a shadow is bothering me. Everyone is so wrapped up in the dancing and welcoming us into the tribe. But I'm not here to dance.

Brendan catches my eye and holds it. He's smiling, but it's a show, and he's the star of it—dancing and singing along to words he doesn't know the meaning of. Then he nods at me once and turns his back. He goes into a freestyle break dance, challenging the guys to join him. As promised, all eyes are on him.

I keep along the shadows and return to my tent. I wash my face in the basin of cool water. I strap on my weapons and look at my elongated reflection. There I am. I can wait until Isi decides to let me go, or I can take matters into my own hands. As crazy as it sounds, I don't think she wants me to go out there.

And so I slink through the trees, stopping at the edge of the forest where I've seen Isi stand once everyone's gone to sleep. I look over my shoulder at the feast. They're still reveling in the night, the music, the sizzle of branded skin.

Then I see her, the veiled oracle. She stares at me from the distance. I feel caught, so I freeze. But she lifts the veil over her face, uncovering those endless black eyes. She turns away, like she understands what I'm doing. Like she's sending me along when the others were pulling me back. I face the forest again and step onto the path.

chapter
TWENTY

I n the dark, there isn't a path.

I trip and bang into the black tree trunks like a pinball. Each time we've come into the forest, Grumble has been careful to lead me west. So I go east. On the way here, the first time when Yara blindfolded us, I smelled the temperature shift, the dew in the air, and the sweet bioluminescent blooms. The water is a thin stream with glass lizards clinging to the rocks. Lights pop up like tiny eyes blinking. Wings flap, tongues hiss, and beaks caw in a chattering that would rival Times Square.

And then it stops, leaving my loud steps bumping in the dark. I see the mouth of a cave, and by the way my skin crawls, I know this is the Naga's home. Fireflies hover above the entrance, and the purple moon is a fat bulb behind the silhouettes of branches that remind me of bones. My heart races as adrenaline rushes through me. The sweet stink of decaying flesh is too familiar, and I take a step back.

Rule number six: There is no going back.

I think about calling the beast out. Throwing some rocks in there like I'm Romeo and she's a hairy Juliet. That plan still ends with someone getting stabbed.

I don't hear the groan behind me until the Naga leaps at me and I run right into the cave.

Rule number seven: Don't run into caves.

There is no exit that I can see. The creature is bigger than I remember. Its snout snarls hot breath.

Rule number eight: Don't get bitten.

The B flat of the dragon-bird rings out from the cave ceiling. It swoops down and tries to peck at my hand.

"No one said anything about a tag team," I say.

I've made a mistake in coming here. Maybe Isi was right. Maybe she wasn't stalling. Maybe I'm just not ready.

I turn around to face the Naga and she moves back, crouched down to the ground. I see her eyes glowing in the dark. The rough reptilian skin. The powerful claws. The seaserpent tail undulating behind it. The Naga opens her mouth and roars, a great scream that carries the lives the beast has taken. The force pushes me against the wall. I roll to the side and pull myself up, shaking the headache away.

I jump on the boulders, using them as a ladder to get to a flat platform where the cave expands like a great dome. I can't see the Naga, but I can hear the talons scratching the stone as she climbs. Nobody said she could do that.

I picture those talons digging inside me, swirling my guts around like a cherry in a cocktail. She jumps at me and I roll to the side, a move I learned from watching Dylan. It takes a lot of patience to wait for the perfect moment to get out of the way, knowing that if it's too soon, she'll have time to recover. If it's too late, then she gets me. It feels like an out-of-body experience, but that's what Karel taught me, wasn't it? To push all of my doubts out of my head. Doubts gets me killed.

The Naga lands in the empty space I just occupied.

"Sorry, beastie—but I need your head." I don't sound as confident as I would've liked.

I jump on her back, grabbing the rough ridges of her neck like reins. I dig my knees into her furry flanks and raise my dagger over her head.

But the Naga lurches and throws me off, and I fall hard on my side. A hot, burning sensation hits my side where something feels broken. My dagger is gone. Panic shoots through me as the Naga breaks into a sprint. No matter how many walls I've climbed, how many pull-ups I've done, watching this thing run at me still freezes my joints. It's massive, with a mouth open to swallow me. But it's the thing that stands between the Sleeping Giants and me, so I push myself to move.

The Naga lands to my side, talons digging into the rock. I see something glint behind her. My dagger! I take a stone the size of a football and slam it into her face. She whimpers and covers her eyes. The dragon-bird swoops down as I run for my weapon. It draws blood from my forearm. I slide on the ground and take my dagger. The Naga shakes her head, a rumble stirring deep inside her belly. She's pissed.

Know what? So am I.

I roll out my shoulders, the adrenaline dulling the pain in my ribs.

No beast is going to eat me. It's just bones and flesh, same as every merrow I've gutted.

I find the spark inside me that needs this more than anything. The part that's been burned and cut open. The bits that had never seen the face of real evil until I watched her take away the people I love.

I hold on to that spark.

The Naga sees the change. She gets up on her hind legs and scratches at the space between us, landing with heavy thuds. She makes the walls tremble. Pieces of the cave come down. The B flat of the dragon-bird echoes. It cries and cries as I charge at the Naga.

She runs at me.

My thighs burn as I run, run, run, and jump. I swipe, and the black stone of Triton's dagger pulses with a dark light. The ancient symbols light up like they're on fire.

I punch the Naga's exposed long neck and she cries out. I hit her cheek with the hilt of my dagger and she slumps forward, dazed. When I hit her, I cringe. This is why I'm here. This is what I've been training for, but I can't shake the feeling that hurting her is wrong. I shouldn't do this. But if I don't, I won't get the clan's help and then I'll never see Layla again.

The Naga recovers, growling at me. Something is different. It's her eyes. I see something so human in the swirl of her eyes, black and brown like melting stone. Something familiar.

The moment of hesitation is going to cost me. The Naga reaches out her claw. I move out of its reach and strike with my dagger, too late. I skim to the right. The blade digs into the flank of her skin until the resistance stops and I'm slicing through air.

At the same time, her talons dig into my chest.

Warm blood trickles from my wound. A numb prickle blooms around the cuts.

A scream.

A groan.

We fall into each other.

Prickly numbness spreads through me. My vision goes blurry.

Beneath the rapid pulse of my heart in my eardrums is the cry of the dragon-bird, like a child after its mother. I roll over and I see her. The Naga, eyes wide open. Mouth drawing in shaky breaths. But the beast's face is changing. Fingers, slender human fingers touching the blackening skin around the cut beneath her ribs. She turns on her side, changing the way the river people do. She closes her eyes—the eyes, lips, face of a teenage girl.

Bloody and cut open and pressed against me so I can feel the cold sweat of her skin. She tries to lift her head but can't, raven hair spilling on the ground.

Sharp pain snakes all over my body and gathers in my head.

When I close my eyes, she says, "Thank you."

chapter
TWENTY-ONE

The numbness on my skin returns. My eyes, still blurry at the corners, focus on Kurt.

He wades out of the stormy Coney Island surf, holding tightly to the barrel of the Trident of the Skies. He has no need to look for human clothes or hide the scales around his waist. The beach is trashed. Sand covers every inch of the boardwalk—or what's left of the boardwalk—in small dunes. Boards are sliced into wet splinters. There's a crack from the Aquarium entrance to the shore, where waves collapse and trickle down. I did that to my own home.

I did that to get rid of as many merrows as I could.

Kurt grabs a handful of sand and runs it through his fingers. I wonder what he's thinking, if he's wishing he could press the Rewind button. Then he dusts his hands, pulls on the yellow disaster tape, and runs up the boardwalk.

The sky is overcast with fat storm clouds. He crosses the street, and I know where he's going—back to Lucine.

He ducks under an archway down the narrow alley that leads

to the Second Circle, the velvet-draped speakeasy operated by vampire Madame Mercury and a sideshow freak. The movement to his side is so fast that I can't see the hands that grab him until it's too late. Kurt is pinned to the red brick wall.

It's Marty McKay, the shapeshifter, with Frederik the High Vampire of New York. They're joined by Penny and the landlocked from the Sea Court, along with members of the Thorne Hill Alliance. The Alliance exists to bring peace among the supernatural creatures in the city. As they surround Kurt, I guess this means to hell with the Alliance.

"You shouldn't have come back," Marty says. I've never heard him sound so serious, but hours before, he was moments from death and I helped save him. So yeah, almost dying will do that to a guy.

"Are you planning on killing me, vampire?" Kurt says.

"Why are you here?" Frederik's voice is steely, controlled.

"This isn't a stake," Kurt says, his violet eyes not wavering from Frederik's black ones. "But it will certainly end you."

You're bluffing! I shout. Me, the ether, the friendly fucking ghost.

But they've all seen the power of our weapons and they give him room.

"Where's Tristan?" Kurt says.

"Don't you know?" Frederik answers, a tiny smile playing on his lips.

Kurt takes in the others, like he's figuring out how best to take them on. But Kurt's not a cold-blooded killer, and he's going to want to avoid fighting them. "We're still on the same side. The side that wants to destroy the sea witch."

"Yeah," Marty says, pacing uncomfortably and rubbing the spot on his chest where he was skewered hours ago. "Only you have to kill our friend on the way. Your kin, am I right?"

"The way of the seas has nothing to do with you," Kurt says.

Frederik bares his fangs. "When your sea ways do this to our home, then you bet your sparkly ass that it concerns us."

My ghost self is laughing.

"Then you've settled it," Penny says, distraught. "You're going to kill Tristan."

Kurt looks at the group in front of him, then at the weapon in his hands. I can feel him trying to draw power from it and failing. But he doesn't falter for too long or they'd notice.

"You say you love this land. You fight for it." Kurt pauses. "Then gather your army because the sea witch wants to watch the world drown from her stolen throne. I will do everything I can to stop her." Kurt walks past Frederik and says, "Do not stand in my way."

Then Kurt barrels into the Second Circle, down the winding steps, along a green velvet corridor, and through a mahogany door. The golden tiles are wet, and Lucine, the split-tailed mermaid, is there. The eldest of the four remaining sea oracles. She swims happily in her golden pool because she's been waiting for him.

Her red hair glistens, and her emerald eyes are beams looking up at him.

"My love. I knew you'd come back," she says, taking his hands and pulling him closer to her. "Now we must hurry. We have much to do."

chapter
TWENTY-TWO

I wake up with that painful numbness when your limbs fall asleep. Tiny clawed feet walk on my chest. It's the lizard-bird. It opens its mouth and throws up on me.

"What the—"

It does it again, shutting me up with a caw. Then it walks over the mushy yellow vomit. The wound cools instantly.

"That's disgusting."

It yells at me and I remember—the Naga.

In her place is a girl about my age. She's on her side, her arms limp and bloody. Dried blood is smeared around her wound, a black mark where my dagger cut her.

"She lied to me," I say, searching for the memory of some hint, some mention that this would happen. That they sent me after a girl, not just a beast. "They all lied to me."

I stare at the girl on the ground and things start coming together. The reason why Isi was stalling. I lift my dagger, dirty with the girl's blood. My wound, on the other hand, has stopped bleeding.

The dragon-bird flies in front of my face, batting wings urgently. I guess we're friends again.

"I got it," I shout.

I pick up the girl in my arms. Her breath is shallow but consistent. Her copper skin is cold. Her eyes flutter, her lips part. I tell her to be quiet, save it. She's going to be fine. Because I can't be the one to kill her. I just can't.

I hurry back the way I came, slowing down at the patch of gnarled trees. The sky is lightening under the white and purple moons. How long were we out of it? I shake from exhaustion before the path looks familiar again.

A tendril of smoke swirls above the trees where the fire pit roared and the villagers danced. Some are asleep on the ground. Others are still talking and drinking. They're oblivious to where I've been and what I've done.

"*Isi!*" I shout her name.

They come out of the river, out of their tents. Whispers become a loud buzz of questions.

Who is that?

Who is the Land Prince holding?

No—it can't be—

I've brought their wolf into the den.

Karel runs at me and Brendan tackles him. I make it to the dais, the bleeding Naga girl in my arms.

Brendan has Karel in a headlock. Dylan and Kai wrestle off two other guards who advance on me. Isi walks among her people. From the look in her eyes, she hasn't been to sleep.

"Call them off!" I shout at her.

"What have you done?" Her face ages in seconds, like a thousand sorrows pulling at her life strings.

"Let's get into that after you tell your warriors to stop."

She lifts her hand, and with the wave of her fingertips, they stop fighting my friends. I shoot a warning glare at Brendan who begrudgingly lets go of Grumble. He falls on the ground and picks himself up, enraged and ready to take my cousin's head off.

I match her stare. "You said a son of Triton had to break the curse of the Naga. You lied to me."

"That is not so," Isi says. "Everything we told you was true."

"Oh sorry, was I supposed to fill in the blanks? The part where the Naga is a girl? I won't kill her."

Isi lifts her chin defiantly. "Even if we refuse to aid you?"

"I told you he was weak," Karel growls.

I look at the shifty people. The scared faces of warriors. What is one girl, one beastie girl, compared to the lives of these people and the future of this tribe? Without their help, how will I awaken the Sleeping Giants?

I know what Kurt would do…

I know that is where we're different.

"I will find another way," I say.

"Very well." Isi turns her back on me. The air shifts around us, rippling with water, and I know we are surrounded. "Take them."

chapter
TWENTY-THREE

The River Clan warriors materialize around us. They wrap around Kai, disarming her and tying her arms behind her back. Brendan screams and tries to run to her, but Karel knocks my cousin on his back with one sucker punch. Dylan is buried under a fury of fists, but there are too many of them and I'm left holding a wounded girl.

I can make out Yara's voice saying, "Mother, please."

But the same warriors I've trained with now advance on me. They go for the Naga first, taking her away as an arm grabs my neck and squeezes. A fist pounds on my bruised ribs until the pain is too much and I'm pushed to my knees.

"These are the court's great champions," Karel says, spitting on the ground.

One by one, they tie us to the dais. My heart thumps in my ears. Everything feels still, muted, as if I'm underwater.

Isi takes my face and holds it in her hands. "You could have been happy here."

She leaves a handful of warriors to guard us.

At first the villagers keep their distance. Then they come by with rotting fruit, and kids make it a game to see which hits on body parts will make us react. But we don't react. Not even when the sky darkens and tiny bugs bite the sweet, rotting fruit off our flesh. Not even when I can hear a girl screaming from somewhere in the distance. Not even when Yara stands in front of me, unable to give me any comfort, to say she was sorry, that she didn't want it to end this way.

And I think, who says it's over?

"I'm going to strangle him," Brendan says, keeping his eyes steady as a sniper's gun on Karel. When the guards change shifts, Karel stays. He walks around the dais like a hawk.

"No one is strangling anyone," I say.

"Really, Cousin," Brendan says.

I test the leather ropes to see how strong they are, but there's no getting out of them.

"They're not going to let us go," Dylan says. "Not until you slay the Naga. And even then, we don't know how to get out."

"Brendan," Kai says, fidgeting with her hands behind her back, "be a darling and distract Karel. I believe he's still angry that you, how do you say, hooked up with his blue-haired mate."

"I'd love to," Brendan says. The moment he tries to stand up, he falls forward. Karel is on him in an instant and so is his backup.

"Leave," Karel tells them. "This one is mine."

"Kai," I whisper, "what are you doing?"

Brendan is shouting obscenities at Karel, and he's eating it up.

"Quiet," she says. But I see what she's done. She's gotten her hand free from her bindings.

"Thank Poseidon for your tiny girl hands."

"Really, Tristan…" she says, but she digs into the pocket of her dress and pulls out a familiar knife the size of an index finger. I won it from Rachel the red-headed demigoddess. Kai widens her eyes and signals for me to come closer. She whispers, "I must cut off your hands."

"*What?*" I hiss.

Her shoulders shake as she silences her laugh. "Are you the only one allowed to laugh in the face of doom?"

"I think you mean danger." I adjust my body so she can cut me loose.

"I like 'doom' better," she whispers.

I can feel my restraints snap, but I keep my hands behind my back.

Karel kicks Brendan in the gut and my cousin doubles over. But he lifts his head, his red hair sweaty and matted over his smiling face, all, is that all you've got? I'm starting to think he likes getting beat up.

Karel doesn't see me until Brendan's eyes flick toward me. The river warrior spins around in time for my fist to meet his face. *Blam!* He's out cold.

"We have to find the way out of here," Dylan says, rubbing his wrists.

But we're not alone anymore. The warriors return and so does

Isi. Even if we make it to the outer ring and somehow find a way out, I'm not leaving the Naga. I can't just hand her over to the people that wanted me to kill her. There has to be a reason I hesitated, something I'm missing.

So in the only way I can think to save my ass, my friends, and a strange beast girl, I say, "I wish to speak to the oracle."

Brendan and Dylan hold on to Karel.

"You don't have the nerve to hurt him," Isi says to me.

"He's hurt me a lot more than the Naga has," I remind her. I look at Yara, stepping beside her mother. "Tell her, Yara. Isn't that consistent with my human code?"

Yara nods once.

Isi looks like she's going to strangle me. I've ruined her veiled paradise.

The oracle has come forth on her own. She is small and wide, and the veil over her face is drawn back around her shoulders. She is fluid, moving effortlessly from her tent to the platform. The bark lines of her face betray no emotion, but the air around her shifts like the moments before a thunderstorm.

The villagers start talking among themselves.

We can't let this be.

He's cursed us again.

"Come with me." The oracle places a hand on my arm. Instant warmth spreads through me. I remember laughing with my parents, swimming with my friends, lying on the beach with Layla.

The oracle sees me not following and says, "I will bring you to the girl."

I start walking.

"Stay," she says to everyone who tries to follow. Even Yara. My friends. Even Isi.

The river people part for us. I follow the oracle into the tent where I was first welcomed. A white flame burns in the center. I sweat the second I walk in.

The Naga is on the leather-clad floor, dressed in white. Her eyes are closed. Her jet black hair is fanned around her. Her nails elongate into claws as she shivers in her sleep. Then they retract into fingers.

"Did you heal her?" I sit beside the Naga girl.

The oracle nods. "When you cut her with Triton's dagger, it allowed her to change into her human form."

"But she's fine, right?"

"This is the first time she's been in her human form in centuries. The weapon hasn't broken the curse. Only a true death will do this."

That's reassuring, I think. "What's her name?"

"Amada."

I nearly jump out of my skin when the Naga girl sits up. She brings her knees up to her chest and holds them with her arms. She looks from me to the oracle then back at me.

"You're awake!" I sit yogi-style in front of her.

She jerks back. Well, I tried to shish-kebab her, so that's a natural reaction.

"You're Tristan Hart," she says.

"How did you know?"

"I've dreamed of you." Amada takes a wooden bowl from the oracle and smells it for a long time before drinking from it. "For so long, my dreams were black. Of screams and blood, and then I saw you, and I knew you would be the one I was waiting for. Thank you for not killing me."

"It was you, wasn't it?" I ask her. "You left me the berries. You caught the fish for me. You sent me the lizard-bird."

"Sun bird," she says.

"Come here, Land Prince." The oracle sits beside us with fistfuls of a green paste that looks an awful lot like my neighbor's dog shit. She slabs the goopy stuff on my face. "You're more bruised than goddess fruit left out in the sun."

"Oh, is that what happens?" I wince when she presses her thumb on my cheekbone.

Then her fingers touch the scab on my chest in the shape of the Naga's claws.

"I'm sorry," Amada says.

"I'm sorry," I say. "I didn't know you. They didn't tell me. They lied to me about everything."

The crackle of the fire is strong. When I breathe deeply, the heat burns my insides, but it feels so good.

Amada looks down at her human fingers. "It's not all lies. I've taken lives. Sometimes the beast would take over and I wouldn't have a human thought for so long. Sometimes I'd stay in my caves so I wouldn't hurt them when they tried to hunt for me."

I kick the wooden bowl in front of me. I was played like a cheap toy. I yell at the oracle before I can think better of it. "*Why did you keep this from me?*"

"Isi didn't think you would do it if you knew the truth," the old woman says.

"Am I so predictable?"

She shakes her head. "Your heart is still open to the world around you."

"That's me," I say, but it hurts more than I'd like to admit. "The open-hearted guy. Kurt isn't worried about doing the right thing, is he? And Nieve didn't create an army of merrows to save the world."

"That is why you will always be greater than them." She steps over me with another wooden cup full of stinky liquid. "My daughter was weak. She could not bear seeing Amada as she was. It is a great strain, losing your children. Watching them suffer."

Amada keeps her eyes trained on the tent flaps, her shoulders hunched as if she's ready to attack anyone who might intrude. Or maybe she wants to run back to the outer ring.

"The Chief is your kid?" I didn't know oracles could have kids.

"We can," she says, reading my thoughts. "Not all of us. Not Chrysilla in her shell. Not Alethea, as you saw her die in Eternity. The oracles and the kings of the sea have always had a close relationship. The first oracles created the trident with their blood.

"We consult with kings during times of war. We shift, as we must. But I will always remain here because, unlike my sisters, I would not advise the kings. I tire of their tempers, their eagerness for destruction. My people still believe the Vale of Tears is a curse. But I believe it is a blessing. Drink."

"What is it?"

She doesn't answer, but I chug it. The bitterroot liquid dries my mouth, like chewing on cotton balls.

"Amada too."

I pass it to Amada who makes a face but drinks it anyway.

The oracle brings out a glass arrowhead and slices the palm of her hand. Her blood pools at the center. She brings it down to my chest.

She nicks Amada's hand. Amada gasps, and for a moment her claws come out. She cradles the hand to her chest.

"*What are you doing?*" I shout.

But the oracle pushes me back on the floor. She holds her hand out to Amada and waits for her to comply. Amada looks at me for encouragement, so I just smile. The oracle guides Amada's bleeding finger in a circle around the oracle's print on my chest.

"To raise the Sleeping Giants," the oracle says, "you must see what they are capable of. For that, you need strength. She is your connection to this plane."

"Is that why I feel like I've known her before?" The room gets hotter, like I'll melt right out of my skin.

"I believe you were brought together for this purpose."

In my drowsiness, I laugh. "I'm fuzzy on my feelings about fate."

The oracle holds my stare. "I fear fate is often mistaken for lack of choice. Our world, the human world, the worlds we can't see are made up of threads, like the web of a spider. Everyone you meet is a thread in your web of life, and you are a thread in the web of the world. Your cousin Brendan led you here. Your friends protect you with their lives. You sought the Naga but chose not to slay her, despite the stories Isi told you. I have dozens of prophecies in my head, but I chose to believe in you."

I lick the dryness from my lips. "He's connected to me too, isn't he? Kurt. And Nieve. Can they see me, the way I see them? In dreams?"

The Tree Mother touches my forehead with the back of her hand. Fever sweat rolls down my face. "Not here. But when you go back, I believe they will. First, you must be here and now. You must see the creatures you are going to raise."

The oracle places Amada's hand in mine. And as we lie side by side in the sweltering tent, I close my eyes.

"What happens after I see?"

I hold Amada's hand like an anchor to this place. She squeezes back.

"Then you must find the seal and destroy it."

chapter
TWENTY-FOUR

The seas are breaking.

Before I shifted into my tail, before all of this, I still felt the longing to be in the sea. My dad used to joke that I took longer showers than my mom. And even though I was doing a little more than showering, I needed to spend as much time as possible in water. The beach. The pool. Running in the park during a downpour. I could feel the torrent of the waves, the angry tug of the tide on long summer nights.

Now, under the oracle's spell, I can feel the sea ripping apart.

It is the eye of a hurricane over a long spread of ocean. The air is thick with salt. I am Kleos, eldest king of the seas, and in my hand is the Scepter of the Earth.

Beneath me, the sky falls away. I'm on the back of the biggest sea horse I've ever seen. It's as big as a ship, and so am I, holding on to its mane as it dives into the waves, its webbed claws parting expertly, its fins pushing us to the surface.

Then I realize the sea is not breaking. The kings are riding the giants of the sea. I can feel the thrill of being on the back of the creature, and a name comes to mind—Doris.

Doris, like the mother of the sea nymphs. I can feel her in my thoughts telling me that the other kings are nearby. Somewhere in my mind I remember Gwen teaching me the names of the kings.

Further out to sea, King Ellanos breaks the surface on the arm of a kraken. His jet-black hair is tied away from his face, while mine blows free in the wind. Ellanos looks so much like Adaro, his descendant. He holds on to the tentacle like a mast. The other tentacles lash out, with skin like rippled armor. I light my scepter and blast them. Doris neighs and a booming laugh comes from me.

Then the third king—Trianos—emerges from the water. I can see my grandfather in his fierce eyes, his golden skin. Trianos holds a harness in his hand around the mandible of a turtle, the other hand wielding the Trident of the Skies. The turtle has spikes all over its shell, and a curved horn jutting out between its eyes. It breaks waves that push us away.

The storm answers the call of the weapons, on and on. Mile-high waves crash over us, and we remain rooted on our giants.

Then I see my chance. I whisper something to Doris. I never was much for languages.

We dive, the sea horse's webbed forelegs and long, scaled tail ripping through the sea, and we break the surface where King Trianos rides the horned turtle. The creature is slow but strong. I jump off and onto the back of the spiked shell. I'm fast and I know it, knocking the king with the Scepter of the Earth so hard that he falls backward, sliding off the shell.

I grab his forearm. The king screams wildly. The turtle heaves. And we both fall back.

My insides ache as tentacles ram into us, knocking me into the waves. A warning screams in my head. *Watch out!* But I don't see until it's too late. A tentacle wraps around me and squeezes. King Ellanos, his golden eyes glittering because he thinks he's got me. I blast energy through my scepter, but the energy goes straight into the sky as the tentacle lifts me higher and higher.

Then a shock runs through me, my heart stopping then racing as the tentacle lets me go. I fall into the sea, but Doris cuts through the water and I grab on to her mane. We break the surface once again.

Lightning streaks the sky. Eight tentacles writhe in pain, and slowly they sink. King Ellanos floats on the surface, barely conscious, the Staff of Eternity gone from his grip. I watch as King Trianos slides the head of the trident into the staff. His hair is white as surf, his violet eyes bright in the darkening storm.

I hold on to the pain in my chest as my blood darkens the seas around me and Doris whinnies from the gash in her flesh.

"Surrender, my friend!" King Trianos shouts from atop his giant turtle. "Live for your people. Our people."

I can feel Doris's consciousness slipping. *Stay with me.*

But she can't. She's too weak. If we keep fighting, she'll die. The power has shifted and I know this.

"Catch, old friend." I throw the scepter like a lance, the quartz a brilliant crystal that pulls on the lightning around it.

Trianos catches it and completes the trident. *The* trident.

When they connect, I'm pulled out of the vision, like getting sucked out and lifted into a vacuum in outer space. I can see the king—my ancestor—as he buries the giants in the sea, deep inside separate caves. The powerful creatures I've been searching for.

The beasts protest, ripping through the earth until they fall asleep. Hearts still beating beneath layers of rock and sea. Sleeping Giants.

Then I'm pulled further out still.

I'm me again, standing in front of Chrysilla—the nautilus maid. I feel like I'm holding my breath. I need air. I try to open my gills but they're clamped shut.

Chrysilla is under water, the pink fleshy tentacles of her hair floating around her like a halo. Her eyes are dazed and wide open. They are mirrors, and in them, I saw the three kings fighting for the trident.

Chrysilla is alone, her hands pressed to the sides of her nautilus shell.

Glass shatters around her and settles on the floating dead bodies of her handmaidens. Someone has slit their throats. But Chrysilla doesn't move. She comes into focus. I can feel the cold water on my skin.

"Don't forget me, Tristan Hart," she says, putting her hand

around my neck and bringing me right to her face. "Please, don't forget me."

Her hand doesn't loosen up and I gasp awake. Here. Now.

There is a real hand around my neck.

I'm in the Vale of Tears. In the oracle's tent. I know where the seal is. I know what I have to do to break it. The same promise I made to the nautilus maid days ago. "Don't forget me," she said. But it isn't her hand around my throat. It's Karel's.

"Die, Land Prince," he says. "Die."

chapter
TWENTY-FIVE

By now I should be used to people trying to kill me.

But somehow, it always comes as a bit of a shock.

I mean, I'm a pretty cool guy. A likable guy. Ask all of my buddies back at Thorne Hill High School. Not my ex-girlfriends so much, but I'm working on that, I promise. Once we're friends, there's nothing I wouldn't do for you.

The minute you try to kill me, it's over.

I grab Karel's throat and land a punch right across his face with the new calluses I have him to thank for.

"You are still weak." He knocks me in the eye, and I know it's going to bruise. "That is why you have failed."

I push him with all my force until he rolls over, spitting blood onto the leather floor and unable to get up.

"I'm stronger than you, Ugly."

The oracle rushes in with Brendan and Yara.

"How dare you enter here!" the oracle says, her voice a deep boom that would send me hiding under my bed.

Yara grabs Karel. "Come with me. Now."

"Amada?" I ask. "Where is she?"

"When she felt you waking, she went to get me."

Now that Grumble is gone, my body trembles with adrenaline. The white fire is gone, and the blood on my chest has dried to a nasty, muddy red. I take a rag the oracle gives me and clean it off.

"You saw," she says.

"I saw." I flex my fingers, working out the pain. "And I know where to go. We have to leave right now."

The oracle nods and nods. "Take what you need."

"I just need my friends," I say.

The oracle puts her veil back on and we go outside. The circle is quiet. A few villagers gather and watch Grumble get taken away somewhere by Yara.

Isi stands on the dais, waiting for me.

I march right to her. "Are you happy now?"

She looks at me defiantly. "I did what I thought was best."

A big part of me knows not to talk to an elder this way. Not just an elder, but the leader of these people. Still, the small part of me that's been tricked and beaten the crap out of is ticked off.

"I can get over the part where you made me believe the Naga was a big threat to you, because at the end of the day, she was the big, bad wolf in your woods. What I can't get over is that you would have me kill your own daughter, and then you stand at the edge of the forest crying every night. Don't look so surprised. I've seen you."

Isi touches her temples, pushing back whatever thoughts make her weak. "I have lost many daughters to the throne. That has not changed. I could not bear to see Amada suffer so. It's been so long that I didn't recognize her face."

"I recognized yours," Amada says. She walks between the villagers who take numerous steps back. Some don't even bother to stay. She takes in their emotions, one by one, but doesn't flinch. The white dress is all kinds of wrong on her. It's like putting a tutu on a wildcat.

"I want to feel for you, Isi, I do," I say. "You all have been teaching me to be strong and push away the things that make me human. And you know what I've decided?"

She lifts her chin, waiting for my answer.

"I've decided that I like those parts of myself. All of them." I look up at the sky. Raise my arms to the violet moon, the murmuring winds around the weeping trees. "The fortnight is ending. I see Nieve and Kurt moving their armies when I dream. You can stay here lamenting the great big detention sentence the old kings gave you, or you can make yourself a new world."

Kai and Dylan come forward. Kai has traded her bow for a staff with an onyx spearhead. Dylan has my backpack over one shoulder, stuffed with God knows what. Brendan takes nothing but the sword he came with. My A team is ready.

"I'm coming with you," Amada says.

We look at each other for a long time. She has these eyes that even her beast form can't hide. Her hair is down to her hips. She has the frozen, careful movements of her days as the Naga. What must it be like to go back to your people after so long and not belong?

"No," Isi says. "You cannot go."

Amada steps forward slowly. "The stories said that a son of Triton would rid the land of the beast. Of me."

"Don't go saying I'm not a merman of my word," I say.

Yara comes running from wherever they put Grumble. I hope they tied him by his ankles from the cliff he pushed me off. "I want to go with you too."

"No," Isi says. *No, no, no.* It echoes deep into the woods where tiny birds take flight.

"But—" The maiden warrior of the River Clan gets cut off. "He's a son of Triton. He can—"

"The seal of the king may be weak, but it isn't gone yet. You are needed here with your people."

I look into the eyes of a woman who's lost so much. Then at Yara's stubborn face, hungry for a fight that she might have a chance of winning. I reach out to her and we embrace forearms.

"Despite everything," she says, "you do have allies here."

"Despite everything," I say, "you still have choices out there."

The river people go back to their fluid forms. I can feel their eyes watching us move across the square and toward the forest. After a few steps, the sun bird lets his presence be known, flying overhead.

As we walk, I tap Amada's hand. "Are you sure you want to do this?"

She rubs her arms, like they are foreign to her. "More than anything."

"Guys," I say, coming to a stop. "Do we know the way out?"

Brendan puts hands on his hips. "I thought you knew where we were going."

I sigh. "I just avoided getting killed by mini-Vin-Diesel. I wasn't about to ask for directions."

"Sometimes I don't understand the things you say." Kai shakes her head. Her hair is braided down her back like the other clan girls.

Dylan raises his hand. "I haven't had any success getting out, clearly."

He looks back at the village. It's not that far. I can make out a thin line of smoke from the communal fire pit. I elbow him lightly.

"You don't have to come," I tell him. I want to make sure that whoever is with me has a choice in the matter. Even though I know that I need Dylan on my side.

I'm glad when he doesn't hesitate. "I do. I owe it to you. To my father."

Amada is the one who holds a hand up next. The movement is so sudden that Dylan jumps back. "I believe I know the way out."

chapter
TWENTY-SIX

A mada takes us through the barren meadows to the same cave entrance where we fought.

Brendan arches his eyebrow at me, and I give him my best reassuring nod.

"This way," she says. She enunciates her words carefully, pleased at the sound of her own voice. I wonder what it's like to not hear yourself speak for years and years. Some people would call that a blessing if it happened to me.

Once we walk past the dome-like cave, we reach a dead end where a waterfall has formed from a source on the surface. The runoff water carves a path that leads to a depression in the stone, like a basin or a wishing well.

As we stand in front of the waterfall, I wish for the sound of one voice in particular, like it's as easy as fishing a penny from my pocket and throwing it in the fountain. I have no pennies. Or pockets, for that matter. Well, I do, but you wouldn't find any pennies in there.

"The island is designed to keep people out. If you make it inside, you stay. Only the king and his children and their children can come and go."

"Then it's a good thing we brought Tristan after all," Brendan jokes.

"No, you're of the family blood," Kai reminds him.

Brendan turns to me. "Where are we going exactly, dear cousin?"

And I don't even hesitate. "The Glass Castle."

"What did you see?" Kai says.

"The old kings. The first battle. It was amazing. I've never seen so much raw power. It's like they each were one being with their creatures, communicating in their minds. Like I was limitless—until I wasn't."

"Like Nieve and Kurt will be, as well," Kai says. "When the beasts rise and travel to their corresponding warrior, you'll be giving them powerful weapons. We don't know where they're buried or what they'll bring with them."

I shake my head. I saw it in the vision. "As long as I have the scepter, I can control the sea horse."

"Kurtomathetis has an oracle on his side," Brendan says, "and a small guard. The sea witch is a force of her own. Tristan is doing the right thing."

Kai nods, but I can feel her mind racing, figuring out what else can go wrong. "Don't forget the connection you have when you dream. Once we're back on our own plane, they'll see you the way you see them. Then they'll know our plans."

"Then it's a good thing I have a head start. How do I get us out, Amada?" The waterfall doesn't exactly lead anywhere.

She points to my dagger, then to a spot on the wall with a circle carved so lightly that you can only see it when you're standing inches from it. "Blood."

Of course, it needs to be blood.

"Both of you," she says to Brendan.

I smirk at my cousin. "Then it's a good thing we brought you along."

He makes a face but holds out his hand. I run my dagger down the center of my palm first, then his. I've had a lot of broken bones in my days, but I don't think I'll ever get used to my own warm blood trickling out of me. We press our hands in the center of the circle.

Nothing happens.

Gwen's voice, unwanted, pops in my head. *Magic is gradual, Tristan.*

And my own response, *So then what's the point?*

The point is to will things to work for me.

The ground shakes, stones falling down like hail. The circle line lights up with a white light, the inside pushing itself back and creating a portal of undulating black water.

"Brendan," I say, "you know the way."

He nods and dives into the dark sea.

I let the girls go next. Kai and Amada shift into their swimming forms when they hit the current. Then Dylan and I bring up the rear. The water is cold and I wonder what part of the world we're in, fearing it's too far from home.

But when we break the dark water and then the mist, we're back where we started. I look at my watch, which still reads 11:53 a.m. We swim down, down, down, and my chest tightens with the pressure. I recognize Arion's ship in a broken mess at the bottom of the sea floor.

Brendan leads us south along the rocky valleys of the sea floor. Amada swims close to my side in her Naga form. Slick gills open at her neck. Her hind legs are hunched up as she lets her serpent tail do the work. She brushes my shoulder every time she wants me to see what she sees—brilliant coral reefs, whales breaching the surface, hundreds of glowing jellyfish floating like clouds. We pass dolphins that swim alongside us for a while until we're too fast and leave them behind. Then the rock formations become tall and broken by a ridge the size of the Grand Canyon.

We swim into it until the light of the surface is long gone.

The break in the ground is narrow. I keep bumping my shoulder on the stone sides. The further we get, the tighter my chest feels, like my lungs are expanding to let in more air. We're surrounded by luminous plankton and fish with forehead flashlights and gaping mouths that are bigger than the rest of their bodies. When Dylan turns around to make sure I'm behind him, his eyes are tiny dots of blue light, his blue scales like reflective mirrors.

We swim as fast as the narrow tunnels allow, making twists and turns that I know I won't remember. The pit of my stomach is in a million knots because I've never been to the Glass Castle.

"Careful on this left!" Brendan shouts.

We turn into a pitch-black, lifeless tunnel for a couple of miles until it gives way and we're in open sea again.

Below us is a structure like I've never seen before. True to its name, the castle is made of black glass. A massive fortress straight out of myth. This is where my mother grew up when she was a mermaid. I think of her swimming out of her rooms and through the patches of green, getting restless and going straight for the surface. After all the stories, I'm finally here. Balls of light burn in the archways made for swimming in and out of. Great, golden statues of past sea kings line the entrance. The spiral turrets form peaks, as if the structure rose straight out of the ground like twisting vines reaching for the sun.

But it'll never reach the surface.

At first, the noise sounds like singing, mermaids and mermen having fun because what's the point of a castle if there aren't feasts.

Then there's a crash at the entrance, golden statues tumbling down, bodies swarming against dozens of armed guards.

"What's—" I start swimming forward, but Brendan grabs my fins and pulls me back.

"Stop! We're under attack."

Part II

Full fathom five thy father lies;

Of his bones are coral made;

Those are pearls that were his eyes:

Nothing of him that doth fade,

But doth suffer a sea-change

Into something rich and strange.

Sea nymphs hourly ring his knell:

Ding-dong!

Hark! Now I hear them—Ding-dong, bell!

—"Ariel's Song," from *The Tempest* by

William Shakespeare

LONG AGO

The Daughter of the Sea would never be free.

Not in the palace of the Rebel King Amur.

Not in the chambers where she swam and swam in circles until the Rebel King summoned her.

Strange they were to her, the people of these warm waters, so close to the surface, so close to the humans wandering in their boats like they owned the seas.

King Amur prided himself on their home made of rose gold, grander than anything they could fashion on land. He hosted nightly feasts, watching from the coral throne made from the bones of his ancestors. He drank in the beauty of Nieve, his Silver Queen.

Nieve waited on her golden seat beside the merman who was her husband king. Her high cheekbones, pale skin, and the silver scales that shone like armor in the great hall made her the center of attention, no matter how long she lived among them.

After the shadow dancers who undulated their bodies like surface smoke, the flute orchestras sweating for the king's approval, the wild shark tamers, and the chorus of guppy children who sang hymns to the Rebel King and the Silver Queen, songs of the moonlight in her eyes—it was her turn.

It was King Amur's favorite time of night, watching his beautiful bride swim to the center of the room, her hair laced with pearls and emeralds. He loved the way the people held their breath, the calm in the great hall, the hungry expectation in their eyes.

Queen Nieve faced the warrior before her and took him in, just as she had others countless times. She held up her palms and sensed the fear in his blood. When she closed her eyes, she could concentrate on the thunderous rhythm of his heart. Fearful, but resolved to stand before the Rebel Court and die. He held up his long sword, a word etched into the blade that Nieve couldn't see. She thought it was probably something that said "strength" or "honor" because the rebels loved their honor.

They were the ones who refused to live under her father, King Elanos. They were the ones who fought against the four cardinal heralds. And yet, after years of being an outsider in her birthplace, these rebels were the only ones who wanted her.

Before the warrior could attack, Nieve summoned her power. She slowed his movement by pulling at the strength of his body. She latched on to the crackling energy that made up his being. For a flash, she could see a memory—swimming with a black-haired mermaid, kissing her as if it was the only thing in the world he was meant to do. Then fighting, slashing, pillaging nearby tribes in the name of King Amur. She wondered what made men like this fight for another. He was no different than her father's soldiers, no different than the men who follow blindly into battle. Causeless. Purposeless. He was the kind of merman she was surrounded by, and it filled her heart with an angry cry.

Sparks emitted from her fingers like fissures in glass. There was a collective gasp in the golden hall, and everyone began swimming backward. King Amur gripped the coral throne and leaned forward, licking his lips as if he could taste the magic in the water the way he tasted the blood of his enemies before he reduced them to surf.

This warrior was bigger than the others. But his strength meant nothing because she was stronger. She swam around him, avoiding his sword. He recovered and tried to wrap his tail around hers. She slithered out of his grip, but his hand grabbed a handful of her hair. Pearls and gems scattered into the sea, and the hands of little mermaids reached out to grab them like trophies, like they too could have a piece of the queen. Nieve screamed and sent a blast of energy at the merman.

For a moment, she considered putting it off. It was an honor to die at her hand, but why should he get it so quickly? The Rebel King hated when they died too quickly.

Mercy, she called it.

She beat her tail and swam up toward the arched ceiling with its floating light-fish, the warrior's hands at her fins. What would it be like if she tore a hole through the ceiling and let him escape? Would he run? Would she go with him?

How fast would King Amur find her?

The warrior grabbed her, squeezing at the middle of her tail until she thought her bones would break. She pushed down on his face, digging her nails into his cheeks, and still he didn't let go, slamming her against the ceiling, scattering the light away.

For a moment, she let him squeeze her. Grip her so hard the life might start slipping away. He only had to reach her throat and close off her gills. Then she'd be free of it all.

But freedom was a small price to pay to feel this—the fire that raged inside her. Live, she told herself. All she needed to do was live and figure out a way.

So she pulled on her magic, on the light of the life around her. She brought it inside her the way she'd seen wood feed fires on the surface. She kept her hands on the warrior's face, and her scream joined his. Her current rammed into him so hard that his arms went slack instantly. She didn't let go—not even when his memories gripped her like a fist around her heart. She saw the black-haired mermaid again, with her black skin and scarlet mouth that caressed his face over and over.

Then she heard his heart burst. Surf bubbled all around her where his body once was.

The crowd's cheers could be heard through the whole palace. The Silver Queen was victorious again. She sank back down to the main hall, settling beside the warrior's long sword. She picked it up and faced her husband king.

"Witness once again the power of my queen! No one would dare threaten us," he said to his people. Then he added in a low growl, "Not even her father."

"You've pleased me once again, my wife." His eyes were drunk with lust and power. He would send for her tonight after he tired of the mermaids from the shore banks, she was sure of it.

"That brings me much happiness, my king," she said.

Around her, the court reveled.

"Does it?" he asked, knowing that her words were full of lies.

She said nothing, only held the sword against her open hands. They stung with power. Her heart stung with hate. It was coiling inside her, and she wondered when it would break like the earth spilling lava and steam. Was it now, with the sword in her hands? With his guards standing there ready to slit her throat at a moment's notice?

No. Patience, she told herself.

Patient, which the Rebel King was not.

"Give it here," he said, pointing at the sword, a spark of nervousness blooming in his thoughts.

She swam to him and handed it over. But first she read the word of honor inscribed into the blade. Gwenivere. She saw the black-haired girl in her mind and thought, What a lovely name.

chapter
TWENTY-SEVEN

NOW

Nieve," I say. Her name is a curse. A darkness I've never known before. She's nowhere in sight, but what we see while we're swimming has her signature of destruction all over it.

"This can't happen," Dylan says. "They can't do this. Not here."

I realize Kai, Brendan, and Dylan all spent part of their lives at Glass Castle. They're mesmerized, like looking at a picture that's distorted and trying to make sense of it.

We crouch below a giant boulder and ready our weapons. Amada growls and rakes her claws on the stone.

"Kai," I say, "can you lead me to the oracle's chambers?"

She stares at the fighting mermen and merrows as the echoes of screams reach us. "Yes."

"The rest of you—"

Brendan doesn't wait for me to finish. He charges down to the castle and cleaves the heads off three merrows. The black, inky blood spreads all over, creating the perfect cover for the rest of us.

Amada and Dylan flank him. Dylan commands the attention of a group of warriors who wear his family's crest on their breastplates. They fight around him, protecting him.

Amada swims fast. She opens her mandibles wide and chomps down on the merrows. The guards, never having seen her before, don't know what to make of such a creature. But they stay out of her way as she fiercely joins the skirmishes inside the castle.

Kai makes sure the coast is clear and leads me through a side entrance. Balls of conjured light float along the halls and up on the ceilings, casting long shadows. It's everything I could have dreamed about seeing and, at the same time, like nothing I've ever seen. The glass itself has the patterns of shells. Now I know why my mom chose that living-room wallpaper.

Then they come through the corridor. A mouth of nail-like teeth chomping at the open sea in front of Kai's face. I grab her and push her to the side. A merrow collides with my chest, and just as it opens its mouth, I sink my dagger into its belly.

"Hurry, Tristan!" Kai says. "If all these merrows are here, I think they're after the same thing you are."

I follow her twists and turns down hallways decorated with carvings of old mermen and women, their likenesses reduced to shattered glass, until we're at what seems like the center of the Glass Castle where the chambers are made of steel. An engraving of the trident decorates the door. It's quiet. The merrows haven't gotten this far in, and I hope we can hold them off.

"The king's chamber," Kai whispers.

She's about to go in, but I grab her wrist and press my finger to my lips. There are people inside there. We lean into the slightly open door and listen.

His voice, demanding and bossy, is instantly familiar.

"You can't go out there," Kurt yells. "You're not strong enough to fight."

I hold my dagger out in the crack of the door and see their reflection. Kurt and the Sea King, his father. My grandfather. He looks old and withered, skinny and weak. He sits on a throne of gold and can barely push himself up to yell.

There is glass all over the floor and Kurt's knuckles are bloody. Kurt turns around and runs one hand through his hair, clenching the Trident of the Skies with the other.

"I came to protect you," Kurt says.

"Because Lucine told you that Nieve's forces would be attacking the castle," my grandfather says suspiciously. "What else has that sorceress filled your head with?"

Kurt growls. "She told me the truth. The truth you failed to tell me for all of my life."

There is a silence full of shattering glass and clanking swords in the distance. The sharp screams of mermaids swimming out of the castle and others fighting back.

"It was your mother's choice. She wanted to raise you as his."

"And you said nothing," Kurt demands.

"Would you have had me force her?" the king bellows. "She

wanted him…in the end. No matter how much I offered. No matter how much I loved her."

Kurt puts his hand through something that breaks like cement.

I wince and Kai puts a hand over her mouth.

"Is that why you sent my father to the dragon wars?" Kurt says. "To get rid of him?"

My grandfather doesn't answer, and the shame of it fills the silence.

"Kurtomathetis, you are a great warrior. A great merman. Don't let this—oracle—destroy that. She's lived as long as me, and she knows how to control minds and hearts."

"If you think so highly of me," Kurt says, "why did you pick Tristan instead of your own son? To protect your shame?"

That's the million-dollar question, isn't it?

"I never meant to hurt you boys."

"We aren't boys!"

"No," the king laments. "No, you aren't."

"Lucine warned you, didn't she?" Kurt says. "She warned you to kill Nieve and you didn't. She told you to pass on the trident to your son. And you didn't. Now everything is broken. The silver mermaid has taken our island, and now our home here. She's more powerful than all of us. We'll have no choice but to follow her."

"Don't ever say that. I will not explain my decisions to you. Know that everything I've done has been because I—"

"Do not tell me you love me." Kurt's voice is deadly calm. "Not when you chose a headstrong human boy who acts more like a seal in heat than a champion of the seas."

Kai snorts then shoots me an apologetic glance.

I can't take it anymore. If they're going to talk about me, I might as well be present. Kai grabs my hand and shakes her head desperately.

"Go," I whisper. "Help the others."

"The latch door is on the ground beneath the throne," she says, taking her sword to do some good.

I pull the doors open. Kurt does a double take when he sees me. My grandfather looks relieved? I can't tell because his brow has always been furrowed and worried-looking.

"What are you doing here?" Kurt puffs his chest like a wet rooster.

"You know me, Uncle," I say. "I just show up and see what happens."

chapter
TWENTY-EIGHT

Kurt and I circle each other, like when you put tigers in a cage and neither one backs down.

"What's up, Kurt?" I say, holding my dagger as tightly as I can. "Finished giving your old lady her sponge bath?"

His eyes widen with shock. I watch him rack his brain as to how I could possibly know that. Then he's back to being angry, because I called his girlfriend old, even if she looks pretty good for being a thousand.

"Why are you here?"

"Why are *you* here?" I say. "I mean, I was supposed to be the champion, right? I was chosen by the king."

I turn to my grandfather, King Karanos. Up closer, I can see withered lines on his face that weren't there a couple of weeks ago. I remember when we found Kai's father in the Hall of Records, dying from a fatal wound to the chest. His eyes faded to the palest blue right in front of us. My grandfather's eyes are fading.

"My dear boy——" he says.

"Don't." I shake my head. "I've been washed away at sea, beaten up, sliced up, poisoned. I have mortal enemies that want my head on a platter. I almost killed an innocent—and I still have to—" I still have to kill the oracle, but I don't tell them that because no one can know. Instead I look at the mermen in my family. "I've done all of this because you chose me. You made me think I was someone important, someone who could change things, and all this time it was really because you couldn't have him."

"Oh you think you were wronged, do you?" Kurt gets up close to my face. "Where would you be if it weren't for me?"

"Not standing here with you in my way." I shove him.

He holds the prongs of the trident under my chin. They dig into my skin, and I can feel his rage, his wanting to shove the trident through my head.

"Tristan," the king's voice carries a deep grumble. Without the trident, his body is weakening, withering to bone. Coral. I can't look at him. My whole life I wanted this—a grandfather. A sense of knowing where I come from. And here I am, yelling at him for things that can't be undone. "Kurtomathetis."

But I laugh.

"Why are you always laughing?"

"I'm sorry," I say. "What do you suppose you're going to do with that?" I swim up and back, pulling my scepter from my sternum harness and holding it up to his face. "They're not working, Captain Dumbass."

Then the sparks flicker from the trident prongs and the core of my scepter. The blast is small, but it knocks the three of us against the walls of the chamber. Perhaps it's the trident and scepter's proximity to each other. Perhaps it's a fluke. Whatever the cause, we're not going to waste it. Kurt's just as competitive as I am, and he's not going to back down.

"You were saying?" Kurt says, a smug smile curving at the corners of his mouth.

"It's been a while," I say, "but I'm itching to finish what we started at the pier."

Kurt's brows furrow when I say it's been a while. Sure, it's been days for me, but for him it's been hours.

"You know my grandfather's right," I say. "Lucine is just filling your head with seaweed. Even her sisters talk smack about her."

"She's the only person who's ever believed in me." He holds the prongs forward and I brace with my scepter.

"What about Thalia?" I swim back. "Do you remember her? Do you remember your sister?"

"You were going to take her away from me." He grunts. "Make her human."

Okay. Perhaps not the best memory to bring up. "It's not the same. She'd still be alive. She'd still be your sister."

My grandfather is still trying to get us to reason with each other. *Down boys, sit. Good boys.*

But we're not good boys, are we?

"She's got your panties in a twist, bro," I say, quoting Angelo. Something he said to me the first time I realized how I felt about Layla.

"You're one to talk," Kurt says. "It's your fault Nieve has the Staff of Eternity!"

We are a two-headed dog chasing after one tail. I'm tired of hearing him talk. I raise my scepter over my head. The quartz fills with a bright light, ready to meet the light of the trident.

Then two hands push us hard against the walls. My grandfather floats above us. For a flash, he looks giant, as if his power never left him.

Kurt has the look that he had when we first met, that strong soldier stare.

"I will not justify the decisions I've made in my lifetime," my grandfather says. "Nor will I allow our bloodline to be extinguished like fire in water. I have been king. I have been a father. I have loved. I have done what was necessary to keep our people alive. I stand by what I said to you the first time you set foot on Toliss, Tristan. I meant every word. You both have very different paths. The seas are vast and ever changing. You will need each other."

"I don't need anyone," Kurt says.

The king looks down sadly. "That is where you're wrong, my son."

In the distance, there is a great crash. I need to get down that tunnel, and I need to do it without Kurt or my grandfather.

"We can beat the crap out of each other later, Kurt. I've got my team helping push back the merrows outside."

"Team?"

"Yeah, the Fintastick Mer Friends, yourself not included."

He faces the large steel doors, because I know what he wants more than to beat the crap out of me is to fight some merrows. Then he looks back at the king.

"You two must go," King Karanos says, sinking down to grab the armrest of his throne.

"What's happening to him?" I ask Kurt.

"He's losing strength too quickly. He can barely swim, let alone lift a sword."

"Then we have to get him out of here."

"I've tried that," Kurt hisses. "He won't listen."

I mutter, "Now we know why our family is so stubborn."

Screams ring out in the halls of the Glass Castle. Kurt and I look at each other, almost like we're a team again.

Then the chamber doors fly open and a current pushes the three of us against the opposite end of the room. My head bangs against the glass wall so hard I'm surprised it doesn't crack open.

My vision is foggy at first but then I see we're surrounded. Gwen swims over us in wild splendor. White blond hair a massive electric cloud around her pale moon face. Those gray eyes focused right on me. Her lips are flushed pink like her cheeks. From swimming. Fighting. Magic.

"Isn't this nice," she says. "The generations together at last."

chapter
TWENTY-NINE

She doesn't let us get a word in.

A dozen merrows swoop in on us in seconds. They're fast and strong with deformed fishy faces. The gaping mouths of sharks and eels. With webbed hands and feet, they're a cross between wild sea creatures and humans. They are the unwanted of the seas, thrown out. They are Nieve's children and they've come to storm the castle.

Their screams are feral, all grunting teeth swarming around the king.

I swim in front of my grandfather. I dig my scepter into the belly of an eel-headed merrow. He chokes on the black blood that oozes out of him and clouds the water. Kurt is as fast as lightning, ramming through the merrows' tender heads with the prongs of his trident.

It happens again—our weapons sparking. I try to hold on to that spark, but the energy slips away as quickly as it arrived.

A scaly leg knocks the wind out of my chest and pins me to

the wall. I choke on air. Water. But all I can think of is Gwen pushing the golden throne with all her weight. Kurt buried under four merrows who taste his blood from a deep bite. Then a merrow going straight for my grandfather.

I shout as teeth rip into my shoulder.

My grandfather screams as he grabs hold of his attacker's face. He snaps the neck of the creature and lets it go, now limp in the dark water made darker by their blood.

I elbow the creature off me and push the pointed quartz of the scepter into its chest. My skin burns where I pull teeth out of my shoulder and throw them to the side.

The king clutches his chest over his heart and sinks backward. His body shakes and his blue eyes keep getting paler. I grab him from the front to keep him from sinking.

He leans into my ear and whispers, "My son."

Only he's not talking to me. He's talking about Kurt, fighting blindly in the dark water. I lean my grandfather against a corner and leave Triton's dagger in his hand.

"Stay with us," I tell him.

But I notice the strain on his face. The hand clutching his heart as if trying to stop it from bursting out.

I click the quartz on the floor. The crystal lights. I can feel its power and I latch on to it, willing it to stay. *Stay.* I remember Thalia's words to my buddy Ryan as he lay dying. *Stay.*

I swim and ram the ancient weapon through a blowfish merrow, its face ready to shoot poisoned thorns. The light glows from within him and he screams as it blazes through his body, lighting up his bones through flesh. Kurt's eyes widen. Is he really so far gone that he doesn't think I'd come to his aid?

The closer we are, and the closer we use our weapons near each other, the more they come to life. He uses the current of the trident, and soon we're back to back taking down every creature that comes at us.

"The king?" he asks, impaling his trident in the meaty head of his enemy.

"We have to get him out of here," I say. "There are still too many."

The wound on my shoulder makes me more of a target than Kurt because the blood is fresh. "I'll get them to follow me."

"I don't think—"

"Get him out of here! Now!" I swim upward, and just as I thought, the horde follows me up and through the skylight in the ceiling. I'm up and above the castle surrounded by echoing screams of mermaids getting ripped to shreds. I see Kai evacuating the people inside. Brendan, a wild man trying to hold back the merrows breaching the front walls. And Dylan, surrounded by an entire guard that wears his emblem. More and more merrows are swarming out of the tunnels with sharp teeth. Their own bodies are weapons, and with so much spilled blood, they're in a frenzy.

As I hoped, the merrows in the king's chambers surround me. I hold my scepter at the ready, but with over a dozen of them, I'm a Happy Meal. One of them, with a human face and sword hands, bites at the air. He hisses and it sounds like, "Alone."

But I'm not alone.

A great set of dragon teeth bite off his head. Amada, in her Naga form, swims like a whip, chomping off arms and limbs. When she's done, she swims to me and licks the wound on my shoulder.

"I'll be fine," I tell her. "The others need you."

She nods and swims back to my friends as they retreat.

Then a jolt goes through my body. "Gwen."

I dive back down through the skylight and into the king's chamber. I open the latch to the trapdoor. A blast of energy knocks the wind out of me and presses like a foot to the chest.

Gwen swims out and keeps her hands up, holding an invisible force on me. It's hard to breathe.

"Don't," I say. "Gwen, don't."

She swims closer to me. Behind her, Archer and another merrow carry a woman. Her eyes are closed and the pink tendrils of her hair hang slack, while her crippled legs float limp. Chrysilla, ripped out of her shell.

"Go on, and don't stop 'til you reach Toliss." Gwen looks to the nautilus maid then back to me. "My mother would like to thank you for this gift."

"Tell your mother to go f—"

"You don't have to be so valiant." She pulses another crushing blast at my chest. My heart skips a beat and my lungs clench. I have the vague notion of being stomped on by an elephant.

"You don't have to be so bitchy," I gasp.

She swims closer to me but keeps the invisible stronghold up.

"You spoke of change. Of bringing the sea people together. But you could never do that, Tristan. No matter how much you try, our people don't change until they're forced. Kurt is nothing but a puppet. The others, they're not strong enough. You, with your human ways, would be dead before the next moon. Don't you see? The old ways are gone."

Her force field is fading. She's pulling it back, readying herself to go. I know I can't let her go. She's too valuable to Nieve.

"Then stay with me," I say. "Help me make a change. If Nieve loves her children so much, why does she send them out as fodder? Explain that to me. Because they're all replaceable. Because she doesn't actually care about anything other than stealing the king's power."

That does it.

I ready my scepter and she readies her hands. With Kurt gone, the power has left my scepter once again, and I get a full blast of her magic. The pillars crack and break. I never knew how much pain one person could experience. I'm screaming, the pillar falling across my chest, but I don't recognize the sounds that come out of my mouth. I hold up my hands to push the weight off but it's too heavy.

"Gwen," I shout.

She swims over to me and I think she's going to help me. Hot shocks pulse through my body as I feel something break. Ribs.

"Gwen."

She looks at me, a white pearly liquid coming out of the corners of her eyes. She shakes her head and reaches down, her pale hands around the hilt of my scepter. It burns and she lets go.

"Gwen."

She touches my face. Then she pulls back and gasps as she sees something that displeases her. She swims away in a white blur through the gaping hole in the castle wall, leaving me alone, screaming her name.

chapter
THIRTY

F orget her!" Kai shouts at Dylan.

They're here.

Amada too.

Dylan is about to chase after Gwen but turns back around. They each grab a part of the pillar and lift. Another set of hands pulls me out from under it. They let the pillar go, and it falls with a heavy thud.

"You court death more than me, Cousin," Brendan says. He pulls my arm around his shoulder and holds up my weight.

I choke back a laugh to spare myself the pain. "Where is Kurt?"

"We've evacuated most of our people," Kai says in a rush. "But the merrows are still coming in through the tunnels. The guard is weakening and we can't hold them back."

"We have to destroy the tunnels," Brendan says. "Kurtomathetis is with the king, safe in the castle gardens."

"We need to go to them," I say.

I can feel them trading glances. "He won't hurt me. It's the only way the trident pieces will work right now."

I wince at the prickling pain that spreads on my chest where the pillar crushed me. Amada shakes her reptilian head, growling in protest. She nudges me to swim to safety.

"Take me to him," I say once more, harshly.

And that's the end of it. I hold on to Brendan and the others follow.

The gardens are a patchwork of tall, thick vines that sway in the current. Flowers with petals that flare like stars emit a soft light. From here, we can hear the shouts of the merrows and watch as they consume the castle.

King Karanos lies in a patch of the tallest plants with turquoise blooms. Kurt swims over him, staring.

When we approach, he turns his head like he's surprised. I let go of Brendan and Dylan and get closer.

"Is he—" But I stop myself. No, he's not dead. If he were dead, he wouldn't look like this.

"Not yet," Kurt says.

"Tristan," says the king. I don't even recognize the hoarseness of his voice. This is happening too quickly, and panic fills me because I don't know how to fix this.

Kurt swims away. He's trying to hide his feelings by putting on that mask of his. But I know him and he can't fool me.

I sink down to my knees.

"Did they take Chrysilla?" the king asks.

I nod and look down at the sand. With a weak hand he lifts my face up. His eyes are the white of pearl now, his once-tan skin fading like an old photograph.

"This is still yours," he says, giving me back Triton's dagger.

I hesitate, but I can't say no to him.

"There are still so many things I wish I could ask you. Why did you choose me?"

He breathes in. "Some things we are not to understand until a stranger reflects it in us."

"We can heal you," I say, thinking there's got to be another place. Another Eternity. Another source of healing water that can undo this. "We can find a way."

I grab his hand and a heavy wetness trickles down my face. It's a white liquid, hot in my eyes. And as it floats away it hardens into tiny pearls. What the f—

He squeezes my hand, a gravelly breath going in and out. "Do not lose each other."

And I nod because I know he's talking about Kurt. How does he expect us to be friends again after we try to kill each other?

Then he calls out, "Brendan."

My cousin is startled, as if a ghost is calling him to his grave. He goes to our grandfather's side and takes my place kneeling.

Kurt stands a few yards away from us, beside a statue. At first I don't recognize the merman depicted. I barely recognize the statues in Central Park unless they have plaques, and this one doesn't. His face is scrunched up like he's mid-battle, and his split tails reach out at an unseen enemy. It's Triton, it has to be.

Kurt's hands grip the hilt of the trident so hard his knuckles are white as snow.

"What did he say?" Dylan asks me eagerly.

Kai elbows him and then Dylan shrugs apologetically. She places a hand on my good shoulder, and I nod my thank-you. Inside, aside from the broken ribs, the bruised flesh, and the bloody raw shoulder, I feel another kind of pain. Inside me is a loss that I can't handle. A part of myself that's breaking, and I know it's stupid because my time with my grandfather has been a blink in time. Parts of me are bitter and angry and betrayed, but despite it all, I wish I could do something to stop him from dying.

Suddenly, Kai is surrounded by a stream of the tiniest pearls. One floats past me and I squeeze it in my hand. When I turn, there are merpeople all around us. Mermaids hold their babies between their breasts, and mermen hold their swords over their heads. Refugees from the castle. As the Glass Castle is taken over in the distance, we form a perfect circle around King Karanos. I don't know whether to stay or run, but in the end, I hold the Scepter of the Earth over my head and take comfort in knowing that he's not alone.

It starts with his eyes, once the same turquoise as mine, now stark white. They roll back into his head. His skin withers and breaks. His scales shed into white sand, his bones twisting and winding until all that is left is a towering mass of coral. The vines and flowers of the garden instantly entwine themselves around it.

Kurt once told me, "We always go back to the sea."

That's all I can think about as I take my eyes off my grandfather and notice that Kurt has his back turned, alone and outside of the ring of refugees—scores of mermaids and mermen—who now turn to me.

They bow.

chapter
THIRTY-ONE

S tand, everyone," I say. "Or, you know, float."

A strong merman decked in the gold of the palace guard swims forward. "You were chosen as the king's champion. The silver witch has taken our homes above and below the sea. We will follow you wherever you will go."

"My guard is also yours," Dylan says, backed by two dozen of what's left of his men.

Here they are, giving themselves to me. Their loyalty. Asking me to protect them. It's what I've wanted, the acceptance of the Sea Court.

"I accept," I say. We embrace forearms and I feel a little more hopeful. A plan is blooming in the back of my head but first…"We must go somewhere safe."

I turn to Kai and Brendan. "We must go back to Coney Island. To the Alliance."

"Where will you be?" Kai asks.

"I'll be right behind you." Then I turn to where Kurt is waiting for me. "There's something I have to do."

Kai, Dylan, and Brendan usher our people through a tunnel behind the gardens. Truth is, I'm pretty nervous about having so many merpeople on Coney Island's shore. But the seas aren't safe, not with Nieve staking a claim in every nook and cranny, and Coney Island is the only place I've ever equated with home and safety.

I swim to where Kurt has been waiting.

"They're reveling," he says, eyes fixed on the Glass Castle. There are places where the structure looks like wrecking balls have gone in and out of it. "Yet it still stands. The castle that both of my fathers built. I remember my father and his men molding the pillars from black sand. I remember my mother waiting for him every night with the day's catch, watching us eat until we fell asleep. When he woke, he'd go do it again until it was done. I remember King Karanos coming to our chambers to speak to my parents. To give us riches for our contribution to the kingdom. And I remember the king holding my chin with his hand and looking into my eyes and telling me that I was going to be a great warrior someday. From that moment, I set down my father's tools and took up a sword."

"Kurt—" I'd like to talk about the great mer-elephant in the room, but Kurt is all business.

He points to the tunnels we came through. "First, we'll close those off, then—" We let the "then" linger.

We swim to the openings of the tunnels. A few merrows are still trickling through on their way to the Glass Castle. I latch on to the power of my scepter, pushing through the pain in my body.

Together, we tear down the valley wall. Boulders break off and cascade in an avalanche to the castle grounds.

Here comes the "then."

"Are you sure you're—"

Kurt lets go first. He holds the prongs of the trident over his head. I join him with the light of my scepter, aiming at the bottom pillars of the castle. The merrows scream as the structure breaks over their heads and crushes them. Some try to escape, but Kurt fries them before they have a chance to swim away.

For a long time, we wait.

Wait for the glass and stones to settle.

Wait for the black cloud oozing out of the castle to clear.

Wait for our worlds to mend back together, but I know they can't. Not right now. Not yet.

Kurt leads the way out through the secret tunnel. The pitch blackness folds around us, but I shine the light of my scepter. There is no life here, not as long as we swim through the twisting passageway. I can feel myself slow down, my wounds taking over. I push harder and harder, and then we're out.

The pressure loosens from my limbs; the water is warmer and lighter.

"*Wait!*" I shout. "Where are you going?"

Kurt looks over his shoulder. "The people have chosen you, Tristan. I have a different path."

He turns around, as if he's realized something. It's like there's another voice in his head, and I realize it's Lucine's. He swims closer to me with his trident at the ready. The lightning sparks. My eyes are heavy. My arm hurts too much to lift my weapons. I'm weak enough that he could kill me if he wanted to.

Then a growl reverberates through the water. A shadow climbs over me, snapping its teeth. Kurt moves back wordlessly and swims away.

Amada swims around me, shifting her top half back into human form. She has strange plants in her hands.

"That's twice you've saved me," I say.

She gives me a small smile and sizes up my wounds. "We must get you to the surface. I can heal you."

When I sheathe my weapons, my muscles and bones burn at a level of pain I never thought I'd reach. Amada shifts into her Naga form and I shift into my legs, getting on her back. I hold on as tightly as I can, and she swims like my life depends on it.

chapter
THIRTY-TWO

When we reach the surface, the sun is setting over the Coney Island shore.

Amada pulls me onto the sand and shoves some of the plants down my throat.

"Chew," she commands.

And I do it. The plants are salty and bitter like ginger, but as the liquid squeezes out of them, my skin warms my whole body. I can feel my chest rising and I can breathe better. She chews on something as well, then spits it out into her hand and spreads it over my shoulder.

"I know you're trying to help, but that is unhygienic."

She laughs. "My saliva mixed with these plants makes a healing salve."

"Oh."

"Yes, oh."

I lay my head back on the sand. The sky crackles with a coming storm. I can smell the recent rain on the sand, feel the swell of the boardwalk. I know I saw the damage through Kurt's mind, but seeing it myself feels like I'm getting kicked in the gut all over again. I take a fistful of wet sand and rub it between my fingers. There's a rusty bottle cap mixed in.

Amada looks at it and says, "I've never seen a shell that looks like that."

I laugh. "That's just trash. They're all over the beach."

"Why would there be trash on the beach?"

"This is your first time on human soil?"

"Since our banishment. So long ago." She nods, suddenly realizing how far away she is from home. I follow her eyes to the old rides—the Cyclone, the Wonder Wheel (still out of service and slightly dented because of certain sea creatures). The graffiti grates of the closed bars and restaurants. The overturned garbage cans that contain decaying food and plastic.

"This is your home?"

I'm about to say that it's not always like this. Except it is.

"Home sweet home," I say.

"How do you feel?" she asks.

"Not dead." I stand and hold out a hand to her on the boardwalk. "The others can't have gone far."

I start heading toward Frederik's place because the Aquarium was totaled.

Then someone shouts my name from behind us. I draw my dagger and turn around, holding it at arm's length. Amada bares her claws and readies herself in a fighting stance.

At the end of my dagger is a lovely green-haired girl. I stand down immediately, and she jumps on me with a giant hug. "We've been waiting for you!"

Amada scratches her head and retracts her claws.

Thalia kisses my cheek with her lip-glossed mouth then holds my hands like she's afraid I'll go somewhere again.

"Tristan," Thalia says, startled. "You've cut your lovely hair."

"The seas are breaking apart and you frown at my haircut. What, don't you like it?"

She studies my face. "It makes you look too serious."

I run a hand over my buzz cut and shrug. "I'm still cute though, right?"

"You're absolutely gorgeous," a dark voice says from behind me. Frederik, Mr. Creeps Up When You're Not Looking Because He's a Vampire Without Manners, stands with his hands buried in his pockets. Then he pulls me into a hug.

"I must be a dead man," I say, because the vampire doesn't hug.

"Not quite yet," Fred says, eyeing Amada curiously. "But you will be if you don't get your folk out of my house."

"They're in your house?" My voice breaks. "I told Kai to bring them here."

Frederik tucks his black hair behind his ear. "In case you haven't noticed, the city has been evacuated because of the encroaching hurricane, thanks to your kind. I couldn't have them roaming the city. Marty took one look at the blond merman and ushered them all into the building."

"I thought the Alliance was staying with you," I point out.

Frederik nods coolly. "The space is big enough, but tempers will get the best of our small army."

I look up at the sky. *Come on, Triton, as your descendant, do me a solid.* I reach for my shirt because it feels tight on my chest, and then I realize I'm naked except for the scales that cover my goods. Right, that's what pressure feels like.

"Before we take care of the room and board for my small army, I have to find Shelly."

Frederik's eyes widen. "She's not in the park. Tonight's a big night for her. She won't want to be disturbed."

"What else do you need from her?" Thalia asks.

I wish telepathy came with the merman gig. If all fails, there are always charades.

"I can't say." I put my hands on Frederik's shoulders. He's cold as hell, even through the black T-shirt. "I need Shelly's help. Can you trust me?"

Frederik wants nothing more than to get the Sea Court out of Coney Island. Ever since it arrived, our little strip on the Brooklyn beach has been terrorized.

"Merrow!" Thalia wields her sword over her head.

Amada is faster, running across the boardwalk and onto the sand. She shifts midair, jaw wide open. Her teeth sink into the creature's neck, reducing it to stinky black flesh. Amada makes a deep guttural sound that's a cross between a hairball and a growl. She sprints back to the beach to get the taste out of her mouth.

"Shelly," I say, pointing at the decomposing pile of flesh. "I don't care if she doesn't want to be disturbed."

"I'll get Marty," Frederik says. "Thalia, you and the—"

"Naga," I offer.

"Right. You two patrol the beach. I'll send help."

Thalia positions herself on a lifeguard tower. My lifeguard tower. The one Layla and I trade off on shifts. Just hold on a little longer, Layla, I think.

"Come on, Sea Prince," Frederik says. "You always know how to put a smile on my face."

"But you aren't smiling," I point out, following a few steps behind him.

"Exactly."

chapter
THIRTY-THREE

Frederik leads Marty, Kai, and me down a manhole on Bowery and Jones Walk. The underground tunnels smell like cat vomit mixed with laundry detergent.

"I must say, Tristan," Kai says, "you do take me to the most interesting places."

"Don't blame the Sea Prince," Frederik says. "The invitation requires us to enter in pairs. And the skeleton brothers prefer to see a lovely face."

Kai smirks but ignores the compliment. "You mean to say there are creatures who live down here?"

"A lot of demons and solitary fairies call the sewers home," Marty says. "There's plenty of room, and they're mostly undisturbed by humans."

He shines an industrial flashlight on the ceiling, and tiny, decrepit winged creatures scatter.

"I can't believe I've lived here sixteen years and never knew this existed."

"There are entire worlds in the in-betweens of human cities," Frederik says.

"Not everyone can pass for human aboveground, you know," Marty says.

"Then what's the point of coming here?" I ask. "If all you'll ever do is hide?"

Our feet splash in the trickle of water that seems to run down every tunnel. Whispers and strange clucks echo around us, and every now and then, heads peek out of their hiding places to get a look at us before going back to their business.

"Some of these people—and I use the term lightly—come from different war-torn dimensions. We call them demons because our world has no name for them. The fairy courts have their own banished and solitary fey. Runaway witches. Lone werewolves and vampires. They seek refuge in the shadows of this city to try to make a new life."

"What about you, Frederik?" Kai asks. "What were you seeking refuge from?"

Then Frederik moves right beside her. "My job is to keep the peace. That's why the Thorne Hill Alliance exists."

No one points out that he totally evaded the question.

Kai shakes her head. "I can't imagine what keeping any sort of peace is like when there are so many different folk."

"I'm not saying it's perfect," Frederik says roughly. "Make a right."

We stop at a lightless tunnel. Even the flashlight is useless. Frederik reaches out into the black wall. The doorbell sounds like it's announcing the end of a basketball game. A shape molds out of the door, like it lives inside the metal. Filmy skin clings to the large skull. It sniffs the air deeply. Then again. And again.

When it opens its mouth, a black tongue slithers out.

I whisper to Marty, "What. Is. That?"

The skeleton thing growls at first. It sucks its teeth, long strings of saliva clinging to the lips like a cat's cradle. "Ah, Frederik. I'm so glad you've finally accepted our invitation. However, I regret that we are about to begin."

"I'm sorry, Qittar," Frederik says, taking on his slow, friendly tone, "but we're here for Shelly. It's a matter of life—"

The skeleton man sucks in his breath again, and this time he chokes on it. "Why, Frederik, are you here to interrupt the sacred ritual of Selene?"

"Not exactly—" I say.

The voice becomes huskier, deeper. "Do you think this is a trivial thing? Some of our candidates only have a hundred years left before they can no longer breed, and you have the gall to stop this from happening?"

"Wait a minute, time-out," I say. "Is this, like, a make-out party?"

Qittar gulps down more air and pushes himself further out of the solid door, bony hands against the black film that allows him to protrude from the strange metal. "I smell something fishy."

"That's racist, bro."

"Tristan," Marty says, "now's not the time to be charming."

Though let's face it, I'm always pretty charming.

I step between my friends. "Listen, Mr. Qittar. I'm sorry we're late. I really need to speak with Shelly. She's important to our cause."

"I know you," he says.

I'm not so sure what he means by that. "This is the first time I've taken a stroll down this neck of the sewers."

"No, I've heard your name. Yes, yes! You, the Sea Prince fighting for the land he loves. For the girl he loves. You, betrayed by your own blood. I have heard of you. What a delectable candidate." Qittar traces a bony finger along his jaw. When his white eyes settle on Kai, he can barely get a sentence out. "I do…I do believe there's still time!"

A second figure pushes its way through the door. He has a small, long skeletal head with pointed ears and two sharp front teeth. His voice is high pitched as he shouts, "Qittar! We must begin while the moon is in place!"

"Don't remind me of things I already know, Qamir!"

The skele-bros pull themselves out of the door.

"They're not buying it," I tell Frederik. "I'm going to break down the door."

Before he can stop me, I slam shoulder first into the metal. The pain blinds me. I swallow a scream and stand back up.

"It's solid steel molded by fairy fire," Frederik says.

Then the door opens and the skele-bros stand beside it. They're the same height with skin that clings to their bones without the imprint of muscle. They're walking, talking mummies. Without the door standing in our way, they smell like it too.

Qittar ushers us into a dimly lit room with plush, black velvet walls and elaborate chandeliers. A quartet of blue-faced men fill the room with deep, vibrating music that gives the room a pulsing effect.

Two dozen or so tables are lined up in rows of three. A silver bell and a long-stemmed black rose sit in the exact middle of each one. Different men—of sorts—take empty seats. A hard nudge shoves me toward an empty table.

I nod at the fellow beside me. He has small tusks protruding from his square jaw. His hair is down to his back in a thick, black twist. He winks a silver eye and fixes the front of his T-shirt.

"First time?" he asks.

In front of me, a large slime-man passes gas and I hold my hand to my nose, nodding. "Yep. You?"

"I was here last month," Tusks says.

"Don't take this the wrong way, but why are you doing underground speed dating? You're a pretty good-looking dude."

He points to the small tusks on his chin. "My mom says it was by the mercy of the Blood Goddess Hecinda that I didn't inherit my father's nose."

I snort then apologize.

"It's quite all right. I'm just doing this for my parents. Our dimension was turned into a black hole by a nasty conjurer. Now most of us live in the Bronx. White Plains. But my mom's all like 'You need to bring home a nice Vasiki woman.' I'm related to all the women in my clan. What about you? What's wrong with you?"

There's an essay I don't want to write. "I'm Tristan."

"Ewin."

Then his eyes fall on someone, and when I turn to see, he's got his eyes fixed on Kai. She sweeps her hair over one shoulder and twists one end over and over.

"Oh," Ewin says. "Oh, I like her."

"Welcome!" Qittar says to the crowd. He has the charm of a used car salesman with a lot full of lemons and a one-way ticket to Mexico in his pocket.

A man covered in hair from head to toe takes a mustache comb out of his back pocket and combs the hair on his neck.

I glance at Frederik one table across from me and hope that my alarm is conveyed in my eyes. He shrugs and holds out a hand that is meant to pacify me but only makes me fidget in my seat.

"Don't be nervous," Ewin says to me.

"Gentlemen," Qittar says. "Ladies. Welcome to the tried and true tradition that is the ritual of the Goddess Selene." He pulls the microphone cord to move with him as he walks through the tables like a game-show host.

"For millennia, our order has created trusted matches. Helen and Menelaus. Catherine and Henry. Brad and Jennifer."

"Those are not very good examples," I whisper to the guy on my right.

"Now! These are the rules. The rotation starts when the lights flicker. Qamir, my apprentice, will hit the buzzer. You have one minute to be sure this is the mate for you."

A nervous rustle of clothes suggests that his challenge has been accepted.

"And when you know she is the one, you give her the black rose. If she takes it, then our work here is done and done. Nothing makes me happier than matches made underground. *Sí, me gusta, xi huan, ani ohev!*" His chuckle drags on but stops abruptly. "If she doesn't—then, not to worry! You get two more nights, not refundable of course. Yes, you with the fur?"

Furry Man twiddles his fingers nervously as everyone turns to look at him. "This is my first time. I know there are three nights. But what if you don't find your match in these three nights?"

Qittar clenches his teeth in a fake smile. "Under the rare and extremely improbable chance that our beauties are not to your liking, then have no fear! We are a monthly ritual. Please see Qamir about a yearly discount at the door."

Someone else raises a hand, but Qittar acts like he doesn't see it.

Then, among the girls, I see her—Shelly! She's in one of her oracle shrouds that remind me of the saris our neighbor Mrs. Patel wears. I know it's Shelly—the pale white of her skin, the deep black eyes so much like those of the Tree Mother in the Vale of Tears. Except Shelly looks different. I only saw her two days ago. Is she taller? Did she lose weight? She sees Marty and Fred, and when she settles her eyes on me, it's like I asked her to smell my armpit.

The lights flicker and suddenly there's a giantess sitting in front of me. She has one blue eye lined with a double cat's tail and a huge fake eyelash. She bats it and takes my hand.

"Una," she says.

"*Dos-tres*," I say nervously, trying to pry my fingers from her viselike grip.

"Strange name." She smiles. Her dress is Pepto pink against her blue skin.

"You look nervous. Do you want a massage?"

Something about the cock of her single eyebrow has me blurting out, "No!"

The buzzer hits and then we switch. Marty does his best penguin impression for a goth girl who doesn't know which way to run. A lady in white skips me completely and goes straight to Frederik's table. The vampire glances at me with a smug-ass smile.

Off to the side, Una and the slime man have made a match. There's radio applause from the DJ station where Qamir pushes buttons.

"Kai!" I say when she sits across from me. "Thank God. Okay. Plan—When Shelly sits here, I'll give her the rose. Then we make a break for it."

"I don't think the skeleton men are going to be too happy about that." She bites her lip. She's still and keeps a hand over the hilt of her sheathed sword. "They take this very seriously."

"Then they should've just sent out Shelly when I asked."

The buzzer makes us both jump, and she gives me a warning glance.

Finally, Shelly is at my table.

"You look beautiful," I say genuinely. "Did you do something with your hair? Not that you don't always look nice."

A lion's grumble sounds in her stomach. "You shouldn't be here. This is an invasion of privacy."

"Shelly, you have to listen to me. I went to your sister, the Tree Mother, and she showed me things. I need you to put up a barrier so Nieve and Kurt can't see me coming. We're all connected. Even Kurt, that son of—Shelly, they could be looking at us right now!"

She purses her lips and glares into my eyes. "They're not. Not this moment, at least."

"Then you see?" My voice is on the verge of squeakiness. "I need you to help me make it stop."

"The oracles are not supposed to interfere."

I laugh. "Tell that to your big sister Lucine."

Bzzzzzzzz.

She stares at the face of the black rose I'm extending. She knows that I'm right. She reaches out and takes it. The radio applause cheers as another couple gets together. Then I realize people are clapping in our direction. I nod my head at Marty and Frederik, who give each other a black rose. Frederik holds his hand out to Kai.

Kai makes it halfway across the tables when a demon man grabs her by the wrist.

"*Hey!*" I yell. "Let her go."

The demon man points a triangular nail at Qittar. "This is my match."

"I think it's supposed to be a two-way street," I say.

Qittar shrugs and mumbles something that sounds like, "No refunds."

Demon Guy turns to me and I take a step back, fighting my gag reflexes when I see his face. Dozens of holes with worms sinking in and out like a stitch pattern.

"Seriously?" I ask. "Even with this thing, how do you expect to get a date?"

He growls, spit hanging between his lips like cobwebs blowing in the wind. A knife materializes in his hand. I lift my dagger to block his, but something—someone—grabs him from the back and flings him across the room.

Ewin from the Bronx.

The rest of the crowd lunges at the skeleton men, demanding their money back.

Ewin motions to the door.

"That's solid metal," I warn him, "forged by f—"

He rams right through it, the door snapping out of its hinges. He winks a silver eye and holds out his hand to Kai.

"All right," I say, waving my hands between them. I lead the way out of the sewers, our feet marching to a synchronized rhythm mixed with the haunting echo of the blue-man orchestra behind us. "We have a barrier to put up, an attack to plan, and two worlds that need saving. Everyone, this is Ewin."

Marty laughs. "Just a regular Friday night."

chapter
THIRTY-FOUR

We march down Surf Avenue past stores covered in graffiti tags and groups of people who wouldn't evacuate if you told them a meteor was headed straight at their homes. They sit under the glass bus stops, drinking booze out of paper bags. When we pass by, they stare, blinking and rubbing their eyes, wondering if we're real or if they're just real drunk.

Frederik and Marty live in the old Childs Building. It's been a restaurant and a roller rink, and now it's boarded up and covered in graffiti.

Waiting outside is a group of the landlocked and the Thorne Hill Alliance.

One of them is Penny, a hardworking mother who's believed in me from the beginning. Her arms reach out into the rain, and she lets her hands shift back and forth between human fingers and tentacles. Each one of the landlocked is different. Some were banished because of something their parents did. Others because they made bad choices. There's a guy with eyes the size of baseballs and a tiny fish mouth. His tank top says Hurricane Gym. Another guy the size of a sumo wrestler, with acid green skin, paces the boardwalk with his eyes trained on the waves.

Someone whistles at me. Up above is Rachel, the demigoddess, sitting on the roof, her crossbow fully loaded. She's flanked by men and women with black retracted wings that make me think of flying Vikings. Howls ring along the deserted beach, a reminder that it's the night of the full moon and they're restless, but they're still here.

When I was little, my dad said I was good at picking up strays because I always brought home a lost dog or a kitten. One time it was a pigeon with a broken wing. Another time, a rat with its tail bitten off. My mom didn't like that one. But we took care of them.

I'm going to take care of my army of strays.

Penny shakes my hand. "I'm glad you're back. The beach has been quiet, minus a handful of stragglers."

"Good. We have work to do."

When Penny notices Shelly, she gasps. Penny gets on her knees and takes Shelly's hand.

Shelly pats her hands gently, but I can tell she doesn't like the attention. "There's no need for that, child."

Shelly points a finger at me. "I hope when this is over, I don't see you for a long time. You hear me? Central Park north of Sixty-sixth Street is off limits."

I scoff. "You can't do that. Can you?"

Frederik and Marty shrug and nod.

"Shelly." I kneel down to her. She gives me her cheek, but I'm used to her being cranky. "This is the reason you're changing, isn't it? Because your sister was killed in the Springs of Aurora."

She doesn't have any quips for me because she knows I'm right.

"I used to envy my sisters and their sight. Now…" Shelly's black eyes concentrate on the space between my eyes. For a moment, she's not there. Worry lines crease her forehead, and I'm afraid of what she's seeing. I reach out, touch her hand, and she jumps. Then her sweet, motherly smile is back. "We're not supposed to pick sides."

I kiss her cheek. "But I'm your favorite, I know."

"We'd best get inside. It's getting too dark." She pushes me away. "Draw an unbroken line of salt around the building. Not a skinny sprinkling over your shoulder. I mean a visible line. When the barrier is up, you'll feel it."

"Where am I supposed to get that kind of salt?"

"You're the champion. Figure it out."

Marty pushes up the gate to let Shelly in. She whispers an ancient language so quickly that it's like someone hit the Fast Forward button on her.

"How are you supposed to put down salt if the ground is wet?" Kai asks.

"It stopped raining," I say. Then it hits me. One of the great things about being a merman who's survived New York City blizzards. "The salt they use to melt snow. It's the same thing as table salt. It just doesn't clump up."

Marty wiggles his baseball cap. "I know where we can get some. Come with me."

Marty, Ewin, and I carry sacks of salt over our shoulders. Marty has a key to every building on the boardwalk. We got into the Cyclone stadium and traded the bags for an IOU favor to a vampire maintenance worker.

"Is it clockwise," Marty says, cutting off a corner of his bag, "or counterclockwise?"

"She didn't say."

Ewin takes a crystal from the bag and pops it on his tongue like candy.

"That's not—" Edible. If he can bust through enchanted doors, he can eat chemically processed road salt.

"I'd go with clockwise," Ewin says, "just to keep a natural flow. Make sure you're inside the circle as you draw it, or you'll have to do it again."

"How do you know all this?" Marty asks.

Ewin shrugs. "My ex-girlfriend is a Wiccan."

Then a car flashes its hazard lights and jumps the curb. Ewin reaches out a hand and places it on the hood of the car. The tires squeak, and the engine cuts off. "State your name and purpose."

The side gate opens and Frederik is a flash beside the passenger door. "That's dinner."

"Not me, right, Fred?" the short delivery guy says. "Just the pizza, right, Fred?"

Frederik shoves an envelope into the delivery guy's hand. The guy tries to help carry the pizza in, but the vampire holds up his hand in a "stay" motion.

"Hey, Fred, when are you going to let me into the Alliance?" The delivery guy pushes his glasses up the bridge of his nose. "I've got skills, man. I'm real handy in a tight spot. What are you planning, huh? An evil force about to take over the city? You're not wearing that, are you? Superheroes need spandex and a big symbol."

"We'll talk," Frederik says with a pained smile. The guy drives away and Frederik mutters, "Soon as you stop calling me Fred."

"Can you guys go inside?" I shout.

I take this moment of being alone to look up at the gray overcast sky. Thick clouds hang so low it looks like they're eating the tops off buildings. Mermaids don't believe in heaven, so what's the point of looking up and giving a shout out to my grandfather? "I won't fail you."

I said the same words to Isi in the Vale of Tears, but this time it's different. I can only promise to try as hard as I can and hope my words find him.

I feel a hot twinge between my shoulder blades and blame it on all the beatings I've taken. Six bags of salt later, I've drawn a thick line around our perimeter. I run to the empty second floor, along the white balcony banister, until I find the empty room where Shelly could be. She floats over the tiled floor as if she's moving underwater.

"Shelly?"

I inch closer. Her black eyes are dilated toward the ceiling, and her lips move rapidly in the language of the gods—that's what oracles speak.

"I wouldn't interrupt," Frederik says.

I jump and put my hand on my heart. "Don't do that."

"We have a problem."

I rub the pain in my skull. "What is it?"

Below, my cousin Brendan is trying to push back a merman who's pointing a finger at Amada. She gets ready to crouch on her hind legs, but when she sees me, she resists the urge to change. The merman punches Brendan, who stumbles into Penny's outstretched tentacles. Kai has her hands up, yelling at them to stop, but dozens of punches fly. Glass shatters and walls are punched to dust. I fear we may kill each other before our enemies have a chance.

chapter
THIRTY-FIVE

What was I expecting?

That the landlocked, the Alliance, and the Sea Court would get along famously? That they would see that we are in this together? That if we start fighting over things that happened hundreds of years ago, we don't stand a chance?

That all it would take would be me to bring them together? And if I can't pull together this army, how will I pull together a kingdom?

I run downstairs, narrowly avoiding a blow to the face. I snatch the golden conch from a guard's neck and blow.

They turn, one by one. I blow the conch again, the hollow noise vibrating against the walls.

"What is going on?" I stand at the center of the room.

Brendan wipes a cut on his lip and brushes his red hair out of his face. He and Amada stand behind me.

Dylan has a white-haired merman by the arms, pulling him away from Jim, one of the landlocked. Jim is shaking so hard that the light protruding from his forehead blinks like a strobe light. Penny puts an arm on his shoulder and begs him to calm down. He points at his attacker. "Stay away from me."

I have new sympathy for my coach after all the times my boys and I started fights with other swim teams.

"Is this why we're here?" I ask them. "To rip each other to shreds? Because you really should save some for Nieve and her merrows."

They erupt in wordless chatter. Their voices are so loud that they sound like a swarm of mutant wasps.

I bang the Scepter of Earth on the cement floor. The sharp sound makes some of the merpeople cringe. "*Enough!*"

I can sense that everyone is ready to grab their weapons, and I know that, for better or worse, I have to end this.

"This is not conducive to defeating the sea witch," I say. "Toliss is overrun. The Glass Castle is destroyed. We have to band together or there won't be a Sea Court to save."

"So it's true?" Penny asks. "The Glass Castle is gone?"

I nod my head. "Kurt and I blew it up with an entire merrow army inside it."

"Kurt?" Penny raises her eyebrows, eyes shifting to Thalia. "Where—?"

"He's gone," I say to Thalia. "He didn't say where, but wherever he is, we know that he's with Lucine."

Thalia nods silently.

"Nieve wants to rule," I say, standing between the people of land and sea and those in between. "She's terrorized you out of your homes. She's taken hold of the island. She has her magic and her army of merrows. But she doesn't have this." I hold up my scepter. "I won't let her."

"Then tell us." The white-haired merman loosens himself from Dylan's hold. "Tell us how you plan on stopping the most powerful mermaid of our lifetime."

I don't answer them. Come on, Shelly, I think.

Nieve thinks she knows me. She'll assume I'll go straight for Layla. It kills me inside, but I have to go to the nautilus maid first.

"I don't suppose the prince knows," says a shrewd-looking, slender mermaid with scalloped braids piled atop her head. "I suppose he'll send us out as bait to give him time to rescue that girl. We don't stand a chance."

"Wait a minute," I say defensively. "I never said that."

"Don't talk to him like that," Penny says.

The scarlet scaled mermaid points a finger in Penny's direction. "Who are you to talk to the prince, you banished scum?"

"That's unnecessary," I tell her.

"Taking their side, are you?" shouts another mermaid. She's shaking and has a bright red gash on her arm. "They said you'd be fonder of the banished than of the true folk."

"I am true," Penny says, but her courage is failing her. It's those years of secret meetings in abandoned subway rooms, led by a man who wanted nothing more than to exploit them. Use them. Always reminding them that they were of the sea but could not be part of it.

"Penny fought side by side with me right on this shore," I say. "Can any of you say the same?"

Some cross their arms, refusing to look at me. Others look torn between what they've always been told and a future that is completely unknown.

"Most of you have known me for the blink of an eye." I point to both sides of the room. "It's a lot to ask for your trust, but know that you are not just bait to me. And if you can't at least be civil with each other, then we're all dead."

The warehouse is silent for a long time. Everyone trades suspicious glances until finally my friends decide to lead by example. Dylan walks up to me and bows his head, then nods to the Alliance and landlocked behind me. He takes Penny's hand and shakes it. His men follow suit, bowing at me on the way to take arms with strangers.

I have a knot in my stomach, waiting for swords to fly, but it doesn't happen. Finally there are a few merpeople left, still on their side. They're older, and under the fluorescent lights their skin is tinged with an algae-colored paleness.

"I'm not shaking hands with him," the old merman says, pointing at Jim with the flashlight dangling from his forehead.

Jim turns his cheek to the old man but doesn't respond. I suspect he's had a lifetime of those kinds of comments.

But the old man persists, walking toward him with an accusatory finger pointed at him. "His father was there the first time around with Nieve. He and his kind should have stayed buried in their caves."

Jim, who I've never seen smile before, bares a hideous set of teeth. His jaw unhinges and elongates further than his upper lip.

The old man draws his sword.

And then so does everyone else.

I bang my scepter on the ground again. "Get. Back."

The old man looks like he wants nothing more than to drive that blade into the closest body he can find. So I stand between him and Jim.

"If you won't consider the things I've said, then the best thing for you to do is leave."

Some of the mermaids gasp.

"Do you know who I am, boy?" the old merman says.

"No, but I'm sure you're going to tell me."

"I am Sulas, son of Tulastian." He puffs up his chest the way I've seen those red-breasted birds do. "I fought alongside your grand-father. What did that mongrel do but come from a long line of banished folk? What did these beasts ever do, other than hide in the shadows of the dry land?"

I get up close to Sulas, son of Tulastian, and he doesn't pull his sword away. The tip pricks my skin. Brendan and Marty step forward, but I hold my hand up and they stop advancing.

"I'm only going to say this one more time. If you won't consider the things I've said, you can leave. I will not force anyone who doesn't want to be here to fight with me. I don't have time for titles or lordships. We're not in Toliss. We're in Brooklyn. I want people who are true and willing to fight for the future, not the past."

It isn't the thing he wants to hear from me.

It isn't the thing many of them want to hear from me.

So, Sulas, son of Tulastian, sheathes his sword. He smiles at me and says, "Then you will die at the hands of the silver mermaid, Land Prince," and walks out into the Coney Island night.

The chill air comes in, along with the stink of rotting flesh polluting the water. The building shakes. A light pulses through the air, the walls, and my skin, right down to my chest. The headache that's been pounding in my head is gone, and I feel weightless.

Then my remaining army of strays gasps in awe at the light coming from the second floor. It's Shelly, floating, her black hair thick and long and moving as if underwater. She descends over us, landing right in the middle of the room. Hands reach out to touch her, just to make sure she's real.

Her eyes trained on me, Shelly says, "Don't ever say I don't come through on my promises, Tristan Hart. It will only last until morning, I'm afraid."

"That's fine," I say, "because tomorrow, we fight."

chapter
THIRTY-SIX

H ow many does that make?" I ask, though I don't want to know the answer.

Marty looks up at the chandelier and counts the people who've left on his fingers. "Twenty-one."

"Seventeen." Dylan corrects him. "When my kinsman learned Shelly favors you, he and his brothers decided to stay."

Dylan sits beside Marty and accepts a slice of pizza. Even though Frederik says the entire city has been evacuated due to a massive hurricane warning, Dominick's Pizza is still open. After our little scuffle, most of the pizza was splattered on the art deco walls. We reordered a hundred large pies—cheese, bacon, and pineapple—because it's my way of getting the merpeople to trust me.

Brendan appraises the newcomer. "Pardon me, but what are you?"

"I am Ewin of the Vasiks clan," he says. "I am not man nor beast. I simply am. I come from the Vasiks dimension, which is now a black hole."

"Do all your kind have those?" Brendan touches his own chin.

"Those who are left, yes. I am indebted to Tristan Hart and his generals. They saved me from a lifetime of unhappiness."

"Generals," Marty says, liking the title. "I can live with that."

There have been zero arguments over hundred-year-old grievances for half an hour. We have enough cliques to put my high-school cafeteria to shame. The court mermaids are fish out of water, touching every surface of the great room. There is not a single vase, portrait, or light switch that is left untouched. Those with children have commandeered all available bathrooms to keep the babies in water because they can't shift yet and scream bloody murder.

The Sea Guard is more willing to mingle with the landlocked and Alliance members. The Alliance is schooling the guard on life on land, and the guard shows the landlocked new fighting techniques.

Some of the older folk stay close to Shelly. Every couple of minutes, she looks over to me, like she's on a date she can't escape. She's not used to being the center of attention, but I think a secret part of her has always wanted to be as powerful as her sisters. It's easier to be humble about the things you have when you've gone so long without.

Me, on the other hand, I've always been in the spotlight. Captain, lifeguard, and all-around stud. Now? The landlocked and the Sea Court come up to me to touch my hands, as little kids run around wielding weapons to be like me and run up just to have a look at the Scepter of Earth close up. I don't know what to do with this kind of influence. One older mermaid with pale green hair that reminds me of pistachio ice cream smiles her wrinkled face at me and kisses the scales at my ankles.

"It's the worship of the king," Kai tells me as the woman walks away.

I want to say that I don't like it, but I don't want to hurt their feelings.

Marty edges closer to where Dylan sits with his legs crossed. "So you were in that Neverland too, huh?"

Dylan's golden face becomes red. He has a mouth full of pizza and mumbles, "Mmm-hmm." I can tell he's burning his tongue but he swallows without chewing. "I found Lord Tristan when he was getting attacked by the—"

I clear my throat and give him a look that says "Shut the hell up." Amada retreats into her seat and I put my hand on her shoulder.

She frowns. "I was not attacking him. I was trying to get him out of the mud pit."

Dylan looks sideways, raking his fingers through his blond mane. "The growling must've confused me."

"Either way, I'm glad Tristan has found a new protector," Frederik says, leaning against the wall with a Slurpee cup. The straw fills up with a deep red liquid, which makes Dylan and Brendan gag, not being used to vampires.

"You did a brave thing, Tristan," Kai says. "The landlocked have never had a voice in the court. Most of them—us—never think of them unless vile stories are being told. Those who've stayed are doing something their ancestors never would have."

I pick a pineapple chunk off my pizza and let the sugar coat my tongue. "It would have been nice to have those numbers."

"Numbers aren't everything," Rachel the Red Menace reminds me. "A true soldier is better than a dozen soldiers who don't believe in your cause."

"I'm not doubting my people," I say. "What if, even despite my best intentions, half of them end up as bait?"

"Wars have their casualties," Kai says, like she's reading a line from one of her dad's textbooks.

"These aren't casualties. They're people. Or merpeople. And vampires. And werewolves."

"And demigods," Rachel amends.

"And demigods," I say. "They're real, live creatures who are caught in something that is my family's fault."

"That's true," Brendan says, eliciting a head slap from Kai. "What? I only meant that each of the three trident pieces has gone to members of the Triton line. Nieve, the first daughter of King Elanos. King Karanos's son and grandson. Except me. He said I'd have my own role."

"And what's that?" I ask.

"To remember my family."

"A shiny weapon would have also been nice," Marty whispers to Dylan.

"And to never let you forget that I'm more handsome than you," Brendan says, reaching for another slice, but I have a feeling there's more to what our grandfather said to him. "Are we finished already? By the seas, you must keep better stock if you want to feed an army, Cousin Tristan."

"Marty," Frederik said "Call Dominick's—"

Then it hits me. "How is Nieve feeding her massive army of flesh-eating merrows?"

"She's not going to do it here." Frederik throws out his drink cup. "We've got our patrols up. I've called our allies in Staten Island and on the Jersey Shore and warned them to post guards."

"I'm going to double ours, to be safe." Rachel conjures her crossbow from smoke. She turns to a group of the landlocked. Points at the green sumo wrestler and the guy wearing the Hurricane Gym tank. "You two. Names?"

"Monty," says the sumo.

"Alligash," say Hurricane Gym.

"Come, you're with me."

The room shakes as they follow the Red Menace out onto the boardwalk.

I rub my itchy eyes. Other than my concussed naps, I can't remember the last time I had solid sleep. I'm too wired. Too crazed. In my mind, I can picture Nieve waiting for me. She's got Layla. She's got the nautilus maid. The full moon is tomorrow, and I'm running out of time. She's got the upper hand, and she's not going to give it up. The next move is on me.

"Guys, I think I should go to Nieve alone."

A dozen eyes fall on me instantly. Swords clink in practice, and there's even some hushed laughter and the buzz of conversation. Then in seconds, my friends are up in arms around me.

That's suicide, Cousin.

That's why we've joined forces!

Yeah, you said yourself that we're stronger together.

What good can come of you dead before you reach her?

"Hold up," I say, making a T with my hands. "Just because I'm going to go into Toliss alone doesn't mean that I'm going to stay that way. I'm going to raise the Sleeping Giants. Then I'll have my power boost. I'll signal you guys, while you wait ready for the attack. If we march up to Toliss together, it'll be ten times harder to get into those tunnels."

Ewin rubs the tusk on his chin. I wonder if it's lucky, like a Buddha belly. "Your proposed plan is sound."

"Still—" Kai starts, but when all eyes turn to her, she stops.

"Still what?"

"It would be useful to see what Nieve and Kurt are up to. The barrier was to block them from seeing you, not the other way around."

"The two-way mirror," I say. "I have to be asleep."

"Then, by all means, Sleeping Beauty," Marty says.

Ewin rubs his hands together. "I can facilitate this with a single blow."

I push myself back. "We are not turning me into a punching bag."

Frederik kneels in front of me. He's usually looking down so I never see him this close up. His eyes are so black. A thick fringe of lashes bats at me, like someone hit slow motion on his face.

"Tristan," he says, "now it's your turn to trust me."

chapter
THIRTY-SEVEN

I've never been hypnotized by a vampire. My eyesight is blurred at the edges. I'm inside Toliss Island, in the king's chamber. Nieve is swimming in her pool again. She takes a silver fish and gnaws the flesh down to the bone. When she's finished, she throws it onto a rotting pile.

Then my heart beats faster as Gwen walks in with Layla.

I feel like I'm stuck in a glass case where no one can hear me as I shout her name. *Layla!*

She is free and her hands are untied—after all, where is she going to run?

She stands with her back to the polished white wall, looking back and forth from one of her captors to the other. Then she surveys the room for anything she can use as a weapon.

"Layla, was it?" Nieve says playfully.

Layla stays silent. She balls her hands at her sides. Her knees are scraped and bruised. Her arms have tons of tiny cuts that are fresh and red. Her browns curls are wild, and her amber eyes are defiant.

I wish I could burst out of this dream and save her.

"Let's try a new game, shall we?" Gwen combs her fingers through Layla's hair, and Layla tells Gwen to do something incestuous to Nieve.

"Now," Nieve says, "is that the kind of mouth the heart of the Sea Prince should have?"

"You really want to talk about mouths, Snaggle Tooth?"

Layla, don't, I think. Please, please don't. I'm going to come for you. Just hold on.

But there's no stopping her. Nieve points a finger at Layla and she flies back against the wall. Her head makes a hard cracking noise that coils my insides.

"This isn't a new game," Layla murmurs, though she's probably seeing stars.

Nieve motions for Gwen to pick her up. She does and has to hold on to her for a few minutes before Layla shakes the dizziness.

"I already told you," Layla says. "I don't know where Tristan is. You took me, remember? If you're supposed to be this all-seeing *bruja*, why don't you just see him?"

"I lost him for quite a while," Nieve says calmly. "But it's okay. My Gwenivere found him, didn't she?"

Gwen says, "Yes, Mother Queen."

At that Layla's head snaps up.

"I see that has gotten your attention," Nieve says. "Now, you're going to tell me what Tristan wants with the nautilus maid, or you will know the true meaning of pain."

"Do you think I'm afraid to feel pain?" Layla asks.

As long as I've known her, Layla has been fearless. She stands up to cops, to teachers, even to her dad when he's being unreasonable. Most of all, she stood up to me, always calling me out when I did something wrong. But this is just stupid.

"I've already told you," Layla shouts. "I haven't seen him! I've been with you!"

"I don't think she's being honest," Nieve says. Something flickers in her eye—a signal.

Gwen holds her hand up and sends a shock right through Layla's body. I can see Layla tremble with it. She grimaces when it's over and spits blood at Gwen.

"I always knew Tristan was an idiot to trust you."

Gwen seems to like that. She runs her hands all over her body and says, "Can you blame him?" She bats her eyelashes and giggles. "He does have the softest lips."

That's a lie. I've never kissed Gwen.

"But as long as you've known him, he has been that way, hasn't he? Always chasing girl after girl while you wondered why he never looked at you. I mean, really looked at you and said, 'You are everything I need.'"

Don't listen to her! I shout, though she can't hear me.

Layla doesn't say anything. She stares at Nieve's cold, white-blue eyes.

"Tell me, dear girl," Nieve says, changing her tone. "And I'll make sure he is spared. I'll make sure you two can be together forever."

"And how do you guarantee that?" Layla asks.

"I'll make you into one of us."

Gwen looks almost as startled as Layla. As me. Is that even possible? It can't be.

"Really?" Layla looks hopeful for a moment. "You can do that?"

"With the power of the full trident to magnify my own magic, I can do anything." Nieve lifts herself out of her pool and sits on the ledge, showing off her scales. "It is a wonderful life, being part of the sea. My Gwenivere tells me you are a fantastic swimmer."

Layla lets herself smile. "I'm okay."

"Mother—"

Nieve sends Gwen a death glare.

Gwen turns around and faces the wall to compose herself.

"But first, you must tell me what he wants with the nautilus maid."

Layla comes closer to them. "My head hurts. I'm a little hungry."

Nieve lifts her chin at Gwen, whose gray eyes are angry little storms.

"How do I know you're telling the truth?" Layla asks. And I know exactly what she's doing. She's stalling. But for what? Oh gods, Layla, what do you think you're going to do?

"When I was young, I was still learning my powers." Nieve likes telling stories. She relaxes her pose, taking comfort in knowing that if Layla were to run, she could fry her. "I was married to the rebel Southern King. He liked to test my magic. He'd heard that my father, the true king, could take human form with the blood and ink of the ancient cephalopod. That everyone in our courts was branded with it, with the symbol of the trident. It gave us the ability to shift out of our beautiful tails and into those terrible things you call legs. But not I."

"It didn't work on you?" Layla asks.

Nieve leans her face, her red lips curling into a smile. "I didn't need it. I could do it on my own. It was painful. I hated it. But my husband king loved watching me do it. And so he wanted me to give him the legs my father denied him."

Layla's eyes go wide. She leans her face in to the silver witch. "Did he get his legs?"

"Yes. But he died trying."

Layla stands back, afraid once again. Nieve realizes the mistake she's made and starts backpedaling. "But with the trident, you won't feel a thing. After all, dear, you can't hide your heart's desire from me."

Layla frowns.

"Let me show you," Nieve says. She shudders as a wave of magic passes through her. For the first time since I've known her, her silver tail parts into two slender legs. She's unbalanced and holds out her arms unsteadily to stand. "It only hurts the first time."

Someone at the entrance gasps. Instead of Gwen, a servant girl returns. She's stitched up the same as Archer, from her clavicle to her belly button. Her skin is a soft gray, like a shark. Her hair is pleated into a long braid and she's got a curved dagger on her hip. The hilt is made of ivory and encrusted with jewels. When she opens her mouth, she's got the teeth of a piranha.

"Avana," Nieve says, "where is my daughter?"

"She went to see about the catch for tonight's meal. Our brothers are taking too long." She places a metal tray at Layla's feet. Layla picks it up and starts eating the raw pieces of fish.

Nieve looks concerned. "The Alliance will be patrolling. Tell them to try one of the shores further south."

Avana nods. "Yes, Mother Queen."

It happens fast.

The second Avana bends over to bow, Layla slams the tray on Avana's face. Layla grabs the dagger at the merrow girl's hip and makes a break for it. Nieve screams a terrible wail, sending shocks in Layla's direction. But she holds up the metal tray as a shield, blocking most of the hit. She runs across the chamber, and when Nieve tries to chase after her, her unsteady legs buckle beneath her and she falls on her face.

Avana rushes to Nieve's side but the sea witch screams, "Don't touch me! Go after her!"

Nieve pushes herself up in time to see Layla jump feet first into one of the pools.

Gwen runs back in. "Mother Queen?" She's startled at seeing Nieve on the ground with two weak legs. She screams as they form a single silver tail once again. Blood trickles from the sea witch's scales.

"Bring her back here!" Nieve shrieks. "No one makes a fool of me. I want to feel her heart stop in my hands. I want to—"

Avana runs out of the room, perhaps to get out of the way of Nieve's wrath. Perhaps to fetch Layla.

"Mother Queen," Gwen says. "If she went down the pool channels, she's either drowning or will be eaten by the shark guard."

Nieve stops, collects herself. She presses her hands on her temples. I wonder if she can hear me screaming Layla's name because the next word she says is "Layla."

She shakes it off. "You're right."

"I don't think she knew anything."

"You told me Tristan would come for her." The sea witch nods. I'm still in her head and she can't figure out what it is, like a mosquito she can hear and not see. "Where is he? I've lost sight of him."

"He doesn't know she's gone," Gwen says slowly. "He doesn't have to."

"Send someone to make sure the sharks have finished her off." When Nieve tries to move, her face contorts in pain.

"Are you well enough to move?"

Nieve groans when she bends her knees. She's not. The shift took a large toll.

"I'll be fine. What is it?"

"We can't get a fresh catch 'til the morning. Not with the Alliance patrolling in such numbers."

"Is that all?"

Gwen shakes her head. "You have visitors in the council chambers."

The way she says "visitors" strikes a chord. Nieve's mood cheers up considerably.

"In the morning, you and your brothers will go fishing. We're so close, my dear. We're so close to having what was denied us."

Gwen doesn't look happy at all. She knew Layla was playing her, but she wouldn't dare speak out to her mother. Still, she bows.

Nieve dives into her pool and swims down the tunnel that leads to the council chambers. She sniffs the water for a scent of the girl, but the water is clean. When she resurfaces, she's in another pool and she's not alone. The light is a flicker of only two sconces, but it is enough to see her visitor's copper hair, her emerald eyes. They embrace like old friends.

"Lucine," says the silver mermaid. "Where is—?"

"I'm here," Kurt says, stepping forth from the shadow of the wall. His violet eyes are glossy and unfocused.

"Good," Nieve says, sizing him up. Her fingers reach for the trident, but one look at Lucine and she stops. I can feel her thoughts. *Handsome, like my brother. With her eyes. If Tristan won't join me, this will do.* "Are you ready to help me rule the seas?"

And Kurt, my friend, my blood, holds his trident up, the prongs igniting with lightning, and says, "I am."

chapter
THIRTY-EIGHT

L et go of me!"

The fuzziness around my eyes recedes. Hands. Dozens of hands grab me. Around my biceps, my forearms, my chest.

"Tristan," she says. The voice is familiar but I can't place it. "Tristan! Settle down!"

And all the while, I scream. I can hear myself screaming at them to release me. I have to find her. I said I would come for her and I didn't. And now Layla is—No, I won't say it.

I feel my fist hit flesh, bodies tumbling to the ground. I open the metal gate, letting in wind and rain. People gasp around me, their eyes wide and bewildered because their champion's gone mad.

And then I'm out the door and running down the streets as fast as I can, ignoring the pouring rain. I run across the boardwalk, hop over the warped railing, and hit sand. Wind whistles and I gasp for air. My thighs and chest burn as I push my way toward the water, my name a distant shout in the background.

And all I see is Layla in my vision, jumping into the tunnels that lead down, down, down into the sea. My blood has turned to ice. My mind is on fire.

I can feel someone fast, faster than me, catching up. He tackles me to the ground. I eat sand. I kick. I punch. But it's like hitting solid stone.

He holds me down with his cold hands.

"You are not going in that water," Frederik yells.

"Let go of me." I try to swing but his iron fists hold my arms down at my sides.

"Weaponless. Blind. You'll die."

"*She's out there!*" I scream. I try to punch but he weighs a fucking ton. "I know she's out there. She has to be."

He lets go of my wrists but doesn't get off me because we both know that as soon as he gets up, I'm jumping into that ocean.

Marty and Kai run up beside us. They're backlit silhouettes against the boardwalk lights.

"Tristan—" Marty tries to say, but he's panting. "Look—"

"No. You don't understand what I saw. None of you—"

Frederik looks up and stands and lets me go as a wave crashes over my head. I push myself up on my knees. From here, there is no separating the black sky from the sea.

"Tristan!"

"Leave me alone." I push the hand away that tries to take my wrist.

Thalia screams and jumps at a creature on the sand. He snorts, shaking his mane. The green scales of his tail wag against the sand. Atticus, Thalia's sea horse.

Then I hear her…

"Tristan." Softer now. Breathless.

I turn around.

She's shivering. Cold.

I fall on my knees.

Part of me is telling me that she isn't real. I'm making her up. I want this so badly that I'm hallucinating. So I reach out my hands and wrap them around her, my head pressed to her belly.

"I was going to come for you." I'm dazed, an electric sense of relief filling all the gaps inside me. "I was going to. I'm sorry."

Layla sinks down too, kissing my wet face with her wet lips. "Didn't I tell you?"

"What?"

"I don't need you to save me."

Her lips are cold and blue. I kiss them and wrap my arms around her to give her my warmth until she stops shaking. "No, but I need you. I always need you."

chapter
THIRTY-NINE

My friends and I sit at a round table in one of Frederik's many rooms. The walls are exposed brick, mostly covered with all sorts of maps. A lot of planning seems to go down here. I trace my finger along the continents. I've been so deep beneath the sea. These maps don't even cover a fraction of it.

I take in the people that have stuck by my side. Frederik, the High Vampire of New York. Marty, the shapeshifter and all-around keeper of the peace. Brendan, my cousin who came back to help me. Thalia, fierce and full of love. Dylan, who is unafraid. Amada, the Naga girl who has saved my life more than once. Ewin, a warrior who is looking for somewhere to belong, just like the rest of us. Shelly, the oracle of Central Park. And then there's Layla. There's always Layla.

Her hair is tied back from her face, and she's holding a blanket tightly over her shoulders.

When Thalia looks at me, I know what she's thinking. We're hours away from the battle that's been coming for days, and Kurt is out there. I saw him with Lucine and the silver mermaid.

Marty spreads sheets of white paper on the table, like the kind an architect or designer would use. He pulls a bunch of pens from his back pocket and scatters them on the table. I take one and chew on the cap.

"You got your compass and eraser in there too?" Layla asks, drumming her pen on the table.

Marty shakes his head, adjusting his black baseball cap. That thing really needs a wash. "This ain't our first rodeo, ladybird."

"Indeed." Frederik clears his throat.

"Tomorrow, we attack Toliss." I take the black marker and start sectioning off land masses. "Okay, this is Coney Island, for those of you who need a geography lesson. I'll say Toliss is south of us by five miles."

"If I may," Frederik says, coming up beside me. He takes my marker and fills in the Coney Island landscape: the beach, the boardwalk, his home, the Wreck, the rides. A red star marks the entrance to the nightclub Betwixt. A II for the Second Circle where Lucine made her home while waiting for Kurt.

"Layla, what did you see beneath the island where the tunnels are?"

She holds her arms around her body, staring at the black ink that bleeds when I leave it on the paper. "Two dozen hungry sharks. The ones with the metal harnesses around their jaws. There are chains that keep them right there. Archer said they hadn't been fed for days. Partly because the king was relocating to the Glass Castle, and partly because Nieve overran the island. Either way, if they smell blood in the water, they'll attack."

Everyone nods, like we're all picturing the same thing—jaws chomping blindly and ready to devour.

"How did you get past the great white beasts?" Ewin asks.

Layla's eyes swivel between Thalia and me. She must have seen Kurt. "Someone was arriving. They parted for them. That's when I saw Atticus hiding. Swam like hell all the way to the shore."

I draw a few sharks beneath my outline of the island.

"Is there anything else you saw?" Frederik asks.

Layla's eyebrows furrow. "Other than the fact that Nieve has more mood swings than my cousin pregnant with triplets? She almost never lets Gwen or Archer out of her sight. You can see that she loves them. Every time they're gone for too long, you can hear her scream for them."

"I can use that," I say, squeezing her hand lightly.

"The beach is full of merrows," Thalia says.

I nod, still thinking of the last order they had from Nieve. "They can't risk losing their numbers so close to tomorrow night's full moon. She told Gwen and Archer to go fishing in the morning."

"Let them try. I want to keep a line here." Frederik draws a line across the beach. "For merrows or any rogue mermaids trying to come ashore."

Ewin seems confused. "Why would the mermaids of your court attack the shore when you're defending it?"

"Because the king is dead," I say. "The trident is severed into three pieces, which means his laws, his bindings, they're all going to be broken."

"It's what has kept the land safe from us for eons," Brendan says.

"And also from us being discovered by humans," Kai adds. "Our laws have changed. Actually, they've been discarded completely."

"She doesn't have Layla anymore, but she's still keeping the nautilus maid. She hasn't figured out what I want with her. She doesn't know about the Sleeping Giants. Big plus for us." I draw Toliss as I remember it—the beach, the forest, the river that leads to a waterfall behind the valley where the Sea Court gathers. The king's throne, marking the entrance to the inner chambers.

"So how do I get me from here to here?" I say, drawing a line with my fingertip from the boardwalk to Toliss.

"What do you mean 'you'?" Layla says. "We're all going. Isn't that the point of having a small army? That you don't have to go at it alone?"

Frederik stands beside me. I'm so used to Kurt being there, lending his suggestions. But Kurt isn't here, is he? I have to keep reminding myself of that because part of me keeps forgetting.

"I have to go in first," I say. "You'll wait for my signal. What's up, Vampire Guy?"

"I'm concerned the night creatures won't be much help until nightfall."

Kai shakes her head. "Not so."

"What do you mean, not so?" Marty asks, jumpy. "Sun equals extra-well-done vampires. And no offense to other supernatural beings in the room, but few things on this plane equal vampire strength."

Ewin smirks and Marty amends his statement. "Except for a warrior of the Vasiks clan."

Kai takes the marker and draws the outline of an eclipse in the corner.

"Remember the prophecy," Shelly says, repeating one line. "'*And in darkness we will remain*.' Everything we're doing is changing the natural weather of this plane."

"This puts me and mine back in the game," Frederik says, eyeing the map like he's trying to sink my battleship.

"Once I free the Sleeping Giants," I say, "I think we can expect thunderstorms with a chance of hellfire. I don't know where the other two will be coming from, but the kraken is inside Toliss." See, Kurt? I think. I did pay attention to some of the things you babbled about.

"That creature hasn't been awake in years," Thalia says.

"Then it's sure as hell going to be cranky when it wakes up," I say, explaining that each trident piece corresponds to a different sea beastie. "I get Doris, the badass sea horse with claws. Nieve, the kraken. And Kurt, the turtle with the spike collar."

"Why are we giving Nieve and Kurt more power?" Layla asks.

"They won't know what's happening. That's where I have the upper hand. I can attack Nieve's merrows and open the field for your entrance. I know we can beat them."

Once again they break into a chorus of indecipherable arguments. That I'm insane to wake these creatures up. That I don't know if I'll be able to control them. But among all of their noise, all I see are Shelly's dark, sad eyes. I hold my palm up so she can see it. There's the scar that bears the promise I made to the nautilus maid. To end her life and set free the Sleeping Giants of the sea. To use them to put an end to Nieve, to start a new world for everyone in this building.

She nods once, and then her voice is in my head. "I know."

Frederik's head turns to the door. "The gates just opened, and patrol isn't due to change for another twelve minutes."

I run after him, leaning over the banister to see what the commotion is about. The downstairs hall is filling up with mermen in armor. I don't recognize their faces, most of them with patches of scars. They shake hands with my army of strays and unload their weapons. One of them looks up at where I stand frozen, staring unbelieving at them.

"Master Tristan," Arion says. "You look like you've seen a ghost."

chapter
FORTY

I pull Arion into a man-hug. "I looked for you, and you weren't there."

He smacks my back affectionately. "The blast severed my rope. I woke up on a strange beach. As soon as I could, I swam to some old friends. They're here to fight for you."

I shake hands with the newcomers. We feed them and give them water. Dylan is fascinated with their weapons craftsmanship. I leave him to prepare the artillery for the battle.

"Come, Arion," I say. "We're going over our strategy."

It's strange and wonderful to see him walking. The black and white scales on his forearms have patches of pearly scars where his ropes used to be, but not anymore. The roundtable welcomes him with open arms. Kai hugs him the longest.

I catch him up on what we've discussed. He agrees with my plan, which makes me feel like I got an A on a test I hardly studied for.

"What about our fin-challenged friends?" I ask.

"I can swim." Marty raises his hand.

"It's best to save that energy for fighting," Brendan points out.

"Master Tristan," Arion says.

"Just Tristan."

He smiles, but I know him better than that. "I have a ship. It is yours."

"Thank you, Arion. We'll load it up tonight." I can see in my team's faces that they're more and more hopeful that we've got this.

"Brendan, Kai," I continue. "Mix and match our troops into small teams. They may have the numbers, but I'd love to watch a merrow figure out what to do when a werewolf is coming at them."

Ewin points to the Toliss drawing. "I understand there is only one beach on this island."

Thalia nods. "Toliss can be entered two ways, through the beach or through the tunnels. The rest of the island is comprised of cliffs."

At the thought of cliffs, I remember Karel pushing me off them.

"There is a third way," Frederik points out. The merpeople are confused as Frederik draws birds above Toliss. "We have wings at our disposal."

"Where will you be, Tristan?" Layla asks. I can feel her jitters. She's good at hiding it, but her nerves smell of smoke.

"After I send out my signal," I say. "Leave finding Nieve to me."

"What about my brother?" Thalia whispers.

I swallow the dryness that coats my mouth. My heartbeat spikes because I have to tell her. "He's already there."

"What do you mean, he's already there?" She gets up, her chair smacking the floor. Layla goes to calm her down. Thalia balls her hands into fists, as if she can take all her anger and choke it. "He wouldn't."

"I know my sister," Shelly says. "She's been obsessed with the boy since he was born. She must know that Nieve would kill him. Joining forces with her would keep him alive."

"She's controlling him," Thalia raises her voice. "She has to be."

"He chose her," I say, though I wish I could agree with Thalia. "I saw it."

Thalia sits back down, her jaw set, her yellow-green eyes full of fire.

"Then it's settled," I say, after a moment of silence. The plan is set. "Now, raise your hand if you don't know how to swim."

chapter
FORTY-ONE

My army of solitary beings and court mermaids sleeps. Or at least they try. After an hour of twisting and turning on a floor that still smells of greasy pizza and fish, I give up. Everything I see is black. There's no Kurt. No Nieve. I wonder if they've finally figured out our connection too.

Wind whistles through the top of the broken window. Rotating shifts patrol the shoreline, but I know there won't be any trouble. Not for a few hours at least.

Off in a corner, Marty and Brendan are having a snoring competition. I'm tempted to take a bit of leftover pizza crust and throw it in their wide-open mouths. Amada is in her Naga form in a hammock because she doesn't know how to sleep in her human body. The merpeople downstairs are still unnerved by her, but no one is saying anything, not after she let the young merboys ride on her back and kept them from crying while their parents prepared for battle.

I decide to go downstairs where every inch of the warehouse has turned into a campsite. Some can sleep better than others. Children cry and mothers shush them. A guard with a trident tattoo leans his head back against the wall. His eyes are shut, but he twists the dagger in his hands over and over.

I start ticking off numbers to have a full count of my army of strays, but it's pointless. Most of the Thorne Hill Alliance isn't sleeping here. They have their own homes right here on Coney Island. They will fight beside me to protect it. I think of my parents, out in Long Island where I told them to go until this was all over.

It's the merpeople I'm scared for. There's so much riding on me, and I feel the weight of it. Each one of their lives, like a human pyramid stacked on my shoulders. I can't let them fall.

The girls have gotten creative and turned the tables into bed. They give canvas and rope to the merpeople for pillows. Layla shows a mother how to make a sling for her baby. It cries out for water so she fills a wash bucket and it quiets down. No one is allowed to go into the water.

Not until I give my signal.

"You need sleep," Frederik says beside me.

I jump. "Did I mention I hate it when you do that?"

He smirks. "Can't help it."

"Do you walk on air or something?"

"Or something."

If someone had told me a few weeks ago that I'd be sitting with a vampire, in the dark, getting ready for the biggest battle of my life, I would have laughed. I'm still laughing.

"How can they sleep?" I say, thinking of Marty and my cousin spread out in the office like we're at summer camp.

Frederik shrugs. "Sometimes the body wins over the mind."

My body and my mind are both warring against me.

"Are you going to ask me to rethink my plan?" I ask him.

He shakes his head and tucks a black strand behind his ear. He leans forward on the railing, fingers touching in that conspiratorial way of his. "No."

It would be weird to confess that I want his approval. He's ancient compared to me. All of them are. They've all had their share of wars, but here they are, backing me up.

"In fact," Frederik says, "it's smart."

"But—?" It sounds like there's a "but" at the end of that compliment.

"But—" He hovers over what he wants to say. My heart tightens like a fist. I feel like I'm getting dumped or something. "I wonder if you've given more thought to what you will do when it comes to Kurt."

"I've been sort of busy," I lie. Kurt is in the back of my head, at the front of my head. He's there when I hold the Scepter of the Earth because the ancient weapon is incomplete, and Kurt and Nieve hold the other pieces. Kurt is there when I look at Thalia because he's her brother. He's there when I look at myself, because we, yeah, okay, Layla pointed out we have the same nose and the same stubborn frown when things don't go our way. He's there when he's not there because I was counting on him and he's missing.

"You should rest," Frederik tells me.

"My blood is pumping like crazy," I say, "not that I should confess that to a vamp. You should go get some sleep."

"I'll sleep when I'm dead."

"You're already dead."

"The dust kind of dead." He looks behind me and smirks. "Though I don't suppose you've got sleep on your mind, either."

And just as quickly as he appeared, he's gone. I see what he was looking at before he vanished. Layla. She cut her sweatpants into shorts. The hoodie she's wearing swallows her up, covering her so that all I can focus on are her sun-kissed legs. Her hair is curled from the humidity, framing her cheekbones in a way that makes my gut fall like it's at the peak of a roller coaster.

"You'd be terrible at sneak attacks," I say.

"Good thing I'm not trying to be sneaky." She sits beside me and my body heats up instantly. "We almost maxed out all the guest rooms. Marty's going to have a hell of a time laundering the sheets."

"I'm going to try to sleep standing up."

She takes my hand. "I think there's still room upstairs."

I let her tug on my fingers, and without even thinking, I follow her up the steps and into an empty guest room. It's all black and red. There's an arched window with a ledge cluttered with old books. I sit on the bed beside her.

Now that it's just the two of us, I let my body deflate. She rubs my shoulder, and some of that pressure eases off.

"That's amazing."

"Jesus, Tristan. You're like overcooked steak."

"Thanks? I'm a little tense, in case you hadn't noticed."

She squeezes extra hard and I pull back. There's this moment where I want to reach out and grab her. I want to hold her in my arms and tell her everything I feel about her. In the dim light of the room, we reach for each other at the same time. My knee is shaking and she puts a hand over it. She touches my chest, tracing her finger on my new tattoo.

"I'm kidnapped for a few hours, and you chop off your hair and get tatted up." She edges closer to me, her warm breath right at my ear. "Any piercings while you were at it?"

I answer with a crooked smile and a wink. She doesn't believe that I'd pierce anything. I have to get belted onto the table when the team does the yearly blood drive. But still, she lets her hand wander from my chest. I hold her eyes, daring her, as she keeps exploring down. My heart is stuck in my throat. When she gets to my stomach, I grab her hand.

It is the most painful thing I've ever done to myself. "Wait."

"Wait?"

"I have to say something."

She sits back and listens.

"Tomorrow," I say, "when this all happens, I want you to promise me, and I mean seriously promise me, that you're going to stay somewhere safe. I can't tell you what to do, because you're you, and you don't listen, even when I'm trying to protect you."

"Not helping."

"I don't care. If something happened to you, I'd—It wouldn't be good for me."

She leans forward, resting her head on my chest. "What about me? I could say the same to you and it'd be like talking to the wind."

"It's different, Layla. I chose this."

She presses her hand on my face, leading me down so we're less than an inch apart. "So did I."

"It's in my blood. It calls to me."

She stands up. The light of the street and the fog fill the room with a strange glow, like we're stuck in an old movie. She takes off her sweater. Her skin is hot to the touch. Her tank top is ripped and has a black stain I'd rather not think about. She bats those thick, black lashes and I forget why we're here and not tangled back at home on a couch. Or on the beach.

"Don't ask me to go home," she whispers.

I smile, pulling on her hands. She sits on me, one knee on either side of me. I want to jump out of my skin, but it's best if I don't move. "There's no telling you what to do."

"Only took you sixteen years to figure it out."

She traces the lines of my face, like outlining where my hair used to be.

"You don't like it." I keep my hands pressed firmly on her lower back. "Layla—"

But she doesn't want me to talk. So she kisses me. It's so soft that I open my eyes to make sure it really happened. It's not enough. Not when either of us could be gone in a few hours. No, I don't want to think like that. I just want to feel her lips on mine. Again. Again. Again. She moves her face to the side and kisses my jaw, my neck. I lean in against her. Her breath hitches when I pull her closer because she's still too far away. I kiss her cheek and then stop because her face is wet.

"That bad, eh?" I try to joke, but I'm nervous. I lean back on the bed and keep my hands at my sides.

She shakes her head, wipes the tears from her eyes, then presses her wet fingers on my face. "I'm trying to not be mad at you."

"What did I do now?" I bark out, laughing, and she puts a hand over my mouth. That pulls me out of our bedroom dream and back to reality. A vampire's home. A storm. A battle.

"You waited too long." She presses her hands on my chest.

"I know." I brush her hair back with my hand and hold her face so she won't look away when I talk. "When I was in the Vale of Tears, I thought about where you were. That somehow I'd come out of that world and I'd have missed it. That she would have won. That I'd never see you again—"

She takes my hands down and holds them. "I'm not going anywhere, Tristan. Not unless you do something stupid."

"I'm trying to have a moment here."

She smiles the kind of smile that makes me forget I'm fighting a war.

"We aren't 'moment' kind of people."

I kiss her wet, salty cheeks one at a time and she jerks back. "Don't kiss my eyes. My dad says it's bad luck."

"Your dad also says I'm bad luck."

"No, he says you're bad news."

"But you're still here." My insides are moving, like the first time I shifted into my tail. Like I'm not done becoming whoever I'm supposed to be. "We're only just starting and I'm not ready for it to be done."

"Listen to me." Her hand cups the back of my neck. "I will *never* be done with you."

And then she kisses me again. I hold her tight against me because I'm afraid if I let her go, she'll be gone for good. I pull her tank top over her head, kissing the dip of her clavicle. Outside the dark is getting darker, but I don't need light to find her mouth. I realize I've never been this close to Layla before. I've thought about it, alone in my bed when the possibility of her feeling the same way was not even an option. I've been with girls because I was bored. Because I wanted to feel this. Because I didn't know how different it could be when I totally completely loved the other person.

She stops for a moment, guiding me with her hands.

I want to shout it out at the top of my lungs. I'm dizzy and giddy. We kiss while we smile and it's clumsy, and we laugh and I know I love this girl. I've never been more sure of anything in my whole life.

chapter
FORTY-TWO

When I sleep, I see her—the nautilus maid. She's weak. Her pale pink skin has a cold tinge to it. The white, shimmering stone of the Toliss chamber is her prison. Two bodies lay limp beside her, and even though I can't look at their faces, I know they're dead.

The nautilus maid snaps to attention, like she heard a noise, her eyes darting right at me.

She says my name.

———————

"Tristan!" Someone is shaking me.

I sit up fast and reach for my dagger. I pat the empty mattress, before I realize my harness is on the windowsill.

"Get up!" Thalia's voice becomes familiar again.

I don't remember the last time I slept so well. Despite the crick in my neck, that is. Then a knot tightens in my chest. When we fell asleep, Layla was in my arms. Now she's gone.

"What's happened?"

"There are people," Thalia says. "On the beach."

Layla walks back into the room. She's changed into her lifeguard two-piece. Her hair is tied back into a long braided rope. A sword draped around her hips. Wait a minute, how long has she been awake?

I rub off the layer of crud that keeps my eyelids shut. "I thought the city was evacuated."

I sling my harness back on and buckle it on my chest.

"I believe it's a mermaid," Thalia says. "She's calling them out to sea. They're sleepwalking, entranced by the call."

I start to follow them out, but Layla stops me at the door. She smirks. "You may want to cover up first."

She turns around and walks down the steps with Thalia, laughing.

When I look down, I'm naked.

"Really funny!" I yell after them.

I close my eyes and wait for the quick burn that comes with raising my scales. My skin is numb where my scales cover my skin, and I resist the urge to scratch everywhere. It's like my entire body is thirsty for water.

When I'm decent, I run downstairs. My small army is pooling out onto the street. It takes me a moment to realize what's wrong. It has nothing to do with the drizzle or the monster rain clouds that cover every inch of blue sky. It has everything to do with the dark circle trying to cover up the sun.

"It looks like a black and white cookie," Marty says.

"Except you can't eat it," I counter, taking Layla's hand in mine.

The vampires step out of the house slowly, reaching out with their pale hands. They don't burn and that gives them the courage to walk out. Even though the day is dark and gray, they squint at the hiding sun.

Frederik is the last one to walk out. Rachel is beside him. He catches my eye, and for the first time since I've met him, I see a look of wonder on his face. It's like even though he doesn't want to admit it, this is the thing he's been longing for.

It only lasts for a few minutes, his face tilting up to the sliver of sun that doesn't burn him. He holds out his palms, like he's receiving a blessing. But it's short lived.

We all turn to the water where someone screams. It's worse than I thought.

Beneath the crashing waves that lap their way up toward the boardwalk, dozens of men tumble out. They walk slowly and stagger, as if their hands are being pulled by invisible strings. One of them walks past me, and his face is both strange and familiar. Then it hits me how long I haven't been home. How my best friends are almost strangers to me.

His eyes are dilated and staring, his mouth open. I grab him by his wiry arms. "Bertie!"

He pulls against me, mumbling and incoherent.

"*Bertie, wake up!*" I shout.

When did he get so strong? He shoves me off him and joins the horde of men making their way to the beach.

I recognize them all—the old Dominican man from the bodega and Jimmy from the Wreck.

"*Coach!*" Layla screams. She runs and jumps on his back. He flips her over, and she falls hard on the boardwalk.

"Don't let them get in the water," Frederik yells, "or they'll drown!"

But the problem is that they're possessed. Their own lives don't matter because they're not in there.

Then I swallow hard. "I'm sorry, bro."

I pull back and punch Bertie right in the face. His head slacks and he crumples to the ground. I hold two fingers in front of his nostrils. His breathing is fine, so I leave him and run out on the beach where the Alliance is trying to hold back the humans.

Layla is screaming, holding back someone's hand. Tears run down her face. I've never seen her so scared, not even when she had a knife at her throat. I run to her and help her hold her father back.

"Don't hurt him, Tristan. Please don't hurt him," she cries. But I know that it's the only way to stop him from drowning.

"Turn around," I say, even though I know that she won't. I look into Mr. Santos's hazel eyes that have the same fierceness as his daughter's. His hair is whiter than I remember, but the mustache is still black. He calls out for Layla, tells her he's coming to find her. Before I can do anything, he takes a swing at me. It takes me by surprise, and he grazes my ear with the ring on his left hand. Then he keeps walking onto the beach, calling for his daughter.

"*Dad!*" Layla yells. "I'm here. I'm here."

We jump on him. He flips over, hands flailing in the air, sand going into his mouth. His eyes are glazed over, bewitched.

All around me, the men of the city trek onto the sand because the Alliance can't reach them in time, and they walk straight into the water where their screams get muffled beneath the waves.

And then the wind shifts. A second voice—strong but soothing. It's the voice that takes me back to being a kid. The utterly impossible memory of being a baby and swimming with a fishtail.

Mr. Santos stops struggling. His arms fall to his sides and he doesn't move.

"Dad!" Layla grabs him by his shirt and shakes him. When she makes a whimpering sound, it crushes me. "Wake up."

I want to console her, but another familiar man is headed our way.

"Dad?" I say.

He walks toward me, eyes totally dazed. He falls to his knees and then on his face. I leave Layla and her dad and run to him.

"You're not supposed to be here," I yell, turning him over and brushing the sand off his face. His glasses are broken and I toss them to the side. How can I be surprised? I should've known that they'd never leave, not knowing that I was right here.

When I look up, my mother is standing on the boardwalk. Her red mane is a beacon. She holds out her arms and the wind picks up around her, listening to her voice as she calls the men back to dry land.

All of the men that fell to the ground get back up again, the bewitched glossiness returning to their eyes. Only this time, they listen to my mother's voice, powerful and true, as if it's telling them their wishes have already been fulfilled, that it's okay to go home.

Layla starts to follow her dad, but the first voice, the one full of anger and longing, picks up again.

"She's too powerful." Thalia is at my side again. "I don't think Lady Maia can hold them back much longer."

My mother hasn't been a mermaid for a long time, and I can see her struggling to sing, to bring the men back to safety. She's like the sun trying to shine when the moon is pushing for darkness, like the sky right above us.

"Who?" But I don't even have to ask. Out in the gray sea is a swirl of water. She holds her arms out and lifts her face to the eclipse.

Gwenivere sings.

Her voice is mingled into the wind that rushes in and out of the shore like a riptide, like the hands of the sea desperately grabbing the men. I felt those hands the first time the wave crashed over Coney Island and I got carried out to sea.

Too many of the men are waist deep in water. The waves swallow them, and when they're washed out far enough, the waiting clawed hands of Nieve's merrows snatch them up and take them back home.

I dive into the waves, flicking my tail as fast as I can until I reach Gwen. She doesn't see me coming at first. Then she loses concentration and her song stops. She teeters on the spiral of water that serves as her tower. I knock her off it and she splashes down. I grab her around the waist and hold her arms down.

"Stop it!" I say. "I know you don't want to do this. I know you're tired of this."

She splashes hard, but I hold on tighter. She screams and the beautiful song she was singing before is a terrible shriek.

"How can you know what I want?"

"Because I saw your face, Gwen. I saw your face when Archer wanted to hurt Layla. You saved her. I know you did." I brush her white-blond hair out of her eyes. She stops struggling against me.

"You can help me stop her," I say. "If you don't, all of the lives she takes will be on your hands."

She grits her teeth and screams once again. We float out in the water, and I wait for her to make the right choice.

"If I do, my brother and sisters—their lives will be on my hands as well."

"Gwen, please," I say, holding her by her shoulders.

She looks back to where yellow eyes lie waiting behind us. There are a few more splashes, and I know if I turn around, I'll see more men drowning.

I keep thinking that if I try hard enough, I'll get her to be the same girl who sailed alongside me, fought alongside me. I have to remind myself that girl never existed. That Gwen was playing me, and I fell right into her stormy gray eyes. I see her make up her mind, a shark ready to strike. She places her hands on my chest and snarls, "You smell like her."

I can feel my heart stop and start as a shock of current hits my chest. From Gwen. I shake as she leaves me in the water. I gasp for air. Try to swim back to the shore, but my muscles are as strong as loose rubber bands.

I push against the weakness and start to swim after her, but someone catches my attention on the shore. Layla's on the sand again, Thalia holding her back from getting into the surf. She's chasing after a guy our age.

Oh fuck.

I put my energy into swimming with the waves toward the shore. The waves take me in, crashing over his head. Angelo, in his stained white underwear.

I loop my arms around his chest and drag him out. He takes a swing at me, but the next wave flips us both over. "Hey, man. It's me. Wake up, wake up."

I grab on to him and he makes it difficult by flailing around. When I get him on land, I smack him across the face. "Remember when we took the Triborough championship last year? How we competed over girls but never let it get in our way? How you beat up a kid from our rival high school for pissing in the pool while I was swimming?"

Something happens to him. Without Gwen, my mom's song is stronger. His eyes are bright again, like he's coming out of a long sleep. "Tristan?"

"Come on." I pull him toward shore. "We have to get out of the water!"

He hangs on to me, trying to take stock of what's happening around him. But all he can say is, "Bro, you have a fucking tail!"

I want to laugh, but I can taste blood in the water. When we're near the shore, I let my fins dissolve and go back into a half-shift.

"You're sleepwalking."

Layla runs to him and grabs him in a tight hug. "Oh, thank God."

"What's happening?" Angelo yells.

"Shark attacks," Layla and I say at the same time.

"Are you on duty? I thought the beach was evacuated. Where are my clothes?" He goes on with questions we don't answer until we get to the boardwalk.

The Alliance and the landlocked are making sure the human men make their way up onto the boardwalk and head home.

"Tristan," Angelo says. He grabs my wrist. His brown eyes are wide, and fat beads of water cling to his eyelashes. "I'm not stupid. You're strapped on like fucking *Clash of the Titans* minus that fly Pegasus. Don't lie to me. I know what I saw. I could hear a voice calling out to me, and all I wanted to do was jump into the water. It was that girl—that Gwen girl. I know she's not your cousin. Those things that got Ryan. Don't lie to me. What the fuck's going on?"

"More than I could tell you and not sound crazy," I tell him.

Because I don't deny him, he relaxes. I can see him fill in the blanks for himself. Then he reaches for the dagger on my chest all, "Cool, can I play with it?"

I smack his hand away. "No!"

"Fine," he says. "I'll get my own."

"Look, something bad is going down tonight. Whatever you do, don't go in the water."

He looks from me to Layla, to the mix of people on the board-walk. "I want to help."

"You can help me by making sure people don't go into sea. Not tonight. Tell your brother—he's a cop. Tell him that you heard about some crazy-ass party that's going down in the middle of the hurricane. Whatever you do, you can't mention me."

"Hurricane party. Block off beach access. Don't tell him about your sparkly tail. I'm on it." He holds out his hand and I take it. Shake, pound, slap, slap—our Thorne Hill Knights handshake.

I turn to Layla. "Where are our dads?"

"Dazed and sleeping. Your mom and I put them in the backseat of her car."

I grab her face and kiss her mouth, then her forehead. I remember that was the last thing I did the last time, when the wave was coming in and I ran right in. Now I'm doing it again.

"I'm going to help the others," she says and pulls herself from me.

"I'll be right there." I hold on to her, right down to the tips of our fingers, and then she's gone. I can see my mom standing at the boardwalk. I fight every impulse to run to her, to go home and let Kurt have at it. A scream is caught in my chest and I push it back down because I have to be strong for her. She's singing one last song, a melody that I know as well as the lines of my face. A sailor getting lost at sea and finding a beautiful castle with riches and a love that is magical and impossible but true, but in the end he comes home.

This is not her world anymore. It's mine.

"Tristan," Frederik says from behind me. "A word?"

I turn to where he stands. "It was Gwenivere. She was calling out to them."

"I saw. Where is she now?"

"Gone." I press my hand over my chest where my skin is red from her handprint. My scabs are bleeding. "I thought she was going to burst my heart out of my chest."

Frederik shakes his head. "She wouldn't."

"I was sure she would come back with me, but I was wrong."

"We lost at least a dozen humans," Frederik says, walking back up the beach to regroup with the others. "Thanks to your mother, we can usher the rest back inland Come on."

When he turns around and I don't follow, he knows what I'm about to do. The sun and moon are stuck, splitting each other in half. As if she's reading my mind, Amada is at the shoreline waiting for me.

"This wasn't the plan," he says. I might be crazy, but I think he sounds concerned. "You said—"

"I have to go now," I tell him.

He nods once. "When I first met you, I didn't think I'd be here side by side in your fight. I couldn't wait to get your kind off the shore."

I grin. "Did my charming ways make you change your mind?"

He pulls his hands in his pockets. "Who says I changed my mind?"

But he holds his arm out for me to take, all the same.

"What should I tell the others?"

"That nothing else has changed." I take his hand. "And remember, wait for my signal."

chapter
FORTY-THREE

Amada breathes in deeply. The air is thick with salt. In this gray noon, I'd never guess it's summer.

"There is blood in the water," she says.

"You can still turn around," I say. "You don't have to do this."

She gives me a long sideways glance, her loose black hair all over her face. In her human form, it's easy to forget how powerful she is. That she's a cursed being. That her talons can rip your head clean off.

"Any other prince would be happy that so many clamor to risk their lives for him," she says. "Yet you would rather risk your own."

"Don't ask me to explain," I say.

"Not asking."

The Alliance has cleared the shoreline, and they're putting themselves in place like chess pieces. Somewhere Layla is wondering where I've gone off to, why I didn't say good-bye. And I know that I couldn't say good-bye to her. When I close my eyes, I don't see Nieve or Gwen. I see Layla on top of me, pressing her hands on my chest, kissing me like she might never get another chance.

Amada nudges my shoulder. "Focus."

"Focus." I repeat the word over and over. Focus on Toliss Island ahead of us and the white room where the nautilus maid waits for me. Focus on not giving up. Focus on being alive.

My body hums with energy and anticipation until I think I'll burst right out of my skin.

And we run straight into a cresting wave. The sea tries to push us back at first, but we push ahead and swim on. My eyes adjust to the dark water. I hold my dagger ahead of me and let my tail do the work. We swim for two miles surrounded by silence and dark. I swallow against the coppery tastes in the sea, the mangled body parts that float back up to the surface. It nearly makes me retch because I can't get the flavor out of my mouth.

Then we see the island. From beneath, it is an expanse of stone. The tunnels are lit with the white-blue light of tiny creatures that cling to the stone walls. Beneath that, the shark guard are chained in a circle, ravenously biting at the space in front of them. Their skin is raw where their chains have drawn blood.

Around them, merrows swim in a circle, taunting the creatures.

Amada and I hold back, watching and waiting for the right time. If we move too quickly, they'll know we're there and we'll lose the advantage of a surprise attack. I swim close to the ground and stay behind the boulders.

"If we go in from different directions, we can create enough of a distraction to get rid of the merrows and then free the sharks."

I wait for Amada to agree with me because this was what we decided on. Distract the merrows and get in through the tunnels.

"Amada?"

She's gone. I look over the boulders, and there she is, swimming in her beast form. Her dragon jaw is open wide; her hind legs retract to let her tail do the work. If I scream for her to stop, it'll give away her position.

The merrows shift around like they can smell something new, something dark and threatening, her roar a deep echo around them.

When I fought her, I know she was holding back. She's faster than I imagined. With her claws, she rips across a puffer merrow's chest, slicing so deep that she rips the heart out before he breaks down into black blood. Before the others can reach her, she lunges with an open jaw, ripping the head off a hammer-headed merrow. She doesn't spit it back out.

They're crazed, and she undulates, swimming toward the sharks. I ready myself to help her. There's no way she can take two dozen of those things and another dozen sharks.

But she cries out and even though I can't fully understand the cry of the river people, I know she's telling me to stay put. With her claws, she breaks the chains that hold back the shark guard. One, two, five, ten. Their teeth are like bear traps closing against bone. They charge straight at the merrows, and within minutes, they've swallowed them whole.

As the sharks swim in a cyclone formation Amada swims between them. They nudge her body in a silent thank-you.

I hover just outside their circle. Then they stop. I brandish Triton's dagger and they part for me. Amada shifts into her human torso.

"You didn't wait for me." I frown.

"I saw an opening and I took it," she says. "The way is clear."

The shark guard swims around the island, but they're not a danger to me or mine.

"I will return to the others. I will tell them I saw you through safely."

And then I swim up into the bright light of the tunnels.

The tunnels are a maze. Thalia said to choose one of the openings on the east, which would lead me to the farthest chambers where prisoners are held.

The problem with looking at an island from underneath is that I don't know where east is.

I take my best guess and decide to not jump out of the pool like a topless girl inside a birthday cake. Nope, that would give away the element of surprise.

The first tunnel leads me to a dim-lit room. I break the surface slowly, keeping my body pressed against the stone. I don't recognize the voices, but there are children crying. The sound is pained and lonely and scared. Footsteps walk in quickly. A girl's voice cooing. "Please don't cry," she begs.

Then another. A softer voice, singing. Gwen.

"They're pretty," the strange girl says. "Aren't they? All things are pretty when they're small. Even us."

Us.

I chance it and lift my head a fraction over the ledge of the pool. Gwen and the girl have their back to me. They cradle babies in their arms. Their faces are distorted, like looking at something through broken glass. They're merrow babies. Dozens and dozens of them in their own cribs.

"Does Mother truly have the power to make them better?"

"Not better," Gwen says. "There's nothing wrong with them. She can only make them stronger."

The girl looks confused, as if everything she's learned is changing in front of her eyes.

"When do we get to name them?" she asks eagerly.

"When they're ready," Gwen snaps, and the girl shrinks back.

A new wave of merrow babies for Nieve to raise.

"I like this one. His skin is like a sunset." The girl rubs the baby's back. "Can we call him Sunset?"

Gwen makes a feral sound and the girl backs away, putting the sunset merrow baby back in its crib. She looks my way and I sink down. I hurry back through the tunnels, keeping myself flat against the stones. When I press on the light creatures, they pull back into the tiny pores of the wall. I take another route and swim upward, breaking the surface up to my ears.

The voice speaking makes me go red with anger.

"I've instructed all my brothers to the head of the island. The beach is the only safe place to land. Are you certain they'll come on ships?" Archer's heavy feet pace around the room. I can't see him but I can picture his scarred face, his teeth smiling cruelly.

When Lucine answers, I shake with anger because I know, I know Kurt has to be here. "I thought Nieve fixed you. Didn't you hear what I said? The Mutt's people will come on ships. I've seen it. If you don't trust in my sight, then you can go cry on your mother's lap and ask her to do better."

"I do not cry," Archer snarls. He bites at the air, and feet shuffle back and forth.

I hear Kurt whisper something like, "I don't like this." And Lucine placates him like he's a child.

"Don't, my darling," she says.

Kurt grunts and walks away, toward where I am. "I'm going to check on my guard."

There's a splash. I press my body against the tunnel and the light scatters around me. I consider making a dash for it, but he doesn't look behind and takes a tunnel going to what might be west. Something about Lucine's tone toward Archer makes me stay and listen.

"You really ought to keep a tighter leash on him," Archer tells Lucine.

"The way your mother keeps you?"

Archer growls at her.

"Once Tristan comes ashore," Lucine says, "it is up to Nieve to take his scepter."

Archer steps closer to her, threatening her space. "And what of your bastard prince?"

"He will see this is the future for us," she says. "I will make him see."

Thalia is right. Lucine is controlling Kurt. How do I make him see? I sink back down the tunnel. This time, I let myself sense the water. East. Shouldn't a good sense of direction come with the merman package? There's a tunnel that doesn't look like the others. The light is fainter, and the water that runs through it is colder.

I take it.

The chill makes me want to turn back, but then I remember the first time I met Chrysilla, the nautilus maid. I went through the well, and the water, like here, was so cold I nearly stopped breathing. My gills refuse to open and I hold my breath, pushing myself up the dark tunnel until I break the surface.

There's a sigh of relief and I step out of the pool. In the center of the white shimmering stone, there is a basin with shallow water. The nautilus maid is not the way I last saw her. Her skin is cold, bleeding where it's dry and cracked. Her rose-colored eyes search the room, but she's dazed, and it takes time for her to focus on my face.

There are two fish in the pool, swimming around her. A few half-eaten fins lie at the bottom and around the floor. Her laria, the tongueless girls that were her handmaidens, are nowhere to be seen. I saw them here in my vision, but they're gone. Long streaks of scarlet blood drag all the way to the chamber entrance. I can picture their dead bodies getting taken away.

I step closer to Chrysilla, the oracle. The water dripping from me is like the heartbeat of a clock.

When I stand directly in front of her, she sighs once more. It takes strength for her to hold her head up, and the long, fleshy tendrils of her hair hang limp at her sides.

"You didn't forget me," she says.

I shake my head. This is not fair.

"Do it," she says, pressing a hand over her heart. "Do it or you die with me."

I shake my head. "Why did she take you?"

Chrysilla tries to smile. "Not Nieve. It was my sister who knew I was hiding something. But we have taken each other's blood and only you can have my secrets."

I get closer to her. She reaches out a cold hand and presses her fingers on my wet face. I take one of the fish that swim around her and put it in her mouth. She bites and nods. "They took my laria."

She chews, shutting her eyes like it's the best thing she's ever eaten. Her last meal.

"Why me?" I want to know. "Why did you pick me?"

Kai's words ring in my ear: they play their games.

She leans forward and presses her hand on my chest, right over my heart. "This is why."

The color is fading from her eyes, like the way it did from my grandfather before he turned into coral.

Do it, I tell myself. Do it because if she dies, I'll go with her, and then what was the point of all of this?

I unsheathe Triton's dagger. My legs feel weak.

"No. The scepter." Chrysilla shakes her head, hand still pressed over her heart. "That is how you will retain control of your beast no matter what."

Her veins are raised and getting darker, like the blood is bubbling inside them and they're ready to burst.

"Do it," she hisses.

I bite down and steel myself, but it isn't me who will feel the pain, is it? It isn't my life that's ending, is it?

"Do it!"

My eyes are closed and I force them to stay open because I know I shouldn't look away, shouldn't hide from my own darkness.

And I take the Scepter of the Earth, look into her eyes, and plunge the crystal into her chest.

Part III

And if the earthly no longer knows your name,

Whisper to the silent earth: I'm flowing.

To the flashing water say: I am.

—RAINER MARIA RILKE

LONG AGO

The Daughter of the Sea would never have peace.

For days and months and years, she swam around the Golden Palace alone. Her friends were few and far between. The old women of the court who marveled at her magic. The leering warriors who longed to feel the strange pulse of her magic on their skin.

The Silver Queen wondered if she was strong enough to be patient. To see her captors dead at her hands. She repeated their names, like promises to the Goddess of the Moon, the Gods of the Sea.

She gave food to the merpeople lingering outside the palace and took her husband's wrath when he heard of her kindness.

"They will never love you," he told her.

She held her hand over the sting on her cheek and waited.

The waiting was the most painful, for she was pregnant once more. She could feel the life of the child pulling at her life strings, her life magic. The first time she carried a child, it came out small and bloody like a broken heart ripped out of a chest. It might as well have been; the Silver Queen wailed harder than the day she was taken from her home.

And then another, and another.

The Rebel King sent a small army to the Sea King's gate. They would pay for a daughter who could not bear children.

Rumors spread through the kingdoms of the Silver Queen and her dozens of bloody children. That she ate them from the womb for her blood magic. That she was cursed to never bear life of the Rebel King. That the magic destroyed her from the inside and she would one day burn.

Not this one, she promised, pressing her hands on her swollen belly. She was bigger than the times before. Stronger. This child was strong and healthy. She could feel it swim laps inside her. This time, the king let her rest. She would not perform at court. She would not leave her chambers.

The Silver Queen asked for her lady-in-waiting, Melaya, and no one else. Just as well. The Rebel King wanted nothing to do with the queen or her child. His forces were weakening in the Northern Seas and he wouldn't return for weeks.

It happened when the moon was gone from the surface. She felt the pain come on too soon, and she held her swollen belly and prayed for the child to stay inside. Melaya took her to the caves south of the Golden Palace where the magic was raw. The king knew nothing of the caves' existence. Life there was strong, rooted deep in the earth. There had been merpeople here once, their markings etched deep into the walls.

The Daughter of the Sea screamed as her fins ripped in half, parting to make way as the white head of her child crowned.

"Shhh," Melaya urged her. They didn't know who was nearby, and so the Silver Queen bit down on her teeth and pushed. She closed her eyes and willed the child to leave her until a small mermaid, no bigger than her fist, came out.

All at once, the Queen felt empty and weak, a black void filling where there had once been life. And the small mermaid child was not a mermaid at all.

Melaya gasped.

"What is it?" Nieve cried, holding her arms out for the child. "What's happened?"

Melaya took a blade and cut off the lifeline that still attached the child to its mother. She brushed the hair away from the child's face and bit her lip to keep from crying because she knew if the Rebel King laid eyes on the child, he would not stand it.

"Let me see her," said the Silver Queen.

In her arms, she could see the girl's deformity. Her teeth as sharp as needles when they drew blood from her mother's milk. The left side of the child's body was smooth as pearl, her hair grew in white tufts, and her scales were white as the stars. It was as if there were two halves to her. The right side was bald, the skin puckered as if it were burned.

"Gwenivere," the Silver Queen said. "I will call her Gwenivere."

The Rebel King had many sons, but none were of his Queen.

They were brown as the earth with eyes like golden suns,

swimming and fighting through the palace. They said after the Silver Queen lost the last child, the king no longer touched her. Her madness was too much for the king to withstand.

And she let them have their whispered stories, as she left the palace every night and swam to the caves where Melaya and Gwenivere waited for her.

Sometimes she came with food, shark fins and tentacles.

Other times she came with a maiden. The first one was young and happy to be in the company of the queen. She took the queen's hand eagerly and followed deep, deep down into the ancient caves. The maiden stared at the creatures she'd never seen before, their sharp teeth and glowing faces. She traced her fingers along anemones that glowed with inner light and tickled her skin.

When they reached the mouth of the cave, she hesitated, feeling the water turn icy.

"What's in there?" the maiden asked.

"My treasure," the queen said with a lovely smile as she put a hand to the maiden's chest and put her to sleep.

It wasn't supposed to hurt. All Nieve needed was some of the girl's life. Just a bit of blood to heal Gwenivere. But the girl woke up and screamed and screamed, and with another touch of the queen's hands, she was reduced to surf.

They tried again and again until Gwenivere had nothing left but a thin scar along the side of her body. She was as beautiful as any mermaid in the court. She laughed and sang with Melaya, always wondering where her mother went off to and longed for her return.

Gwenivere never noticed where the pretty maidens went, but she woke to the burst of bubbles in the sea and reached out with her tiny hands to touch them.

They noticed.

Mermaids missing from the harems, mermaids missing from their homes.

The Silver Queen sat silently on the throne, knowing she had to stay away from her child to keep her safe. She kept her secret treasure close, marrying her to a strong merman, a herald of the Eastern Seas who relished the magic of Gwenivere's hands.

"Patience," she told Gwenivere, "for soon we will rule the entire seas."

"My king," Nieve said. She had not spoken in so long that the Rebel King marveled at the sound of her voice. "You know quite well who is behind these disappearances. For who else would want to take the daughters of our court except the man you took me from?"

It was easy, stoking the fire that was already lit. The Rebel King armed himself with his best men and his golden armor and charged the true king.

The Silver Queen was left alone on the throne, and she watched it carefully, patiently. She resumed the feasts, but this time, no one would die. Instead, she gave them gifts—shark skin armor and jewels from the king's caves and food. There was always food for the people on the outer lands, the ones as skinny as coral. They praised her kindness, her beauty, and they loved her.

When the Rebel King Amur did not return, they loved her still, bowing and willing to give their lives for their generous Silver Queen. And she drank their love the way they drank her gifts. From miles and miles came strange tribes of the sea, uniting with her against her father, the true king. They heard of his heir, King Karanos, leading his father's armies. But Nieve did not fear her father or the brother she had never known.

When her father came to the Golden Palace, he demanded she unite with the northern kingdom.

"I am your eldest child, Father," she said. "Will you take the trident from Karanos and give it to me?"

She waited, staring at the frightful face of the man who sent her away and now wanted her back.

"I didn't think so," she said, when he answered with silence.

They came from the shadows, each and every one of her army. They surrounded the king and his small fleet in the great hall of the Golden Palace.

"What are you doing?" he said, succumbing to the fear he'd always felt around her. "My son is on his way. He's bringing the entire Sea Guard."

He babbled, twisting and turning. But the king was too old, and the sword in his hand weighed him down.

"Let him come, Father," she told him. "I've been waiting."

chapter
FORTY-FOUR

NOW

Chrysilla doesn't scream.

But I do.

I know I shouldn't because if they hear us, we're dead.

But I do.

I grit my teeth as I feel the crystal of the scepter break her skin. Her blood flecks my hands, gushing from the wound.

And then brilliant light floods the core of the crystal, hot and red and blinding. The floor is the ceiling, and the ceiling is the floor. My head spins like I've been shoved down a whirlpool, like I've been swept into a dream.

It has to be a vision because I'm still me.

I'm me looking at me.

I'm king, sitting where my grandfather sat the first time I stumbled onto Toliss Island. The people are somber and there is no singing. At first, I don't recognize my face. I'm old. Like thirty at least. Considering how merpeople age, I might look thirty, but I could be one hundred.

There's a woman beside me on the throne, and she talks and talks. She's beautiful with hair the color of corn silk and amber eyes. Her lips are as red as roses, and she places a hand over mine. My stomach is all knots when I look at her, and the me that is king leans over to kiss her. Then I lean back and she's quiet, as if all I wanted to do was shut her up.

I realize that the court isn't sitting idly. They're all dressed in armor, waiting for me.

I hold the trident in my hands. Thick white scars decorate my skin. In the king's chamber, I fiddle with a picture. It's faded and wrinkled like it was left in water for too long.

Someone walks in behind me and I drop it.

"It's only me, Cousin," Brendan says. He doesn't look as old as I do, but white streaks his hair. "The guard is ready."

"I'll be right out," I tell him, but my voice is so distant.

"It wasn't your fault, you know," Brendan says. "You warned Thalia not to go fight him, and she did so on her own. Her death wasn't your fault."

"Is that true of all of them?" I start naming people I haven't met yet. Then I get to the ones I have. "Dylan and Layla? Are you going to tell me those weren't my fault?"

Tendrils of lightning circle the prongs of the trident. Brendan steps back.

"We must go," I say and walk past him.

Brendan doesn't follow right away. Instead he picks up the photograph. It's of me and Layla, but her face is nearly washed away. He puts it back in the hiding spot I took it out from.

The dream changes, vertigo returning. I'm charging headfirst in the water, my guard behind me. I can't see my enemy's face, but the fury in my eyes scares me. I'm a wild thing, cutting down mermen. They turn to surf and become part of the wave that takes me to him. His hair is long, down to his hips. A white scar marks his face like a crescent. But the violet eyes are still the same.

Kurt wields another trident. It's one piece and solid and new. The silver catches the sun.

I'm shouting. The dream-me. Not the king-me.

I tell myself to stop because I know that this is the wrong thing. This is not what is supposed to happen. Not to me, not to all of us. Not after we've worked this hard.

The image dissolves and I stand on my shore. Toliss. The white sandy beach. Bright blue waters that you can see right through. Something about the way I stare at the sky unnerves me. I'm waiting for something. Or someone.

She comes out from the patch of forest that leads inland. I didn't expect her. A leaf is caught in her crown. I look back at the water.

She wraps her arms around me and I let her, but there is no warmth. She talks to me. Her voice is sweet like a songbird. Pleasing, consoling me over my stalemate with the bastard king. We'll get him soon enough.

Who is she? Where is Layla? Why do I keep looking at the sky?

Something in her hand glints. I want to reach out to stop her. I can feel the stabbing pain in my side. Her blade digs deep into my skin. She twists the knife and stares into my eyes as I fall back onto the sand. I'm not surprised. I'm not anything.

I'm lying on the sand, bright red blood tainting everything around me. I try to stand but poison spreads in blue lines across my skin. I reach a hand out to my queen, but she keeps on walking.

chapter
FORTY-FIVE

Maybe it's watching myself die.

Maybe it's the chill of the room or the painful pulse that runs through my body. But I can feel a change. I roll over on my side, sure that I'm not going to make it out of this room alive. Maybe I'm already dead.

I taste copper in my mouth and I spit it out. My tongue is dry and my lips are swollen.

In my hand is the Scepter of the Earth. I'm afraid to look at the end of it, but I force my eyes to open. The nautilus maid is gone. In her place is a tall coral the same shade of pink as her eyes. A lone fish is swimming in the shallows.

I hold my side where I saw myself get stabbed and replay the vision in my head. It couldn't have been a vision because that's not how my life is supposed to be. And then I think really hard about what another oracle—Lucine—showed me the time I watched her give Kurt the Trident of the Skies. She showed me the same thing. Me, dead, with a crown on my head.

Thalia's words ring like a bell: killing an oracle is a curse.

And then I feel it. The ground is shaking, trembling like an earthquake. The quartz in my scepter lights up, and I know I've done it. I've released the Sleeping Giants.

The sensation is thrilling, pushing every thought of death out of my head. It is the lightning and current that flows through the earth. I hold my scepter horizontally, and the energy that flows through it is like ten shots of adrenaline in the chest. I could swim for miles, for days. I hold out my scepter, and a blast of light crashes into the wall, breaking it down.

I concentrate on pushing the lightning straight through the rock of the ceiling until it's a single beam into the sky. The room is flooded white and the walls are crumbling around me, but I don't care. I hold the beam as long as I can.

The island trembles all the way through. Pieces of stone break away from the ceiling. I have to get out of the chambers and find Nieve and Kurt. But I'm high on adrenaline and the power of the scepter. The ground is shaking so hard that it knocks me off balance and I fall forward, right on top of the pink coral.

That sobers me up.

Focus, Amada said. Focus.

I dive back into the main artery that leads to the tunnels and swim down. The shark guard is all gone. Instead three prongs wait for me, pointed right at my throat.

Kurt's violet eyes glow fiercely; his mouth is an angry snarl.

My mind flashes to us fighting in the vision Chrysilla gave me. I shake it away because that can't be how we end. Not after all we've been through.

Chunks of the island break off from the tunnels, and the hungry chatter of merrows echoes through them.

"You can't go that way," Kurt says, lowering his trident. "They're coming for us."

He swims along the base of the shaking island. The ground beneath us is also trembling, splitting like a hairline fracture across glass. First a nick, then with every shake, it keeps going and going.

When I don't follow, Kurt turns around. "Please."

This could be the worst idea I've had in a while, and I have a lot of bad ideas. But when Kurt gives me his back, I know he's not worried that I'm going to skewer him. So I follow him where he leads, back to surface that is overgrown with vines and trees. It's a part of Toliss where I've never been before. A waterfall breaks the landscape and rushes into a narrow stream full of multicolored fish. We trip over broken branches and scratch our legs on jagged rocks until we're under then behind the waterfall. It's relatively dry, and a hole in the ceiling of the cave provides some light.

"Why are you doing this?"

"I have to!"

I shield my eyes as birds take flight around us. "That's a non-answer!"

But we keep running through the Toliss jungle, and I fluctuate between wanting to bash him in the face and hug it out like bros because he came back to me.

"Where are we going?" I shout as branches and boulders fall all around us. I duck out of the way as lightning strikes the ground near us and three trunks fall sideways, narrowly missing me. A few hours ago, I couldn't get the quartz scepter to conjure any power, and now it's made us target practice for the angry sky gods. Kurt's screams get drowned out in the rumble of thunder, the ripping apart of solid rock.

"Kurt?"

He falls forward, flat on his face.

"What's wrong?"

"She's calling to me—" He grits his teeth and screams through it, clutching the Trident of the Skies. His unfiltered power blows through it in sparks of lightning. His breath is labored, like someone's got their hands on his lungs.

"What do I do?"

He shakes his head and pushes himself up, like he's wading through cement. "I have to go to her."

"No!" I pull on his arm.

He wavers on his knees, gasping for air. He gulps it down and it sounds easier. He grabs my shoulder for support. "It's like she's squeezing my lungs."

"She can do that?" I hope I've never seen Kurt complain about pain before. "As your friend, I'd like to point out that this is what we call an abusive relationship."

"Lucine wants what's best for me." He leans on a tree trunk for support, pressing his hand to his chest like he's making sure his heart is still beating.

"We have to get back to the others," I say. "Shelly'll know how to make it stop."

"No. We have to finish this. Nieve has weaknesses just like everyone else." He breathes normally again.

The sky is dark and so are our paths. We follow the light of our weapons and the animals that scatter away. I scream as I feel the ground fall beneath me. Kurt grabs on to me by the back of my harness and pulls me back. With one foot out to sea, I'm a step away from free falling off a cliff and into the crashing waves.

"Only way out is down," I say.

And he goes, "Together."

"On three," I say, retracing our steps and getting ready to jump.

"Tristan, I'm sorry," Kurt says.

The wind is screeching in a fury, bringing the sea over the cliff.

"One—" I say, but neither of us waits. We run, run, run, and then jump.

It feels so long since I've taken a dive. I've come a long way from Karel pushing me in the Vale of Tears. I tuck my head between my shoulders and straighten my legs.

But I don't reach the sea.

Searing pain digs into my shoulders. Something warm runs down my chest and back. In the dark, I see a slick body and massive wings flying beside me. A sea dragon. It wasn't the wind screeching; it was the sea dragons. Thick black talons grab Kurt by the shoulder and fly away. Talons, cutting me and dragging me away.

I scream, and as I feel my body being lifted into the sky, I know no one can hear me.

chapter
FORTY-SIX

My body is cold. There's a void that is getting bigger and bigger. It's like losing a part of myself. I can feel a piece of me missing. Gone. The scepter is gone.

I try to lift my arms. Feel my chest. Move my legs.

Except I can't move my legs.

I hold my breath and brace myself to look down. My vision is doubled and my temples pound. I lift my torso up and even that's a challenge. The ground has stopped shaking, but I feel a wave of nausea hit me and I turn my face to the side and puke last night's pizza.

When I see my tail, I could cry tears of joy that it's there and I'm in one piece. I search the room and I must be dreaming because I see Adaro. His face is right in front of mine.

I shut my eyes to make his face go away and it does. When I open them again, I see Gwen. She presses something warm and smelly on my shoulders. I blink and she's gone.

Off to the side, Kurt's hands are chained against a wall. His blood is smeared all over his torso so that with my fuzzy vision, it looks like he's wearing a shirt.

"Don't say it," Kurt says. He shuts his eyes and I picture him trying to retrace his steps to see what he could have done differently.

"Say what?" It hurts to talk.

"I told you so."

"I didn't say it, you did."

He closes his eyes and leans his head back. "They've been coming in and out. Gwen healed you. She loves you. She won't let Nieve kill you."

The combinations of being without my scepter and the beatings I've taken have left me quiet. I did it. I killed the nautilus maid. I can feel the sleeping giants stirring awake. I signaled my army.

But I messed up badly. "How did we get here?"

"My father told me that if we follow our hearts to the very end, we'll find what we're looking for."

I laugh and it hurts. "If what you're looking for is death."

"You don't believe that."

He's right, I don't.

"What made you change your mind?" I ask. "What made you come back?"

"Lucine herself." Kurt lifts his legs and swallows the pain. "She told me to give the Trident of the Skies to the sea witch so we could be together in peace, away from all this. All I had to do was kill you myself. Now she has it anyway."

I sit up like I've been set on fire. In the back of my head, I can see Kurt and me as mortal enemies. We can't end up that way. Perhaps this is how it starts. Perhaps this is how it ends.

"Where was this when I was warning you, huh?" I could kick him. "We were together, Kurt. We were together from the beginning, through all of this. We watched your father die. And then you still went back to her."

"Do you think I wanted this?" He leans forward, pulling on his chains. "I've spent my entire life doing what the king asked of me. Then I find that he's—was—my father, and despite that, he chose you. Forgive me, Tristan, but that hurt me more than I'll ever want to say. You have been in a land where time is unmoving, but it has only been a day of mine."

Look at us, the mighty champions.

"Nieve promised me that my loved ones would be alive at the end of this," he says. "And Lucine—I've loved her since I met her. When I was searching for vengeance for my parents' deaths, she gave me a path. She gave me a reason to live for that was all consuming and wrong, but I wanted it. If she had told me to chop off my limbs and give them to her, I would have without question. Then she cast me aside because her mind isn't right. I know that. When I saw her again, it was like she had never left me in the first place."

"To be fair, you seemed to enjoy it," I say, laughing.

He squints and gives me his cheek.

"The king was right," he says, "in the end. You and I are not very different."

I agree.

"Though now I have better hair."

I point to my head. "This is your fault."

"Tristan, why did you go to get the nautilus maid again?"

How do you change a future that seems to be laid out for you? Here I am, looking at my friend turned family turned enemy turned ally once again. He's asking me to trust him. I've had too many misses with the trust thing recently. I never knew how much it would hurt to have someone betray me.

"Because I had to kill her."

The fog lifts from my head when I say that.

"No one can do that." He's startled. "There's a curse. If you kill an oracle, you'll die a young king."

"Well…I did. With the scepter." I reach for a weapon that isn't there and the emptiness grows tenfold. "She was in bad shape when I got to her. After you and Gwen came to get her—"

"That's not why I went." He looks away, ashamed. "Lucine told me to go to my father because he was dying. She told me to help Gwenivere rescue her sister oracle." A bitter laugh leaves his lips and he looks to the hole in the ceiling. "Because you wanted her, that's why. I'm such a fool."

"Layla says it's part of being a guy," I say. "The fool thing. I don't think she means that."

Kurt nods. "I'm sure she does."

"Thank you," I tell him.

His brow creases. "What for?"

"For protecting her. From the sharks."

The earth rumbles harder.

I shake my head. "You warned me that the people I love would get hurt."

"It's the best kind of way to hurt your enemy," he says. "By taking away the things they love."

"What does Nieve love?" I wonder aloud. "Besides her power."

We say it together. "Her children."

chapter
FORTY-SEVEN

Steps echo outside our chamber prison. Kurt and I remain silent as Gwen comes back in. She ignores Kurt and touches the bloody gashes where the sea dragon grabbed me, and I scream bloody murder.

She flinches and looks me dead in the eyes. "You're awake."

"Gwen." I take on a lighter tone. "Enjoying the weather?"

"You don't have to put on a brave face," she says.

"Is that what you're doing?" I will her to look at me. "Because you don't have to heal me. You can let me bleed out. I've been wondering lately what will happen to me when I die. You know, since I'm half human. Humans leave behind their bones, no matter how old they are. It's the one thing that we have in common at the very end. But then there's the fishy part of me. What if the bottom half of me washes away in little bubbles and from my waist up I'm all human bone? What if it's the other way around?" I cough and laugh, making a terrible choking sound.

"Say something," I whisper.

The white stone walls bounce my words back at me. *Say something.*

She squeezes the towel soaked with a green liquid. Then she throws it on the floor. The green ooze trickles from the broken shell bowl and spreads out like the Finger Lakes on a map.

"What would you have me say?" Gwen lowers her face to mine. "That I love you. That I love you so much I'd betray my family for you?"

She laughs a bitter laugh and turns away so I can't see her. "We have worked too hard and too long to stop now. Don't you see? Mother will bring our people together when we take over the land that once belonged to us."

"That world doesn't belong to you," I say. I pull at my bindings, my joints screaming in pain. "Is that what you really want, or your mother?"

She traces her fingers on my face, down my neck and along where the cuts on my shoulder have started to scab. Her magic leaves a dirty trail on me, and I think I'd rather feel the pain.

"I don't know what I want anymore," she says softly. Then she turns around and leaves me, walking out into the dark corridors of the Toliss chambers.

"Gwen, don't go," I say. "Don't go."

"Leave her," Kurt tells me.

She stops at the door, but she isn't talking to me. She's talking to someone out there, waiting in the hallway. "He's ready."

Leomaris walks in. It wasn't Adaro I thought I saw; it was his father. His long hair is pulled back, and the thick golden band frames his forehead. He's joined by a slender merman with a face that looks like a jigsaw puzzle of skins.

Leomaris raises his hand and the binding ropes loosen. My muscles are cramped and I fall hard on my face. They're on me at once.

"Gwen!" I shout her name but she's gone.

Leomaris and the merman pick me up and drag me out into the hallway.

"You're making a mistake," I tell the herald. "You can't trust her."

"I don't have to trust her," he tells me. "I can't defeat her. No one can. Someone has to pay for my son's death. That someone is you."

They throw me in front of the great white throne where I first met my grandfather. Kurt falls beside me on his knees, his head bent forward. Wet strands of hair cover his face.

Then there's Nieve flanked by Archer and Gwen. She smiles wide as a shark, her teeth a waiting trap. Her legs are covered with bright silver scales that look thick as armor, right down to the ankles where her slender feet touch the ground. Her crown is gilded gold with woven pearls as if they're floating on her white hair.

The pool was once bright and laughing with mermaids singing and swimming. The paradise welcomed me to my life as a merman. Now there is only the smell of death. Merrows in clusters adding to the destruction. It's gone, broken in half. The gash down the lake has created a connecting rush of water from the shore. It's like a wrecking crew ripped out the lake and went straight for the sea, crushing the valley wall that used to block the surrounding trees.

Now, that's all demolished. From here, there's a direct path where trees were crushed to mulch. The sea is dark and I squint my eyes for some sign that my army got my signal, that I wasn't too late—

No, it wasn't a wrecking crew that did this. Not even Nieve. Not the merrows. It was the Sleeping Giants. Well, wide awake now.

With a shove, I'm on my knees beside Kurt, facing the Silver Queen. The pieces of the trident are suspended in the air for her to take. Hands push our heads to the ground. My cheek presses against the top of her foot. She lifts my chin with her toes. Kicks me in the face.

First, she holds the Staff of Eternity. She twirls it between her hands like a baton. Her merrows holler and shout in a discordant chorus. Then she takes the Scepter of the Earth. My scepter. I tug on my ropes, summoning the energy that ran inside me moments ago, but it's gone. She slides the handle into one of the openings of the staff. The core of the quartz lights up like a headlight shining in my face. I have to look away.

Then she takes the Trident of the Skies. She holds it alone first, raising it to the sky, pulling on the power of the heavens until it circles her in a shower of sparks. Kurt can't look, but I force myself. I force myself to get angry. I force myself to hate.

Finally, she connects the missing piece. The lake of the Sea Court is full of stomping feet and shouts of victory.

Then she walks forward to face her merrows. She raises the trident into the sky and blocks out the sun.

chapter
FORTY-EIGHT

Without my scepter, I don't know what to do but watch the silver mermaid wield the Trident of the Seas.

Her exterior changes. She looks taller, her hair as white as the lightning that courses through her body. She stares straight into the eclipse, and in turn, we all stare at her. I don't want to. But she's a force of nature, wild and fierce. Her arms look like they're holding up the sky.

The waves around Toliss are so tall that I can see the white surf rising high.

"Today we take back our oceans," she says.

Kurt lifts his head to look at me, his eyes glowing. He doesn't have to say it. No matter what, Nieve can't win. Even if it means our lives.

Merrows flood out of the court and into the sea. Terrible moans and roars mingle with the whipping winds. The giants crest with the waves. The sea horse stretches its forelegs, its slick mane shimmering in the starlight. Then it dives back in, its tail a prism of colors. Sea dragons screech above us, ready to sink their talons back in our flesh. They fly a careful distance from the giant tentacles that curl and stretch toward the sky. The only creature I can't see is the turtle with the spiked shell, but when a long angry noise rips through the sky, I know that it's close by.

"Hey, Leomaris!" I call out to him. "How does it feel to kiss the feet of the mermaid who murdered your kid?"

Nieve snaps her head at me. She's drunk on power and she smiles with her shark teeth. "Don't listen to the half-breed. He was there. He could have saved Adaro and he chose not to."

I get on one knee and face them. Then I stand, my hands still tied behind my back.

"Do you know how I found him?" I ask.

He doesn't want to hear it. It's cruel of me to do this to someone's dad. But he has to know. "Adaro was on his ship, writhing in pain."

Nieve hisses at me. She sends a threatening bolt at my head, but I throw myself to the side.

"Archer's knife was stuck through his chest so he'd die slowly, and for as long as he held on, he told me not to cower to her. But here you are. Because you're weak. You disgrace the memory of your own son."

Leomaris lunges at me. He unties my bindings and pulls me up because he wants me to fight back. I jab and cross. His jaw doesn't even snap to the side. I kick forward but he doesn't budge.

"You're pretty solid for an old guy," I say, readying my fists.

Rowdy cheers egg us on. Beneath the noise, I can hear Gwen.

"Mother," Gwen says, "do something."

"I promised you I wouldn't kill him," Nieve answers coldly. "And I'm not the one doing the killing. Not yet, at least."

I find the nearest rock and throw it at him. I miss and double over when his knee hits me in the gut. I've lost Kurt from my sight. I hope he's gotten free.

Then I see it—the ripples in the great lake. They're distorted, like something is wading out of there. Tiger eyes appear in thin air. In her translucent phase, Yara carefully makes her way onto the bank.

"Mother…"

Yara nocks her arrow.

Leomaris raises his sword over his head, thinking I'm too weak to get up. "It should have been you."

I roll out of the way, listening for the snap of the bow. The onyx arrowhead breaks through his shoulder and he cries out. Leomaris's sword cleaves two inches into the ground, and I'd hate to think that if I'd been slower, that could have been me.

He tries to yank it out but it won't give. I uppercut him in the jaw and, as he staggers back, kick him square in the chest. He moves back so quickly that he falls into the pool and doesn't resurface.

Adrenaline thumps in my ears, and I can't make out the commotion. Yara lands beside me. I can see through her like glass. The river tribe emerges from the water undetected. The merrows are confused, attacking enemies they cannot see.

Nieve fires away with her trident, but she risks hitting her children. Yara is as fast as lightning, a whirlwind of her own. Beside her is Karel with his axes, cleaving heads and rib cages until he's covered in black blood down to his elbows.

"You're late to the party," I tell him when he runs past me. I've never been so happy to see him.

He grumbles, but I catch a smile as he throws a dagger my way.

"Kurt!" A hulking merrow is ambling toward him.

I don't think it. I just do. The dagger in my hand spins in the air and hits its target between the eyes. As he decomposes, I see Gwen's face standing behind him. She's seen me do this before and had to hide her displeasure at killing merrows. Now, she takes up a sword and holds it at my face. The tip follows me as I stand, retrieving the dagger from the stinking pile of black flesh.

"You can't trust him, Gwenivere," Nieve says, her voice slithering between the fighting bodies.

And then Gwen, who patched up my wounds and begged for my life, lunges at me with the sword. Sparks fly when our metals meet, the sharp sound of blades slicing against each other.

"Your heart isn't in this," I tell her.

"You don't know what's in my heart."

I tap her solar plexus with the ball of my palm and she staggers back.

"I'll show you," I say, getting on my knees and holding my arms out. My whole self is exposed to her. "Do it."

She looks horrified and takes a few steps back.

"Your mother might love you," I say, "but as long as that trident is in her hands, she'll love it even more."

Gwen shakes her head.

"Do you remember how beautiful this place was?" I say, motioning to the screams and bloodshed. "You say you don't have a home but you've always found yourself here in this place. Now look at it. Look what she's done."

"Gwenivere, if you don't do it, I swear I will. Do it!"

And then Gwen steps aside like I knew she would.

"I don't know what kind of future I can give you," I say, "but I wouldn't use you."

"Mother, I won't."

Nieve pushes her daughter aside with a wave of her hand. I lunge for my sword, but a force grips me and squeezes the wind out of my body.

"You don't deserve your scales. You don't deserve the blood of kings that runs through your veins."

Even as I choke, I say, "Tough luck, Grandma."

She blasts me with the trident. I catch the current with my dagger until it's so hot that I have to drop it and my fingertips are black.

There is so much fury in Nieve's eyes that they're stark white. She throws the trident at me. I try to move out of the way, but a dark force holds me in place. My feet become a tail. She's pulling it out of me in the most painful way. It's like I'm cooking from the inside out, stretched out in midair.

You know, when you're about to die, things really do go in slow motion. My heart races like the pulse of thunder in my throat. My name is shouted from so many different voices I can't tell who is who. All I know is that they say it, over and over.

Tristan.

Tristan.

Tristan.

There's the blow of a conch shell followed by the warrior cry of an army of strays.

I want to close my eyes but I can't. They're trained on the three prongs of the trident coming at me like a harpoon.

Gwen jumps in front of me. Her magic crackles around her like a shield. Her lips are open, and a thin line of black blood drips from the corner of her mouth. The trident is stronger than her shield and rips through her body. She looks down at the golden prongs covered in her own blood, then at me. Her eyes wide as full moons, black tendrils spreading from the wound in her chest.

A cry starts at the bottom of my heart and can't get out.

No, no, no, no.

She holds out her hand to me, the dark veins spreading beneath her porcelain skin. Black blood pools out of her mouth. *Tristan.* She closes her eyes and then is gone.

A jolt runs through me like a cord wound so tight it snaps.

When Nieve screams, the heavens rip open.

chapter
FORTY-NINE

Nieve screams so loudly that a white light descends over the island. I hold my arm up to block it. The rumbling starts again, and this time, something in the water moves. The lake is one big ripple as a horn breaks the surface, followed by the massive head of the turtle. It swallows two bodies whole from the water, making its way down to the shore.

The creature bursts out with a gallop and rattles the whole island, knocking everyone to the ground.

All except for Nieve, who raises herself into the air, the wind forming a cone around her. She holds her hand out and the trident flies to her open palm.

Her eyes are a white film, the air thick with her magic. It's not enough that she's blocked out the sun. She wants to bury the world under the sea. Great waves crash over us, pushing some out into the sea where awaiting tentacles reach hungrily.

"Tristan!" Marty is running under the heaving turtle. "This thing is huge!"

A merrow attacks me. I kick him in the chest, but I'm not up to my full strength and he falls on me. I hold his sword hands and push them away from my face. A blade rips through its head and the merrow breaks away on top of me, chunks of its flesh going in my mouth.

"Thanks for showing up," I say.

"We were waiting," Marty says, throwing me a weapon. "Brendan's ship can't anchor. The water's too rough."

"Stay close," I tell him.

He nods and runs to the aid of one of his allies. I'm trying to find familiar faces in the mix of merrows. In her beast form, Amada runs alongside her sister, forming a tag team that's fluid one moment and solid the next.

Something deep in my bones tells me that Nieve is heading straight for Coney Island. It's my home. It's the best way to hurt me. I can sense her urging the giants toward land. The turtle crosses the Toliss forest, flattening it to the ground as it nears the shore.

I throw things at her, but she's turning into a storm at full force.

I try to remember what happened after the sea dragons grabbed us. Where is Triton's dagger? Nieve thinks the Triton line is hers. I'm not worthy. She'd keep it at the throne. I run for it, but so does a merman from Nieve's ranks, his forehead inked with the symbols of the court. I stop running and let him reach for it. He smirks then is confused as to why I'm laughing. When his hand starts burning, the skin black as coal, he drops the dagger and it slides right at my feet.

"Mercy," he says.

I hesitate. This is war after all. The merrows aren't showing mercy to any of mine. Would he do the same? I don't have time to answer as the wall behind him crumbles, what's left of the throne crushing him into surf.

As Nieve floats higher into the air, she hisses a command to her army. A mass of them dive into the lake. "Land," she says, her voice a hateful slithering thing, "land."

The turtle has reached the Toliss shoreline, and it steps into the water. I jump over boulders and fallen trees.

"Duck!" someone shouts.

It sounds like one of my men so I drop to the ground and a cannon blasts from the massive wooden ship bopping in the water. The turtle walks past it, creating a small wave that pushes the ship precariously to the side. I can see Layla on the deck, grabbing hold of the mast. She's joined by Shelly and some of the landlocked.

Then from the sides, silver bodies slither out of the waves. The island is sinking, the water edging closer and closer. The lake is getting so high that it goes over the banks. Arion marches with a group of landlocked warriors and they run into the lake.

"Behind you." He points.

I throw myself on the ground as Archer's fist grazes my cheekbone. He's joined by four of his brothers. In the dark, all I can see are their yellow eyes, and I hear their screams as four winged men of the Alliance swoop down and pick them up. They go higher and higher and them throw them back into the sea as piles of black ooze.

"You," Archer says. It's the only word he can seem to get out. He blames me for Gwen. I blame me for Gwen too.

A hand rests on my shoulder and pulls me back. Kurt, wielding a sword he seems to have stolen from the enemy. It is curved and bloody. His violet eyes are focused and trained on the tall merrow.

"He's mine," Kurt says, pushing me aside and meeting Archer.

I run back in the thick of it, back to back with Yara and the River Clan. Their arrows never miss a target.

Then I can feel a voice in my head whispering in a strange tongue.

Shelly? I ask. She was the last one to speak in my head before. But the thoughts are distorted, like they're not even human.

Above me, Nieve screams like a banshee, directing her chaotic orchestra. The tentacles of the kraken are long gone, the turtle swimming straight for Coney Island. It's the sea horse that is unaccounted for. It's the sea horse that's in my head.

Doris? I say, unsure of myself.

I can feel her happiness at the recognition of her name. I remember what the nautilus maid told me. I could control my beast, no matter what. Chrysilla knew this. I think this was her own way of stopping her sister from taking the future into her own hands. Chrysilla left me with the connection to the sea horse.

This is so weird, I think. Doris neighs in response.

Uhh, where are you?

"Tristan!" Ewin from the Bronx yells at me. "Why are you standing so precariously close to danger? Seek cover!"

He shoves me behind a boulder where Kai is nursing a nasty cut across her ribs. Marty takes off his shirt and rips it to make a bandage.

"Jesus, Marty," I say, "you're paler than Nieve."

Then he shifts into me and goes, "Better?"

"Cut that out!" I hate it when he does that. But he's got me down to a T, for Tristan. Every cut and bruise, and the nose that didn't get set properly.

Ewin pushes both of us away and picks up Kai.

"I'm fine," she says. "Give me my sword back."

Ewin turns to me for some support but I shrug. "I wouldn't argue."

The tusked warrior smiles at her and says, "You are perfect."

She turns beet red but takes her sword and steps out from behind the boulder that shields us.

"Marty!" I say. "Don't change."

"I don't intend to."

"No, I mean, stay me." I take the dirty cap off his head and throw it into the lake. He whimpers, probably contemplating if it's worth his life to go jump into a lake infested with merrows. "Take off your pants."

"Thought you'd never ask," he mumbles.

"With your scales on," I say. It's like standing in front of a mirror.

A black shadow races toward us. "This was not part of the plan," Frederik says when he sees what we're doing.

"Can you tell which one is which?" Marty says.

Frederik looks back and forth at us, a wrinkle forming between his eyebrows. Then finally, he points at Marty and says, "Marty. You ate that tuna and it's coming out of your pores."

The good thing is that it took enough time for him to figure it out.

"Of course," Marty says, his voice coming out of my mouth. "That's your backup plan."

"I need you to get her attention. Do something that makes her want to chase you. I need her to come down from up there."

"What'll you do after?"

"I'm not sure," I say. "Making this up as I go along."

"Good." Marty/Me nods. "I'm glad my whole life is dependent on your whims. I'm so glad I met you."

I wait as he runs out into the lake area, his feet splashing ankle deep in the rising water. He waves his hands like he's trying to land a plane. Then he throws some rocks at her.

I squeeze the bridge of my nose. "Oh, Marty."

A moving shape catches my attention. A fin stuck beneath a boulder.

"Well, look at you," I say. "Big bad oracle got squished by a rock?"

Lucine hisses at me, using her free fin to try to get me. "It's a curse, you know, killing one of us."

"I think you made that up," I say. "The same way you made up those prophecies to Kurt. You never told my grandfather to choose him, did you? You told my grandfather to pardon his sister."

She snarls at me, her emerald eyes as bright as beams. "You don't have the nerve to hurt me."

"Oh, I'm not going to hurt you," I say. "She is."

Thalia, who's been standing behind Lucine, is caked in black blood.

"Kurtomathetis will never forgive you," Lucine says, starting at the sword in Thalia's hand.

"Kurtomathetis will never forgive you either." I point to where Kurt is channeling all of his pent-up rage on his enemies.

Then I do a double take when I see me yelling, running backward as Nieve comes down from her whirlwind and races toward Marty/Me.

I break into a run. Marty/Me holds his sword up at Nieve's face, and she stares at the blade curiously. She knows. She knows it's not me.

Doris neighs in the back of my head, and this connection to the giant sea horse is like trying to pat my head and rub my stomach in the same direction at the same time. *Waiting for you,* she tells me.

I'm coming, I think. *Hang on.*

Rachel appears beside Marty in a puff of smoke. She raises the crossbow at Nieve's face, the arrow snapping straight to her forehead.

Nieve blocks the arrow with the trident and the arrow's trajectory switches, landing straight in the heart of a female vampire. She gasps with the shock of the wood sticking out of her chest. Rachel screams and reappears beside the girl. I didn't know her name. I should've. She burns from the inside, her mouth still open, ready to take in a breath that isn't there. In the breeze, she gets carried away into dust.

Nieve sees me, the real me. She looks back and forth between me and Marty, and that's when I jump, grabbing her around her waist. Her nails dig into my back, but I push her into the lake where a whirlpool has started.

I need to take her away from here, away from my friends.

She holds on to me as we spin in a rush out of the Toliss tunnels.

Doris? I ask. *Are you there?*

But I'm met with quiet. Nieve pulls back the trident, her scream a long echo through the dark sea. I try to back away, but the currents pull me closer to her.

Nieve is confused as a neighing sound answers her back. I push upward toward the surface and Nieve follows. I hold out my hand, reaching for the creature swimming straight for me. Its skin is like a prism, part reptilian, part scales. Doris flicks her nose up and pushes Nieve away from me.

When I saw the original three kings ride the animals, they were the same size. It was true, that we used to be bigger. Doris is the size of a whale.

Hold on, her strange animal voice tells me.

And I do. I grab on to the slippery mane, bracing my knees against her neck as she rips through the surface. Above, the storm is worse than before. The sea is teeming with yellow eyes marching toward the beaches.

A sea dragon screeches nearby, swooping down toward us for a good bite of me. When I turn around, squinting against the sea spray, the sea horse's tail bats at the sky and takes out the dragon.

Its wings flap in the water. With another kick, the screeching beast loses consciousness.

Then Nieve is right beside us, grabbing on to the spikes of the giant turtle. She holds on as the creature swims toward the Coney Island shore. She aims the trident and blasts at us. Doris is quick and dives. The force of it almost knocks me sideways, but I hold on until we're on the other side of the turtle.

"I have a faster ride than you," I yell at Nieve.

I want you to get as close as possible. I need to get on that shell.

Doris shakes her head.

I have to get on that shell!

She makes a terrible sound but takes me closer. The storm has moved with us, Nieve controlling its forces. I remember once my grandfather told me that the old kings shaped the seas, the land masses, all with their storms. Nieve could do the same now. All she has to do is bury the shore beneath the waves.

You take care of that turtle, I command her. This she likes. *See? We make a good team.*

Doris kicks out with her claws, grinding against the shell like nails on a chalkboard. The turtle is slow because it's so huge. When I'm on its back, I press my hand to the rough skin of its neck, the part exposed outside the shell. He's bleeding where my sea horse has cut him.

"It's not like you to hide," I yell, turning in a circle. I can feel her near me, but she keeps herself out of sight.

"I do not hide from you." Nieve holds on to a spike, the trident in her hand.

She's worried. I can tell she's worried because her pale blue eyes watch the surface of the water.

Now? Doris asks.

Not yet, I say.

I walk behind a spike, giving her enough time to strike me, but she doesn't. She's trying to figure out how I could command one of the giants without the trident. She's trying to figure out why the full power of it isn't hers.

Now? Doris asks.

Not yet, I say.

"You've got nothing left, you know," I say. "You killed your own daughter. Kurt is with Archer. The rest—you don't care about their lives, do you?"

She blasts me with the trident, but I stand sideways behind a spike. The turtle, on the other hand, feels it and moans.

I keep my back pressed to the rough bone. "I told Gwen this is what you were. I told her."

"She was everything to me," Nieve said. "Everything I have done was for her."

"No, it wasn't. Everything you've done was for you."

"What do you know of our world?" She moves between the spikes, the smack of her feet getting closer, the mist turning into drizzle. "You have never known the wrath of the kings. You have never been on the other side of love."

"You're right," I say. She's surprised that I agree with her, but she's right about that. "I have never known. All of my life, I've been

302

pretty content not knowing. All of my life, I've had everything. Then it was taken away—by my grandfather, by you, by my own choices. But I'm going to get it all back."

She laughs, a sound that sends the blood running through my veins, a laugh that threatens to swallow the whole world. "You are powerless, Tristan. I have the trident."

I step out from behind the shell.

Now? Doris asks.

Nieve holds the trident over her head, and the three prongs reach up to the sky. The quartz crystal is full of light and angled at my face.

Now!

I don't move out of the way.

Not right away at least. I'm not that crazy.

I don't move for a breath, the quartz coming straight at me.

I grab it, and the light pulses in tune with my heartbeat. The turtle heaves as Doris crashes into him. Nieve and I tilt toward the sea but I hold on. I have my hands around the Scepter of the Earth and then I twist.

The weapon slides out and the trident breaks.

Nieve slips and falls at my feet, as if I've taken the wind out of her. That's how it felt when I woke up in the Toliss chambers after the sea dragon grabbed me from the cliff. That's what it felt like when I woke up and the scepter wasn't there. Like something inside of me was missing, couldn't be filled.

"This is still mine."

She pushes herself up, but the turtle giant is unsteady and we both heave. She thrusts the trident to the sky and pulls on the lightning. But I'm faster. I can feel my sea horse's power inside me. I push the quartz scepter through her heart.

The silver mermaid gasps, tendrils of lightning wrapping around her in bursts. Her bright red blood stains her white skin, and the silver scales dissolve instantly. I hold her wrist. Her flesh hardens beneath my fingers. Her head rolls back in a scream that scares the sky into silence.

chapter
FIFTY

When Nieve dies, the coral of her bone solidifies around the crystal of my scepter. Her hand around the rest of the trident. When I pry the weapons out of her hands, what's left of her snaps into brittle little pieces. There is no garden outside the Glass Castle; there are no tears of pearl. The sky trembles above me. Waves rise to meet my touch. I slide the quartz piece back into the trident and it's complete once again. It's like the world falls apart, like everything is rushing past me all at once, heavy on my shoulders. Is this what Nieve felt? Is this what my grandfather felt? It's like thousands of voices linked around me. The cries of the sea people, the waves, thunder and lightning, and the deepest ends of the ocean. It's part of me. For a moment, I can't breathe.

The turtle giant moans, a long sad noise. I can feel its anger, its confusion. It's been asleep for so long, and believe me, I know what it's like to get woken up before I'm ready.

"It's okay, boy," I say. "Stop right there."

Even though I've got this awesome trident, I'm not ready for the turtle giant to hit the coast. Its steps shake the ground and I nearly topple over. It kneels forward, lowering its head so I can walk off. Its eye is not as fierce as I saw in the vision of their battle.

"You must be tired." I press my hand on its nose. The tide washes around us. "We just have one last thing to do, okay? Then you can be free."

I don't speak ancient turtle, but he opens his mouth and a deep horn blast rings out.

Behind me is the shore I've known forever. Ahead is the open sea that calls to me. When I close my eyes, I can feel the waves listening to me, pulling back from land. I search and search for the thoughts of the kraken. He's off on the Jersey Shore, plucking out a group of crazy guys who thought it'd be fun to go body surfing into the middle of a storm.

"Alleas," I tell the kraken, his name like a faint memory in the back of my thoughts. "Come back, we still have work to do."

"Doris," I say out loud. "Can you hear me?"

She neighs.

"The merrows. Stop them from coming on land."

Together the turtle giant—his name pops into my mind, Krios—Krios and Doris dive back into the stretch between Coney and Toliss. But the merrows that don't make it into their awaiting jaws still make it onto the shore, and I know this is far from over. The line of troops we kept to protect the shore is led by Dylan. Mermen and vampires fight with fang and sword against the intruders.

I take my trident and aim it, one, three, six, twelve. Lightning strikes, breaking the merrows into black, fleshy piles that get pulled in by the waves.

Dylan runs over to me and starts to kneel, and I press my hand on his shoulder.

"No time for that," I say. "This isn't over yet."

Dylan and I swim into the waves. I shift into my tail and this new power is a turbo boost. I reach the Toliss shore in minutes. My legs rip when I break the surface.

After all the pandemonium, the silence on the beach is unnerving. I take in the momentary quiet of the beach, the darkness of the sky. I can feel the giants returning. Their steps shake the earth. All three of them touch my mind with quiet good-byes as they make their way into the ocean, free.

When I hear my name, I smile. Dylan's finally caught up.

"Tristan, watch out," he screams, wading out of the water.

Behind me is Leomaris, raising his dagger. I slam my trident at him like a baseball bat and he falls back, blood dripping out of his mouth.

"It's over," I tell him.

He spits on the white sand. "As long as you live, we will always fight. Every day, every night, we will come for you."

I stare at him for a little bit. He doesn't get up, his amber eyes so pained from losing his son. I was wrong about merpeople. I always thought they didn't care about death, just because they didn't leave traces behind. Except they do, and they will remember for ages.

"You will never know the truth of our ways," he says. "You will never know, and you will die a young king."

Bodies surround us now.

"I know," I tell him, taking the trident and piercing his chest. I force myself to look at him, even though what I want to do is close my eyes, just close my eyes for a little while.

He crumbles into coral.

"Report," I say to Frederik.

Black smudges cover his face. "It seems that when you defeated the silver mermaid, what was left of her army ran away."

Surrounded by the landlocked, the Alliance, and what's left of the Sea Court, I know what I have to do. I know that I've never been one to believe in prophecies. I believe that my fate is my own. I did this. I chose this. I wanted to fight for these people.

And I have fought.

And I have won.

I hold the power of the trident, the power of the king. Layla takes my hand, and in that moment, I am certain.

"This isn't a congratulation speech," I say. "This isn't a congratulation speech because I'm not the one that's won anything. Our homes are safe for now, if a little more crunchy than usual. But we will rebuild. We will rebuild the Glass Castle, this time with metal of some sort and hope for the best. We will rebuild the lake here, and the throne, and it'll be better than it was before." I turn to Penny. "The landlocked are free of their bindings. I release you and your children.

"For as long as I've been a merman, I've had other people tell me that 'the sea people are responsible for their own demise.' They aren't wrong. Not from where I've been standing. It's time that we take that back. And the only way to move forward is with a king who truly knows you."

I turn to Kurt, and he takes a step back. "What are you doing?"

I hold the trident out for him to take. "My grandfather was right. I was meant to change things. To make you see that humans aren't so bad, that the landlocked can be forgiven. You don't have to be afraid of the unknown. But the kingship? That was meant for you."

"Tristan—"

"I'm only going to offer the one time," I say, the power of the trident pulling me. It's tempting, it is. I saw how power was a living force that fed Nieve. I never want to be like that.

Kurt takes the trident from me. He stares at it for a long time, and I know in my bones I've done the right thing.

"King Kurtomathetis," I say.

He laughs, taking my arm. "Just call me Kurt."

chapter
FIFTY-ONE

For days, I stay on the island.

Along with the Alliance and the landlocked—not so land-locked now—we help rebuild Toliss as much as we can.

Most of it is on Kurt, whose formal awkwardness as my guardian has translated into being a king. Sometimes he forgets that he can smite people if he felt like it, and he bows at the end of conversations.

"Can't you just whip up a giant statue of me?" I say to him. "I think I'm pretty statue-worthy."

He's using the trident to rebuild the wall the Sleeping Giants crushed. Instead of a huge structure that needed to be climbed, it's now a line of pillars that give a view of the thick forest. Beyond the forest is the white beach.

"I wouldn't want to scare anyone away," he says.

"Funny."

It goes on like that for a few days in preparation for the official coronation. Part of me is all jitters, thinking about the visions I've seen—me dying, Kurt and I mortal enemies. Even if I've avoided that version of the future, who's to say something equally violent isn't going to happen?

Slender hands wrap around me. "Worrying again?"

I sling an arm around Layla's shoulder. "Me? Never."

She tilts her head up for a kiss and I take it eagerly.

"Thalia says she needs you in the nursery," she says.

This is when my heart tightens. I walk into the Toliss chambers where one room hasn't changed. During the aftermath, I told Kurt about Nieve's nursery. We decided it was best to raise the baby merrows.

"This has never been done," he said.

I picked up the one with skin the color of sunset. "The creatures we were fighting didn't stand a chance. They were literally fed hatred and dark magic three times a day."

It didn't go over well with some of the elder mermen, but those who didn't want to be ruled by the throne had the option of leaving. Our numbers now are small, which I guess makes us an endangered species.

Now in the nursery, Thalia feeds one of the children. "You wanted to see me."

She nods, her long, greenish hair loose around her body. She wears a tulle skirt. Her scales cover her breasts like a bra. I wonder if I can do that. So I close my eyes and try to make the scales rise, but they don't. Must be a chick thing.

"Thalia—" I know what she wants to ask me.

"Why didn't you change me?" she asks, trying to keep her voice down so as not to wake the kids. "You kept your word to everyone else. To the landlocked, to the river people. Everyone except for me."

"The reason I did that…" I say.

"Is because I asked him to," Kurt finishes for me. He walks into the chamber. His cheeks are sunburned from a week of pure, unadulterated sun. "I owe this to you."

Thalia puts the baby down and stands in front of her brother.

He takes her chin and tilts her face so she can look at him. "I wish I hadn't left you. I wish I'd been a better brother to you. But know that I love you, and if this is what makes you happy, this is what I will do."

He takes his trident and points it at Thalia. A pulsing blue light hits her chest. Her eyes and mouth open wide as if something inside her is breaking. Her gills disappear, leaving the faint pearly scar. It has to hurt. I know it does. My mom said it did when it happened to her. But when it's done and Thalia wobbles to take her first step as a human girl, Kurt holds out his arms and catches her.

The coronation is an all-day thing.

With all the elders turned to surf and coral beneath the Glass Castle, Kai is the only one left to fill their shoes. She takes in every detail, from a specific leaf that has to be wreathed around Kurt's hair to the direction he holds the trident to the sun. It's like she's posing a model for a photo shoot. She guides the new members of the Sea Guard, lead by Arion, to flank the new king.

She nicks his finger and holds it over the great lake. Kurt repeats after her, "As blood of the sea, I swear to serve thee."

Then she pops a crown over his head, the same one my grandfather wore the day I met him.

"Jealous?" Shelly asks beside me.

"Like the new 'do," I tell her.

She touches her hair self-consciously. It's long and black, no longer a handful of thin wisps. Now that she's one of the two remaining oracles, she's been trying to "get out there" so her line doesn't die with her.

Shelly struts to the throne where Kurt takes her hand and kisses the back of it. Her fairy handmaidens flit about her, fixing strays from her hair and wrinkles from her dress.

Kai calls my name and the lake gets quiet.

I look around as if there is another Tristan Hart.

Layla gives me a push and I walk to them. When I try to bow, Kurt stops me. Shelly holds a golden box and opens it for me. Nestled on a lining of red velvet is a strange weapon. Seventeen inches or so of glistening platinum with HART etched in a fine cursive, and a sharp piercing white crystal at the end.

"For defeating the sea witch," Kurt says, "and never forgetting where you come from. Tristan Hart, I declare you Protector of Land and Sea."

"I forged it myself," Shelly says with a wink.

I take it and feel the instant connection to the core of the crystal. I turn to the cheering crowd and hold up my weapon to the sky.

chapter
FIFTY-TWO

I stand at the Coney Island pier. In the distance, a storm moves toward the horizon and I know that's where Toliss is moving on to its next destination.

The boardwalk is reopened, and with a little help from the Sea King, the beach is patched from the holes we put in it. The sky directly above me is silky dark blue without a single threat of a cloud. The Wonder Wheel and other rides are up and the beach is open for the public once again. Frederik lies on the beach, a line that could pass for a smile brightening his face. He's surrounded by giddy vampire girls and demigods. They look up at the moon and soak up its light—moonbathing.

Marty and Layla run up on either side of me. We lean on the new wooden railing. The old one was blasted to bits. I grab for Layla without thinking twice, taking her hand in mine and trying not to think that this is the same pier she got taken from.

"Your parents are wondering where you are," Layla says. "Everyone is celebrating."

"I know," I say. "I'm just taking it all in."

"Marty misses Dylan already," she snorts. "Now that Dylan is the King's advisor guy."

Marty pulls down the beak of his cap. He's got a new one, though he's still pissed at me for throwing the other one out.

"Not my first heartbreak, ladybird," the shapeshifter says. "There are plenty of fish in the sea. Isn't that right, T?"

I shake my head, bringing Layla closer to me and biting down on her neck just to feel her shiver. Then she pulls away and says, "I'm not a chew toy."

"More for me," Marty says.

"I don't know, guys," I say. "I know it's been a hell of a couple of weeks, but I'm feeling kind of antsy, you know?"

Marty picks up a newspaper that blows against his legs. The *Brooklyn Star*. The headline reads: Local Swim Team Captain Saves the Day. There's a picture of Angelo saving a homeless guy from a fuzzy shot of a merrow. Then a smaller article that reads: Kraken Attacks Local Celebrities. Well, it's not wrong. Marty crumples the paper and dunks it in the garbage.

"You're just saying that because you have a new toy," Marty reminds me. "You're like Aquaman. No wait, that's taken. Mighty Merman? How about—"

"How about, you all shut your clams and come with me for a bit of fun." Brendan is standing on the pier.

"How the hell did you get up here?" Layla says, hugging him.

Brendan smirks, and we follow his eyes to where a ship bobs

in the distance. On the deck I can make out Amada and Arion talking. I wonder what it's like being free after so long. I could go on board and ask them.

"I happen to recall," Brendan says, "our grandfather telling me not to forget about my family. You helped me remember that. So I'm going to repay the favor."

"Where are you going?" I ask, edging closer to where he balances on the railing.

"Nowhere." He stretches his arms to the clear sky. His red hair is like a flame in the wind. "Everywhere. But I can guarantee it will be dangerous."

Perhaps I share in Brendan's desire to discover new worlds. Adventure is like adrenaline in my blood. So much for sleeping until school starts again.

I look back at my home. Take in the brilliant lights of Luna Park, the sweet smell of corn dogs and cotton candy. A little storm wasn't enough to stop Coney Island from bouncing back.

I look at Layla, biting her lip playfully. Marty gets up on the ledge beside Brendan.

"What about the whole 'protecting the land and sea' stuff?" I yell at them.

"Believe me, ain't nobody messing with this Coney Island shore any time soon," Marty says.

"Although Arion has told me of some displaced landlocked in Australia," Brendan says. Then he looks at Layla. "Or Galapagos, if Lady Layla prefers. The seas are vast and they're ours."

I smile. I smile for every person we've lost on the way here. For my grandfather, for Kai's dad. Blue and Vi. For Ryan.

I look at the white of the moon, for Gwen.

No matter what, I'll always come back here.

Brendan and Marty backflip onto the sand. Layla and I hop over after them.

"Last one on the ship swabs the deck," Brendan yells as he sprints into the water.

Marty pulls up his sagging shorts and shouts, "Cheat!"

I take one last look at Layla. She leans up to kiss me. We run, her hand still in mine. And as we dive into the welcoming wave, I don't let go.

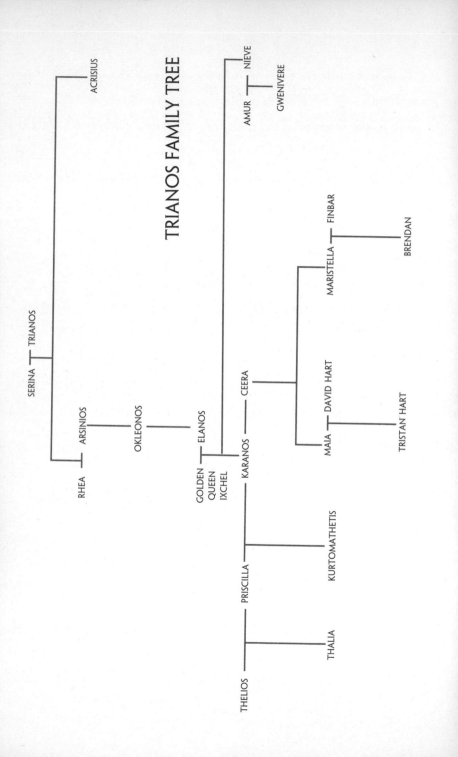

TRIANOS FAMILY TREE

KLEOS FAMILY TREE

TRIANA ——————————|—————————— KLEOS

RHEA

ELLANOS FAMILY TREE

MEMET ——————————|—————————— ELLANOS

SERIANA

ACKNOWLEDGMENTS

As always, thank you to my Ecuadorian and Sicilian tribe. I'm incredibly lucky to have a family that supports and shares my books with others.

A gigantic thanks to everyone in my Sourcebooks family. Jillian Bergsma, thank you for your great notes that made this book better. A huge thanks to the stellar production team for putting up with me. Derry Wilkens for all that you do for me. Aubrey Poole for truly getting Tristan and his friends from the beginning. We made a trilogy!

Tony Sahara for another kickass cover.

My Goodies—Adrienne, Nat, and Higgs—because all of our adventures keep me sane.

Lauren McCall, thank you for reading the first draft of this book and lending your notes. T.S. Ferguson for helping brainstorm the killer title.

To my writing groups—the Apocalypsies and #write-o-rama—for being there along this journey.

Kelly Skillen, for letting me use your house as writing den.

I am truly the luckiest mergirl in the world.

THE VICIOUS DEEP SERIES

Zoraida Córdova

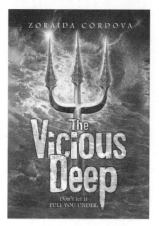

Tristan Hart was gone for three days. Sucked out to sea in a tidal wave and spit back ashore at Coney Island with no memory of what happened. Now his dreams are haunted by a terrifying silver mermaid with razor-sharp teeth.

His best friend, Layla, is convinced something is wrong. But how can he explain he can sense emotion like never before? How can he explain he's heir to a kingdom he never knew existed? That he's suddenly a pawn in a battle as ancient as the gods.

In the quest for the Sea Court throne, Tristan has already watched one good friend die. Now he must lead the rest on a dangerous voyage in search of the trident that will make him king.

While Tristan chases his destiny, the dark forces raging against him are getting stronger, and the sea witch of his nightmares is getting closer. But his allies each have their secrets, and a betrayal will force Tristan to choose between loyalty and ambition, friendship and love. In the race for a throne, all's fair in the savage blue.

THE EMBRACE SERIES

Jessica Shirvington

Embrace

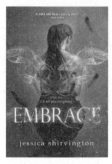

It starts with a whisper.

*"It's time for you to know
who you are…"*

Strange dreams leave her with very real injuries and there's a dark tattoo weaving its way up her arms. The guy she thought she could fall in love with just told her he's only half-human—oh, and same goes for her. And she keeps hearing a distant fluttering of wings.

Violet Eden is having a very bad seventeenth birthday.

But if angels seek vengeance and humans are the warriors, you could do a lot worse than betting on Violet Eden…

Entice

The war between exiles and angels is on— and Violet Eden is wanted by both sides.

Suddenly everyone she knows has something to hide, including the one person she's always trusted—her partner, Lincoln. No matter how bad things get, though, Violet doesn't run and she doesn't quit. Even if it means asking her enemy for help…

Emblaze

Her choices are harder. Her enemies are stronger. And no one can know how much she's hurting...

Both sides—angels vs. exiles—are racing to decipher an ancient scripture that would allow anyone banished to the Underworld to return. And at the very center: Violet. She only has one chance to make the right choice...

Endless

In the war between angels and exiles, Violet is about to take on her most dangerous adversary yet.

When Hell unleashes its worst, Violet must embrace every facet of her angel self to save the people she cares about and the world as she knows it. But death is not the worst thing that Violet will face. For her, the question "Can love conquer all?" will finally be answered.

Empower

It is time to make the final surrender. But who will Violet surrender to?

It has all come down to this, the final battle. Violet is the rainbow, a bridge, and now there are those who would use her to travel in the wrong direction. She will learn who she really is and what she is capable of. The angels created a weapon in her that is now being turned on them and Violet is all that stands in the way of the end of the universe as we know it.

THE SCORCHED SERIES

Mari Mancusi

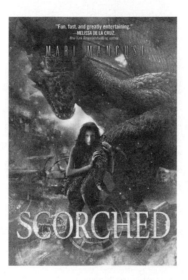

Sixteen-year-old Trinity Foxx is used to her grandfather's crazy stories, so she doesn't believe that the latest treasure he brought home is a real dragon's egg. Not until their home is invaded by soldiers trying to steal it and a strange boy telling her the world as she knows it will be wiped out in a fiery dragon war—unless they work together to stop it.

Meanwhile, there's a different voice whispering to Trinity, calling to her, telling her what to do...because the dragon in her egg is not ready to give up without a fight.

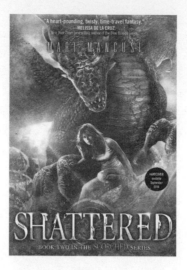

"A heart-pounding, twisty, time-travel fantasy."
—MELISSA DE LA CRUZ,
New York Times bestselling author of the Blue Bloods series

MARI MANCUSI

SHATTERED

BOOK TWO IN THE SCORCHED SERIES

Trinity, Connor, and Caleb are trying to stay under the radar, holed up in an abandoned West Texas farmhouse. Their only problem is Emmy: a baby dragon that's growing like crazy. When Emmy is caught on tape and the video goes viral, they find themselves on the run again. Their only hope comes from an old map leading to a man who has come from the future to help them.

But with the government hot on their heels and Caleb's growing addiction to spending time in the Nether world, will they be able to reach him in time? And will keeping Emmy safe end up being too high a price for Trinity to pay?